Trials of Artemis

BOOK 1 ⚭ THE HABERDASHERS

SUE LONDON

Trials of Artemis: Book One of the
Haberdashers
by Sue London
bysuelondon.com

Graythorn Publishing
Copyright © 2013 Sue London
All rights reserved

Cover Design and Interior format by The Killion
Group
http://thekilliongroupinc.com

PRAISE FOR SUE LONDON'S
HABERDASHERS SERIES

Delicious…

"Captivating tale of complex characters exploring uninvited relationships, battling preconceptions and discovering twists and turns of human nature and a satisfying plot with equally satisfying intelligence. Can't wait to get to know the other Haberdashers!"

~Amazon UK reader

Enjoyable…

"I enjoyed seeing the relationship play out between the two main characters, especially since the author decided to make them both forthright and honest with each other, being able to pick up on emotional cues, instead of relying on misdirection and misinterpretation to lengthen the story, as is usually the case in this genre."

~ Amazon.com reader

Looking forward to the next book…
"Their characters and their relationship develop at an almost perfect pace as the book progresses (with bumps along the newlywed road, of course). If you like a strong female, this is the book for you."
~ Amazon.com reader

DEDICATION

To my husband Devin for being supportive and helping me to believe in happily ever after. Without your kiss Sleeping Beauty would have never awoken. Nor would she have made it to that marketing class...

ACKNOWLEDGEMENTS

Considering that so much of a book requires hiding away and typing it's amazing how many people there are to thank when it is all said and done. As was evident from my dedication, if it weren't for my husband Devin I probably wouldn't be writing romance at all. Thanks for being my sweet, romantic partner. And for being half of the Dev and Susie show that keeps everyone laughing.

Enormous thanks to my sister for being my first fan and also giving me the necessary boot in the pants by saying "I'm not reading anything else until YOU FINISH SOMETHING." This wasn't the sci-fi epic she was hoping for but I know she still loves me anyway.

Thanks to my good friend Steve who never missed a chance to say, "What you really ought to do is publish a book." Thanks for the advice and coffee talk. And for lending me your Michael Connelly books. I promise those are coming back some day.

There are not enough words to express my thanks to writing buddy extraordinaire Kris Silva who went through my beta draft with a fine tooth comb, and a fine wit, to point out opportunities for improvement. And who also supplied me with a collection of her Muppet fiction to keep me entertained while she was reading. (It's good stuff!)

Tremendous thanks also to Jen Sylvia whose insightful comments in beta review helped to make this book so much better, and so much more, than it was. (Did you see all those 'so's Jen? I took them out of the rest of the book but had so many left over it seemed like a waste to just throw them away.)

Thanks to Elizabeth K. Hinds for Regency history pointers, including how to find the Parliamentary debates online. Who knew?? She did.

Thank you so much to my Facebook "fans" (yes, fans before publication, how 21st century!), especially Mike Worthan, Lydia Ondrusek, Neil Shurley, Dan Gage, Dusk Pennington, Jeremy Warach, Jen Stayrook, and Ed Rafalko. You guys are awesome.

Last but not least, thanks to my twitter buddies who make 'the writing life' not so lonely (well, and maybe not quite so productive, but what are friends for?), especially those mentioned above for Facebook plus Kerry Schafer, Jeffe Kennedy, Jenn Spiller, Steve Huff, Wendy Sparrow, J.C. Gregorio, Suzanne Gale, Kelly Breakey, Kristina Martin, Bill Cameron, Luis Vazquez, Amanda Alley, Dayton Ward, Rick Gualtieri, Matt Forbeck, and Lindsay Buroker.

Many of the above are awesome writers and bloggers. You should go look them up now!

*And thank **you** for taking a chance on a new writer. Hopefully we'll have a lot of fun together.*

"But, the bravest are surely those who have the clearest vision of what is before them, glory and danger alike, and yet notwithstanding, go out to meet it."
~ Thucydides

"Jack be nimble, Jack be quick, Jack jump over the candlestick."
~ children's rhyme

A cool summer rain pelted the rolling green grounds of the Bittlesworth estate. Rivulets of water dripped outside the folly claimed as a clubhouse for the afternoon, beating a staccato patter on the soaked earth. But all three of the youths inside were focused on the ceremony that Sabre was performing, cutting thin wounds in first Jack's and then George's palms. Jack looked a bit skeptical but George shrugged. Sabre had older brothers and seemed to know about these things. Joining their hands together, palm to palm, they sat in a circle while Sabre intoned, "Blood of my blood. Flesh of my flesh. We are now and forever the Haberdashers." And that was how three little girls pledged an oath of friendship the summer they were eight years old.

CHAPTER ONE

February 1815, London

Jacqueline Walters barely suppressed a sigh as she looked around the ballroom. She knew that Sabre had picked the name Haberdasher because it sounded daring. When Jack had learned that haberdashery was the term for men's accessories, hats and gloves and the like, she had argued that they needed to change it. Now she could admit that Sabre, or more precisely Miss Sabrina Bittlesworth, was nothing short of prescient in selecting the name. Ten years later it seemed that Jack's entire family was bent on making her some man's accessory.

"Oh, Jackie, isn't it quite the thing?" Her younger sister Samantha squeezed her arm. This was Sam's first formal ball and Jack was sure that her sister would walk around gawking at the decorations if she didn't think it would mark her as a complete unsophisticate.

"It's lovely, though I hate to think of how many peacocks are roaming around completely naked in service of it." The ballroom was grandly done in bright blues with peacock feathers displayed to excess. There were also quite a few trees from the orangery, the bright fruits making complementary splashes of color in the room. "Lady Wynders certainly knows how to make an impression."

Sam continued to gush. "I think it's the most amazing thing I've ever seen. I want to pinch myself to make sure I'm not dreaming."

Jack smiled down at her little sister. "Surely if it were your dream there would be at least one kitten."

"Oh, don't be such a goose, Jack!" Sam said with a nervous laugh.

"I'm just saying that your love of kittens is renowned," Jack continued. "Why, when you are Lady Such-and-such and throw your first ball I shall expect to see kittens there."

"Don't tease me so, Jackie," Sam admonished. "I shan't aspire to a title."

How like Sam to disparage the idea that she might snag a titled husband. However, if one of the Walters girls were to elevate her station it would undoubtedly be the petite, golden, and sweet-natured Samantha. Tall, serious Jack had been on the marriage mart for two years now and had been marked as a bluestocking, too intelligent and outspoken to be a good Society wife. She had slowly faded into the background as a wallflower, accepting that she would most likely be firmly on the shelf in another year. In the meantime she could be a chaperone for her sweet sister in the hopes of helping Sam make a worthy match. Perhaps, she thought, someone that she could stand since she would most likely be living with them as a helpful maiden aunt one day. Of course Mama and Papa still expected Jack to make a stunning match, but she was sure that as Sam blossomed in her first Season the pressure regarding Jack's own marriage potential would wane.

"You know," Sam said, tapping her fan on Jack's arm to get her attention. "Men would be much more interested in you if you didn't look at them all like they were Lord Lucifer."

Jack frowned. "Don't be ridiculous, I don't look at them like that."

"You were, just now. Staring at that poor little man over there as though he were a disciple of the devil himself."

Jack's gaze swept the room. "What little man? I was thinking about something else entirely, I assure you."

Sam gave a delicate sigh. "Yes. You always are."

A handsome young man of Jack's barest acquaintance approached them for an introduction to Sam and Jack knew that it had begun. Four introductions and two glasses of punch later Jack was certain that her sweet little sister was already beginning to take in a way that Jack never had herself. Did she look at men as though they were that reprobate Lord Lucifer? Certainly not. To the best of her knowledge she didn't look at men at all. Few of them took the opportunity to speak to her and fewer still asked for a dance. Not that she was surprised since she matched the height of most of them and towered over others. As such she spent most of her time at these events lingering along the wall and thinking.

During one particularly long country reel that Sam had been invited to dance and Jack had not she took the opportunity to find Lord Wynder's famed classics library. Even level-headed Jack had to admit that being ignored for two years to then be sought out as a conduit of introduction to a debutante had a certain sting to it, one that she was certain could be relieved with a quick peek at a rare book. Perhaps he would even have some tomes on weaponry. She was quite sure that Lord Wynder wouldn't mind. Too much. Especially since he would never find out.

After perusing the shelves Jack finally chose a book, setting the lamp on a shelf high enough to shine its light down onto the pages. Greek was difficult to read in the best of conditions and the combination of dim light and cramped writing in this particular text almost made her give up entirely. An arm sliding around her waist from behind interrupted her focus on the text. She stiffened as she felt the warmth of another person pressing up behind her, accompanied by a smell that was a mix of mint, cloves, and leather.

"And here you are," a deep voice murmured in her ear. "You're early."

It was one of Jack's peculiarities that she wasn't the type to jump and scream. Both Sabre's and George's brothers had made it their mission over the years to get a girlish, squeamish reaction out of her to no avail. In this particular instance she was frozen like a statue while her heart sped into an erratic beat in her chest. Who was this man? Who did he think *she* was? She felt his breath on her neck as he nuzzled closer to her, his fingers tracing lazy patterns on her stomach.

"What are you reading?" he asked, voice low and husky at the side of her neck.

"Thucydides," she managed in a strangled whisper.

He chuckled, his breath stirring the strands of hair at her nape. "Planning a war instead of a seduction? What am I saying, you probably consider seduction to be a war."

Planning a seduction? Good gracious, who *did* he think she was? Why would anyone be planning a seduction in the library of all places? Her mind turned frantically like a moth trapped inside a jar. She had never done more than hold a man's hand before, and that only briefly. This wasn't only wrong, it was *forbidden*. Rather than panic her that thought relaxed her. She enjoyed doing forbidden things. Climbing trees, racing horses, practicing swords. Perhaps this forbidden activity would be just as invigorating.

Jack felt as though he were drawing her into a cocoon of his warmth and scent. His lips touched her neck and her own blush in reaction added to the sense of heat so that she almost felt she had walked into a fire. His other arm came around her and pulled the book from her fingers, laying it aside. He had eased her back against himself and her shoulders now rested on his chest while he continued his slow journey downward of touches and kisses. Her initial shock had worn off and her body was languidly surrendering. His nearness was new and thrilling and surprisingly relaxing. She melted back into him and was rewarded with another chuckle and a gentle nibble on her ear. She shivered in response and his arms tightened as his fingers became bolder in their exploration, one hand sweeping under her breasts while the other traveled down, pressing her back so that her derriere fit snugly against him. With that the sensations went from soothing to alarming and she tried to wriggle away.

He murmured in her ear again. "You are just as luscious as you look. More so. Let me taste you."

Becoming outraged she pushed away and turned to address him. "Sir! You - "

He took her lips, covering her protest. Tasting, indeed. He sampled her lips with gentle suckling and licking. His errant hand had made its way to palm her breast and on her gasp he took the opportunity to plunder her mouth with his tongue. Jack shivered again. She had never felt anything like this before. Had never thought that it was even possible. Her body throbbed with hope and want and need but her mind was beginning to rebel even more at the outrage. She gave him a savage push and managed to lever away from him. The damnable man was the size of a house!

As her seducer drew back from the kiss and looked down at her face his own was illuminated by the lamp on the bookcase. She saw unfashionably long dark hair and dark, heavey-lidded eyes. The eyes widened with shock.

"Who in the bloody hell are you?" he choked out.

He was withdrawing his hands from her when the side door of the library opened and Jack heard a woman's voice, a throaty contralto, coming in from the hallway. "No, Lord Wynders, I don't need an escort but it is lovely of you to ask."

"Well, my dear, it wouldn't do for one of my guests to be left unattended at our soiree."

Jack turned toward the door and her seducer took a step back as the woman entered the room. Outlined by the light from the hall all Jack could see was a tall, curvaceous figure cutting a rather fashionable silhouette. It was apparent the woman had seen them because of her surprised but understated, "Oh."

Within a moment of that shock the woman began to withdraw but Lord Wynders had scented scandal and pushed the door open further. The light from the hallway spilled a feeble ray across the floor and dimly lit the occupants at the bookcase and Wynders drew himself up. "Harrington," he said shortly.

"Wynders," Jack's seducer replied with a brief nod.

"Miss Walters," Wynders said, with a nod in Jack's direction. Jack could feel the tension in the room rising as the four occupants eyed each other.

Jack dipped a quick curtsy. "Lord Wynders."

Another voice in the hallway, this one a woman with a higher and more patrician tone. "Darling, whatever are you doing in the library?"

Lord Wynders moved aside to allow his wife into the room. "I suspect..." he said.

Harrington grabbed Jack's hand and pulled her forward, cutting off Wynders. "Congratulating us on our upcoming nuptials." Jack looked at him in panic and he pulled her tight against him. "Although we would appreciate your discretion since the particulars haven't been worked out with her father yet."

They had drawn close enough to their unexpected audience for Jack to see their faces. Lord Wynders looked speculative, Lady Wynders looked delighted about this *on dit,* and the mystery woman looked sympathetic. Upon closer inspection Jack could see that she was the widow Lady... Spencer? Spinner? Undoubtedly the woman with whom Harrington had planned to rendezvous in the library this evening.

Lord Wynders broke the silence. "Miss Walters, perhaps you would like for me to fetch your father so that they can discuss this?"

Jack glanced up at Harrington and then back to her host. She mustered a smile that she hoped wasn't too sickly. The year she had spent recovering from a broken arm after falling off her horse came rushing back to her. Sometimes things were forbidden because they were dangerous. "No thank you my Lord. Don't worry Papa with it now."

Returning to the main ballroom they made their way around the periphery in a slow stroll, absently nodding to acquaintances in a typical display of a potential couple. It maintained the fiction presented to the Wynders while not making a clear commitment to the other attendees. Jack was desperately trying to remember where she had heard the name Harrington before. He was an aristocrat, that was clear, but what kind? Younger son of a titled man? A baron himself perhaps? It was rare to find a man a full head taller than herself but she didn't remember him from the soirees she had attended in her first two seasons. Perhaps he had only recently returned to Town. It was still quite early in the season so perhaps he only attended smaller affairs. Her mind churned through possibilities while he seemed content to maintain the silence between them.

Presently he stopped and spoke to someone Jack very much recognized, the Duke of Beloin. This was a surprise to her since the young duke was known to be a bit high in the instep. As the duke turned to address her escort with a friendly smile Jack remembered. Harrington. Bloody hell, it was the *Earl* of Harrington. She pasted a false smile on her face and began to wonder how on earth she would be getting out of this tangle.

CHAPTER TWO

Regardless of his desires to the opposite, the next day did dawn for Gideon Wolfe, Earl of Harrington. He looked up at the Walters townhouse with some trepidation. He had already avoided the early morning hours, convincing himself that he shouldn't assume Walters would be up and about like himself. But there was no avoiding it any longer. Gazing at the black lacquer door he thought it was like his future, an interminable black void. Marriage had not been something he was planning imminently, perhaps never. His solicitor pestered him periodically about the succession and as a result Gideon knew exactly which cousins were to inherit and in what order. Why should he want a wife? In his experience women were only pleasant in the beginning of a relationship, after which they became clingy, demanding termagants. His mother had been an excellent example of the species, nagging his father into an early grave. Firmly shoving aside his morose thoughts he grabbed the brass knocker to rap smartly at the door. It was opened by a butler of middling years who had that peculiar talent of seeming both subservient and dismissive at once.

"How may I help you, sir?"

Gideon offered his card. "The Earl of Harrington to see Mr. Walters, if you please."

The butler accepted the card and bowed Gideon into the front hall and preceded him through the hallway. The townhouse was what Gideon would have expected for a gentleman of some connections and inherited wealth. A subdued decor, aged but with a timeless quality. The Walters were cousins of the present Viscount Whitemarch, if he recalled correctly, from the branch of a younger son some generations back. Certainly enough of a pedigree that no one should be surprised by the selection of his countess, provided they could keep the particulars of the reasons for the engagement from the society papers. He had been surprised when there had been no mention in the morning papers and had to credit the Lord and Lady Wynders with more discretion than he thought them capable. For a brief moment he had considered the danger passed and he did not need to offer for the chit, but the moment had been fleeting. Truth would often out, and the more unpleasant the truth the more likely that it would get tongues to wagging. Honor dictated that he couldn't leave any woman without the protection he could offer in such circumstances. If the story were to get out, at worst the *true* story, then not only would the girl's reputation be ruined but perhaps that of her entire family. Nor would such a salacious tale help Gideon's own standing, especially if he were to act without the honor expected of any gentleman of his class. Maintaining his reputation in Parliament dictated this action if nothing else did.

The butler stepped into an open door and bowed to the occupant. "The Right Honorable Gideon Wolfe, Earl of Harrington, sir."

Gideon's first impression of his future father in law was the voice saying, "Very good, Villiers. Show him in, please." It was a tired voice, resigned. Not the voice of a man delighted that his daughter had finagled an Earl by whatever means necessary. Villiers bowed Gideon into the room, a large study with maple-paneled walls and warm sunshine spilling in from tall windows. A figure stood by the desk, a slender man of perhaps forty years who stood at about the same height as his daughter, and shared her pale brown hair. The family resemblance was unmistakable. But where Miss Walters had forest green eyes, a detail Gideon had noted when she had turned to him in surprise at introduction to a duke, her father's were a watery blue. Gideon bowed. "Thank you for receiving me, sir."

That caused Mr. Walters to quirk a small smile. "Yes, I'm famed for my tendency to toss out all the nobility that comes by."

Gideon hesitated. When he had imagined this exchange it certainly hadn't featured a potential father in law who was both resigned and sarcastic.

Walters waved a hand. "My apologies for the attempt at humor. Please, have a seat. Brandy?"

"Yes, please." It was all he could do to not suggest that Walters hand him the whole bottle.

Returning from the sideboard with two glasses Walters sank into the guest chair next to Gideon after handing him his drink, rather than sitting behind the desk. "So," he said without preamble, "you think you want to marry my daughter."

Choking a bit on the swallow of brandy he had taken, Gideon managed. "Of course."

Walters had crossed his legs and begun jiggling his foot while staring down into his own brandy glass. "I have to warn you that Jacqueline is not in favor of the marriage."

Gideon frantically searched his memory. Was Jacqueline the daughter or the wife? He couldn't recall that he knew either name so stayed silent.

"My wife is overjoyed of course. Her father was a merchant and now her daughter will be a countess."

A-ha! Jacqueline was the daughter. His future wife and he hadn't known her name. Nor that her mother had come from the merchant class. And her father didn't seem inclined toward the match either. Perhaps Gideon *would* ask for the bottle.

Walters' pale blue gaze rose to meet his own again. "From all that I've heard about you, Harrington, I wouldn't have thought you to be a man of few words."

"I'm, ah, overcome with the event."

"So, here I have a daughter who spent the whole of the night trying to convince me to reject your suit, and a potential son in law who behaves like a man marching to the gallows. Certainly not the recipe for a happy marriage, do you think?"

Struck by that unexpected comment Gideon asked, "Is that important to you, that your daughter be happy?"

Walters foot stopped jiggling. "Of course it is." He looked off toward the sunny windows and sipped at his brandy. "Perhaps one day when you have children of your own you will understand."

"I can only hope so, sir."

Walters looked at him again. "When you hadn't arrived by nine this morning Jack decided you weren't going to come and finally went to sleep. She was relieved."

Gideon now stared down into his drink. "I didn't want to assume you would be up early."

"On a day when our eldest daughter is to become engaged? I worry that you aren't showing a great deal of wisdom or insight."

The man wasn't intimidated by rank in the least and his acerbic comments were getting on the earl's last nerve. "My apologies, sir," Gideon said stiffly. "I didn't think of it that way."

Walters sighed. "So, the particulars. Jacqueline has a dowry of three thousand pounds which will be rendered to you upon the completion of the wedding vows."

"If you don't mind me saying, sir," Gideon interrupted, "you don't seem enthused by the idea of this marriage."

"Enthused? No. But is it necessary? Yes." Walters tossed back the remainder of his brandy and then his pale blue gaze settled on Gideon again. "Let me be clear about this. If I didn't think it would do more harm than good to her reputation I would have called you out this morning for even thinking of touching my daughter. As she does not seem inclined to this marriage, no, I'm not in favor of it. But I want my younger daughter Samantha to have a chance at a good match. I want my wife able to go out in polite society. Neither of those things will occur with the barest hint of scandal, our family simply isn't important enough to withstand it. I will say that I'm disappointed in Jacqueline for putting us in this position, but there is very little choice in the outcome now, is there?"

Gideon shook his head. "No, there appears to be no choice at all."

Both men were startled from their brooding by the door crashing open.

When Jack heard that the earl had arrived she raced down the stairs and threw open the door of her father's study. And there he was. Not to be inconvenienced by rising early, he had dragged his dissolute, arrogant carcass to her house on what had to be going on two of the afternoon, and now sat drinking her father's prized brandy for what probably served as his breakfast. If she had something close to hand to throw at his head she was fairly sure she would do it. After her shock had worn off the night before, she had spent hours trying to convince her father that the marriage wouldn't be necessary or a good idea. It was the one time in her life she had regretted her natural honesty. If she had kept the full truth of the situation from her father he might have been more pliable, but upon hearing even the sketchiest description of what had happened earlier in the evening he had been consumed with a cold rage, the likes of which she had never seen. Her frustration had led to crying and pleading, but her uncharacteristic behavior had seemed to make her father more intractable. Her only relief had come when Harrington hadn't arrived in the morning. No earl, not even a note. Surely he had realized that backing away from a hasty engagement made due to silly social pressures was the best course! Now he was here, cozened in the warm room as though he were a treasured family friend. It was outside of enough.

He rose to his feet and bowed to her as though she weren't standing in the door breathing heavily from running down two flights of steps. "Miss Walters."

She gripped the door handle tightly, a solid anchor in a world that was very much off-kilter. "Harrington."

He raised a brow at her more casual use of his name. His gaze traveled up and down her length in an appraising way. "You look well today."

She nearly snorted. She full well knew she was flushed, most likely with wisps of hair flying around from her headlong flight down the steps. It was tempting to return his bland compliment, but he truly was looking well. A man with such a dissolute reputation shouldn't look so... well. He had the physique of a horseman, with broad shoulders and a narrow waist leading to solid thighs encased in buff breeches. Realizing that her gaze had wandered to his breeches Jack felt herself blush. When she looked back to his face he smiled knowingly at her and she wanted to throw something at him all over again. Instead she took a deep breath and said, "Perhaps you would like to take a walk in the garden?" If she couldn't convince her father about the perfidy of this match then the next best course of action was to convince Harrington.

CHAPTER THREE

Upon Miss Walters' invitation to walk in the garden Gideon looked to her father, who shrugged tiredly and nodded his consent. Offering the girl his arm she had looked at it like a snake, then after a deep breath had taken it without comment. At this point he was a bit put off by the Walters family. It wasn't like he was a pariah! Most young women would be *beyond* delighted at being offered marriage to an earl regardless of the reason. Once outside in the back gardens Miss Walters towed him down a path. Their destination became clear as she slowed at the sight of a stone bench under the shade of an old oak. The view included an arbor and a bed of roses still dormant for the winter.

Stopping in front of the bench Gideon took both of her hands in his own. Not the easiest thing since she seemed disinclined to surrender them or to turn to look at him. Frustrated by her obstinance Gideon did something he hadn't expected to and dropped to one knee in front of her. "Miss Walters, would you give me the pleasure of being my wife?"

She began tugging to get him to release her hands. "No."

At her flat denial Gideon did release her hands and rose back to his feet. "No?"

Miss Walters brushed some dead leaves off the bench before seating herself and carefully arranging her skirts. "No, I don't think we need to marry at all. I understand that a public engagement may be necessary, but after a suitable period I can beg off."

Gideon remained standing since her voluminous skirts left little room for a companion on the bench. "That is not acceptable. Honor dictates we marry, otherwise your reputation, and most likely that of your family, will be ruined."

She raised her chin to address him directly. "No."

"No?"

She seemed absorbed in smoothing her skirts again. "Simply that. No."

Gideon held his breath for a moment. It wouldn't do to lose his temper. Just because neither of them wanted this match didn't mean that either of them was to blame. Miss Walters turned her head away from him to look at the arbor, her chin tilted at a defiant angle.

"What do you expect me to do? Propriety demands –"

She whipped her gaze back to him, her green eyes like chips of emerald. "To hell with propriety! I wasn't planning to marry at all, much less..." she waved her hand at him, from his Hessian boots to his barely tamed hair, *"you.*

Life as a spinster due to my 'reputation' would be a far happier life than one where I am married to you."

He stepped closer, crowding her with his height and bulk. "As though I would be getting the superior end of the bargain?"

She huffed. "Undoubtedly! At least you won't have to worry about me planning assignations at social events."

"Bloody hell, woman! Not just stubborn, but a harpy as well?" Gideon threw his arms out in exasperation. "This marriage is getting better by leaps and bounds."

"Stating facts makes me a harpy?"

"Facts? You do not know me madam. If you were a man and questioned my honor thus-"

She poked a finger toward him. "You don't know *me* and-"

"Zounds, woman!" he exploded out. "Will I ever be able to finish a sentence in your presence?"

Miss Walters opened her mouth to reply and then shut it closed again. She went back to staring at the arbor as though the vine-wrapped structure were the ultimate source of their problems.

Gideon straightened his cuffs. "If we are to get on you cannot constantly contradict me."

This time she looked at him as though he had sprouted another head but her lips remained firmly sealed.

"It wouldn't do to have a countess who cannot conduct herself appropriately," he added.

That seemed to unglue her lips. "No one is asking you to!"

"This is not a negotiation! We are getting married and you need to resign yourself to that!"

This caused her to surge from the bench. She placed her fists on her hips and narrowed her eyes again. "Even if I *do* agree to marry you I will not become a simpering mouse and you will need to resign yourself to that!"

Realizing that it was best to quit the field before he did something hideous, like throttling his new fiancée, Gideon sketched a stiff bow. "Good day, madam." As he walked away he could hear her irritated huff and something that sounded suspiciously like "bloody bastard." Stopping by her father's study briefly to ensure that the announcement would be in the morning's paper, Gideon took his leave of the Walters' home.

For the first time in her life Jack retreated to her bedroom, threw herself across the bed, and wept like her best friend had died. All of this trouble because of her love of Greek? It was unfair! There seemed to be no escaping the engagement. But perhaps she could still avoid marrying him. If only Sabre and George were here they would help her come up with a plan. She wiped her tears and went to her writing desk.

My dearest Haberdashers,
I send you both a copy of this letter as I desperately need you here with me now. It

seems that I am to marry soon. Yes, it is rather sudden. My betrothed is Gideon Wolfe, Earl of Harrington. Although I would be against the match myself, my family seems in favor of it. Father seems resolute, if you can imagine that. My mother is over the moon of course, and also sure that my elevation to countess will assure Sam making a good match. Meanwhile Sam, softhearted and dare I say softheaded girl that she is, has been trying to convince me that it could be a love match. Oh, how much I need you at this time! Sabre, you could help me to set and stay on the right course. George, you could help me see what all my options are. I have only seen two - rejection of Harrington which will lead to my ruin, or acceptance of his suit which will chain me eternally to what seems an overbearing, arrogant, uncompromising man. What am I to do? Fulfill my duty to my family to marry him? Or follow the best course for myself and reject him? I desperately need your counsel.

Together forever,
Jack

For the next three days everywhere Gideon went someone wanted to congratulate him on his engagement. At his club, at Tattersall's, even at Gentleman Jackson's. It was enough to make him consider retreating to one of his country manors. And while it was difficult enough receiving the felicitations with grace, the comments... the comments would be his undoing. "Charming gel," said the Marquess of Bath. "All that is demure and graceful." Then the diminutive Baron Hastings with his almost worshipful praises, admitting that he'd been too intimidated by her to ask her to dance. It was all Gideon could do to not shout at the man, "Then you marry her!" It was as though none of them had even met the same woman he had. Sensual and attractive, yes, but she was possessed with the tongue and humors of an asp.

On the night of that third day he knew that he was to see her. They were both invited to the Wittier soiree and it would be their first event as an officially engaged couple. Gideon spent extra time dressing for the event, partially because he wanted to look his best and partially because every extra minute spent on preparation was another minute where his travel was delayed. Then he became annoyed as this was the second time he was avoiding dealing with what he was now calling "the Walters problem." His valet was tying his cravat for the second time when he heard footsteps from the hall, his butler Dibbs followed by another, familiar set.

"Announcing his grace, my lord," Dibbs intoned from the doorway.

"Hullo, Giddy," said the duke as he entered and flopped down on the lounge chair in Gideon's dressing room.

"What are you doing out slumming, Quince?"

"Slumming? Indeed not. With the announcement of your engagement you became as respectable as any earl might hope to be. Although I am concerned that this marriage disease might be catching."

"Worry not, Quince, you will marry precisely the perfect woman at precisely the perfect time. Your perfection is part of your charm."

"Yes, I think thirty is the perfect age to marry. That means I have at least another two and a half years of freedom."

"By your theory I am marrying two years early? It feels a great deal earlier than that."

"That's part of why I came to see you, old boy. There is talk afoot, what with your engagement being so sudden. It would do for you to at least hint at a sudden *tendre* for this girl."

"Who is to say that we haven't formed a *tendre?* I don't remember talking to you about it."

Quince fixed him with a droll stare. "Unlike the others I actually know you quite well. When you introduced me to her you were furious and, if I'm not mistaken, she was in shock. Now I come here tonight to intercept you and end up cooling my heels in your library for an hour while you fiddle with your cravat."

"You were downstairs? Dibbs didn't inform me."

"I told him not to bother since you are usually quite punctual and I wanted to catch you on your way out. I then found myself staring at your family portraits until I began to fancy I knew them all quite intimately. But the point of this being that you aren't acting like yourself and it won't be long before others notice that as well."

Gideon frowned. "Men in love are known to act quite strangely. Who's to say this isn't due to love?"

"Simple, my dear boy. The look on your face. Were that the look of love there would be more duels twixt the bride and groom at weddings."

Gideon continued frowning while giving a final inspection to his coat. "There aren't more duels at wedding Quince because by the time you arrive at the chapel you have quite given up on life."

"Oh yes," the duke said drily, "I see that you are already practicing your 'young man in love' mien."

"Being neither young nor in love I don't see the point in bothering. Are you coming to the Wittiers?"

"Indeed I see I must, if only to prod you to the proper behavior to save you and your *fiancée* from embarrassment."

CHAPTER FOUR

Jack looked out across the ballroom, absently fanning herself. She knew that the earl was supposed to be here tonight but hadn't seen him yet. Both Mama and Papa were ensconced in the card room and her sister Sam was dancing a reel with a dashing young Captain. When the family had arrived there had been a stream of well-wishers on her engagement and a few gentlemen had politely asked her to dance. She had saved the first waltz for Harrington, since that seemed appropriate, but its time had come and gone and there were no new dance invitations. That meant Jack was lingering along the wall, wishing she could just plead a headache and go home. Watching her sister, she realized she wished she could be more like Sam. Silly, good-natured Sam who looked to be having the time of her life, spinning on the arm of her partner. Sam, who found joy in all that life had to offer. Jack was smiling indulgently at her sweet little sister when motion at the entrance caught her attention. At last the earl had come, resplendent in black and white. His too-long hair was tamed back into a queue and his clothing was fitted to perfection. He was holding her gaze from across the room. She suddenly realized she was staring and went back to watching her sister dance, picking up the tempo of her fanning. Shortly before Sam's dance ended Jack felt, rather than saw, the earl approach her.

"You're looking lovely this evening, my dear," he murmured, as though it was a compliment he didn't want anyone else to hear. He bowed over her free hand, and then kept it in his grasp as he looked around them. "Where are your admirers?"

Jack stopped fanning her face to look at him blankly. "My admirers?"

"Yes," he said, still looking around the room and sounding peevish, "all those men who have been singing your praises to me for the last three days."

"I'm sure you're quite mistaken," Jack said tartly. "It was very clear that I never quite 'took' in the *ton*."

The earl brought his gaze back to hers, his brow furrowing into a frown. "Oh, I'm quite sure I'm not mistaken. If one were to listen to Hastings over there it is apparent that you're some rarified combination of the Virgin Mary and the Queen."

Now Jack's brow furrowed and she looked around. "Hastings? Who the devil is Hastings?"

That caused the earl to smirk. "Poor chap. Smitten with you and you don't even know who he is."

"Don't be ridiculous, no one is smitten with me. It is ungracious of you to tease me with such an idea."

The earl's expression went from amused to irritated. "If you don't-"

"Hullo, Giddy," the duke's voice cut in. "Miss Walters," he said, stealing her hand from the earl and bowing over it. "How sublime you look this evening. This shade of green brings out your eyes."

"Thank you, your grace. You are all that is charming and fashionable."

The earl, his hands now clasped behind him, rolled his eyes to the ceiling. "Yes, you're both bloody amazing. I was having a conversation with my fiancée, Quince, which any idiot could see."

His Grace kept a jovial expression in place but said, "No, any idiot could see that you were having an argument. If you aren't going to go about this properly you might as well give up now."

The earl's expression darkened into a scowl. Based on how freely he had spoken to the duke, Jack had to assume the two were fast friends. It didn't seem right to have such a friendship strained by this awkward engagement, and it was quite magnanimous of the duke to bolster their relationship with his attention. Jack knew that she was ill prepared to smooth the waters in such a case, since it was unlikely that a recitation of Greek or Latin would have a positive effect. Both of her friends would be better at navigating this. Heavens, even her sister would be. In fact, what would Sam do? Playful Sam. Whom everyone adored.

She tapped the duke's arm with her fan. "Oh la, your grace, it wasn't an argument. Harrington was telling me how jealous he was of my admirers." She gazed up at the earl from under her lashes. "I'm sure he was about to ask me to dance."

Harrington looked down at her as though she had taken leave of her senses, which honestly was exactly how she felt. But she was willing to brave her way through this to settle a discord between friends. She attempted to look winsome but assumed that with all the lash batting she was doing she just looked like she had something in her eye. At last Harrington held out his arm to lead her out to the dance floor. Ironically they were just in time for the second waltz of the night and something of the humor of the situation must have registered on her face.

"What is amusing to you now?" the earl prompted as they settled into the rhythm of the dance. He held her at an appropriate distance but she could feel the heat of his body from her head to her toes. Everywhere he touched her burned like sitting too close to a fire on a chilly night.

Jack looked up at him. Really looked, as she hadn't before, and considered him as a man. His face bordered on craggy, all sharp cheekbone and aristocratic nose, and his dark blue eyes were expressive. At the moment they expressed curiosity tinged with a bit of bewilderment as she continued to smile up at him without speaking. As tall as she was, he was one of the few dance partners she'd had where she truly had to look up which was novel in and of itself.

"Why does the duke call you Giddy?"

His expression cooled as though he were disappointed that was what she was thinking about. "It's his attempt at humor."

"Sarcasm then?"

"I suppose," he said with a small shrug, losing interest in this line of conversation.

"In truth that wasn't what tickled me."

"Oh, and what was that?"

Jack lowered her gaze to Harrington's cravat. "I saved the first waltz for you but you hadn't arrived yet when it was played. I found it amusing that here we are dancing the waltz anyway."

"It seems I shall always be in trouble with you for being late."

Jack looked back up at him. Those deep blue eyes spoke not only of defensiveness but some apprehension. "Of course not," she answered blandly, in order to minimize the issue. "Where were you, anyway?" Jack nearly winced when the question came out of her mouth. It was never good to ask a question when you weren't prepared to hear the answer. Further, he might be insulted by her intrusiveness about his activities. Honestly, she thought, it would probably be better if she weren't sent out in public at all.

"Quince was lecturing me about how important it is that we make a good showing of our *tendre* for each other."

Jack stumbled a step, causing Harrington to pull her closer to steady her. "Our what?" she gasped.

"Our *tendre*. The sudden romantic interest that caused a confirmed bachelor and bookish maiden to announce an engagement before anyone even realized they knew each other."

"Surely no one is going to believe that."

"We need to make sure they believe that." He leaned closer, until he was whispering in her ear. "Especially if you have any hope for the rather outside chance of breaking this engagement. You can be assured that I will not let you go if your name is sullied by knowledge of how our attachment actually occurred."

Jack shivered with the memory of the last time he had whispered in her ear. As much as she was against this engagement, her body still yearned to feel him pressed against her, touching her as he had in the library. She might, she thought, have a lifelong affection for Thucydides simple due to the scene his name aroused in her memory.

Gideon felt the shiver go through Miss Walters and drew back to look at her face again. Her eyes were closed, her chin tilted back as though expecting his kiss. For a moment he had a crazed notion to do just that, kiss her here on the Wittier's dance floor in what would undoubtedly be the *on dit* of the season. But that would hardly be beneficial for her reputation. Upon reflection it might even push her father to do something reckless after all. The fact that they were now dancing scandalously close and the imperious Miss Walters had melted into a pose of feminine submission was probably enough for the biddies to start gossiping behind their fans. And bloody hell, when had the music stopped? Gideon swept Miss Walters off the dance floor under the speculative and smirking gazes of half the ton.

"I should return you to your parents," Gideon said, feeling rushed and out of sorts. "Where are they?"

"What? Oh. They are in the card rooms I think. You need not worry about returning me to a chaperone."

"Have you not seen the look in the eyes of those around us? I very much need to worry about it. Neither of us acted with much decorum on the dance floor once we were... distracted by our conversation."

Miss Walters looked around and blushed. "Oh. I see."

"I wonder if you do."

Jack indicated the south wall of the room. "That is my sister is over by that palm tree, you can leave me with her."

"The young blonde surrounded by swains?"

The petite blonde practically beamed at them as they approached. Miss Walters made introductions between Gideon and her sister's bevy of hopeful admirers, the younger men acting with some satisfying deference towards him. Having regained his composure he fetched the elder Miss Walters a lemonade, danced with her one more time as was appropriate, asked to take her up in his curricle on the morrow, which she accepted, and then took his leave for the evening. His invitation had been spoken well within the hearing of at least two society matrons who would most likely spread the story of the ongoing romance. He told himself, as he boarded his carriage at the unfashionably early hour of eleven o'clock, that he wasn't fleeing Miss Walters' company, he just had things he needed to do. Although at the moment he couldn't remember what those might be.

CHAPTER FIVE

Jack woke up early and lay in her bed watching the room slowly lighten. She felt unaccountably content, as though things were going well when she knew that the exact opposite was true. Although perhaps this was the right thing to do, to enjoy this short-lived engagement. To enjoy the attentions of an attractive man, even if he was acting under pretense for the sake of honor. These days could become treasured memories after she became the spinster she planned to be. After all, this would be the first time she went on a ride with a man younger than her father. All of her suitors had been older gentlemen who needed a young second wife to give them heirs. This year she hadn't drawn any suitors at all. Now she was being courted by an earl. What stories she would have for her nieces and nephews some day. 'Why yes, I was engaged to the Earl of Harrington at one time. We would dash through the streets in his racing curricle, cutting quite the picture I assure you. Who did he marry?' A good question. Who, indeed, would Gideon Wolfe, Earl of Harrington marry? He was by all accounts very active in the House of Lords. He counted a duke amongst his friends. A duke who liked him well enough to tease him with the nickname Giddy. Jack snorted a laugh. Giddy was, in fact, a horrible nickname for the overbearing and downright dour earl. Which was what made it perfect. Who would be the perfect wife for Giddy? A sweet, charming butterfly like her sister Samantha? Most likely not. She would make an excellent hostess, but his mercurial moods and bad temper would be a strain on poor Sam and she would wilt like a hot house flower. A bossy termagant like her friend Sabrina? Sabre wouldn't give a hang about Giddy's disposition, but the two of them would fight like cats and dogs. And the first time he tried to be autocratic with her he might find himself skewered by her namesake sword. Perhaps the wily, artistic George? She would certainly avoid the pitfalls of conflict with Giddy but his volatility would probably make George withdraw altogether.

Honestly it was no wonder he wasn't married yet. He needed a woman strong enough to withstand his temper, and to stand up to him when necessary. She needed to be a good hostess in order to help further his political ambitions and, well, really a countess should always be an incomparable hostess anyway. She needed to bear and raise a future earl. And it would be best if she were a person of character, with interest in doing good works. Thinking through the young women on the marriage mart Jack couldn't think of one who even came close to meeting the criteria she had listed off the top of her head this morning, and surely there would be more requirements of a countess.

For instance, how many estates and holdings did he have? Were any of them in need of refurbishing or having staff replaced? Did he have family that he was most likely ignoring? Those were the sorts of things a wife looked to when an earl didn't have time. She was almost inspired to get up and begin making a list. Perhaps she would do that, create a list of criteria for his countess and begin looking on his behalf. Just because she didn't want to marry him didn't mean someone else wouldn't. It was only appropriate to think of his welfare since she was the one who wanted the engagement ended. Giddy most likely wasn't thinking about these things at all. She perceived he was a bit thick headed in that way. Even in their short acquaintance she could see that. Smart, certainly, but stubborn about things he had already decided. It was evident that if honor hadn't dictated that he offer for her that he wouldn't be thinking about marriage at all right now. According to Debrett's Peerage he was coming on thirty years old and had ascended to his seat years ago. She also had it on good authority that he was an active politician. How could he not see that a wife was an essential ingredient to the life he was leading? This morning she would start to make a list. Certainly she could find a viable candidate before the season ended.

Gideon pulled his horse to a stop at the Walters' front door and waited for his tiger to grab hold of the leads before he sprang down to the ground. The invitation to take Miss Walters riding in his curricle had come out of his mouth before he'd had time to think about it, but it seemed appropriate. That was his favorite word these days, appropriate. It was appropriate to ask her to marry him after pawing her in the library. It was appropriate to court her like a gentleman since they were most likely to be married, regardless of his fiancée's beliefs to the contrary. Appropriate, appropriate, appropriate. He'd never realized before exactly how loathsome the word really was.

He rapped smartly at the door, idly wondering what parlor they would stow him in as the estimable Miss Walters finished her preparations. Would they ply him with cakes? Would Mrs. Walters and the younger Miss Walters entertain him by asking the sly and leading questions all families used when assessing the man their daughter was going to marry? His ruminations were pulled up short by having the elder Miss Walters open the door. "I've got it, Villiers," she called out over her shoulder. She was still tucking stray hairs into her bonnet and veritably bounced out on the portico, pulling the door closed behind her.

"Good morning, Giddy," she said. "Fine day for a drive, don't you think?" She had turned her attention to the buttons on her gloves, leaving Gideon staring down at the top of her straw bonnet covered head. Where was the vitriol?

Where were the bitter recriminations, the catty and sarcastic comments? And why was she still calling him by that detestable nickname? Satisfied with the fit of her gloves she finally looked up at him again, her green eyes sparkling. "Well, are you coming or do I need to drive myself?"

Gideon offered his arm and they walked down the steps together. "Were you caught off guard by my being timely today?"

"Precisely. You're lucky I wasn't still abed drinking chocolate and reading the papers, not expecting you for hours yet."

"Still here you are, turned out to a tune and literally waiting by the door. You had some faith in my reformation."

"Even dogs can learn, I should hope that earls can."

"You have been singularly unimpressed with my title, but this is certainly a first to be compared to a dog."

He lifted her into the curricle and she was looking down at him with her hands still resting on his shoulders as she replied. "And potentially finding you lacking in the comparison had you been late today."

"You vicious minx."

She laughed, a throaty burst of joy that lit her expression and made her eyes twinkle before she settled onto the high bench. She was a strange yet refreshing creature. At turns serious, ferocious, and now light-hearted.

Settling in to take the reins Gideon said, "I thought to take us through Mayfair and around to Gunters for ices."

Miss Walters wrinkled her nose. "How pedestrian a trip for a high flier. I should think we would want to take the road through the park."

Gideon laughed. "Are you hoping to find a young buck who will race us?"

"I've won a race or two in my life, I'll have you know."

"Curricle racing?"

"Yes, though not in town."

"Who on earth gave you permission to race curricles?"

She gave him a droll glance. "That isn't the sort of thing one asks permission for, especially if one is a girl."

"Where did you even get a curricle or horse to race?"

"Sabre's brothers Robert and Charles. Though Robert doesn't let me race anymore."

"I should hope not!"

"Since I beat him at a quarter mile," she added with a self-satisfied smile.

Gideon stared at her for a moment. "I'd best hope we don't need to make a marriage of this, shouldn't I?"

Miss Walters laughed her full throaty laugh again. "Undoubtedly. Only an eccentric spinster can hope to sail through the park in a high flier of her own. What would an earl do with such a wife?"

Gideon shook his head. "What indeed?"

Her expression changed, becoming once more the prim and serious young woman he was used to seeing. "I was wondering, " she said, "how many properties you have?"

Gideon's eyes narrowed and he felt his jaw clench. At last, his wealth was appealing to her regardless of what else she might say. "Quite a few," he said tersely.

"Can't you be more specific? That's rather careless of you. How would you know if a solicitor or steward was siphoning funds off of one of your properties for their own purposes?"

"Be careful where you tread, madam. You border on insulting me."

"Indeed I thought that I outright insulted you. But how else to pry the pearl from the oyster? It rarely yields to sweet whispers."

Glancing at her again he saw that she had an eyebrow raised and the ghost of a smile on her lips. Vexing wench.

"Are you suggesting that I have been withholding of information?"

"You certainly haven't been forthcoming."

"In my defense I don't remember any sweet whispers either."

"*Touché*. But certainly you expect me to be at least curious."

"You want an accounting then? Very well. There are fourteen properties in all. Two townhouses in London, I currently reside in one and lease the other. I also have townhouses in Bath and York. The primary manor attached to the earldom is Kellington Hall in Kent. The remaining properties are in Cornwall,

Staffordshire, Cumberland, Wales, Scotland and Italy."

"You have a property in Italy?"

Gideon looked over to see that the cheeky chit was scribbling it all down in a tiny journal that she must have pulled from her reticule. "Yes, I have an estate in Italy. Would you like an inventory of the furnishings?"

"Do you know that?"

"No, I'm not going to give you a bloody inventory of the furnishings. Why are you writing all this down?"

"I'm working on a project."

"What project could you possibly have that requires an accounting of my properties?"

She gave him a mischievous smile. "Since I must break our engagement I thought to find you a proper wife."

Gideon nearly drove the curricle off the road. "You mean to find me a what?" he asked, his voice rising in surprise and, if he was honest, horror.

"A proper wife. It's actually harder than it looks."

"I don't want a wife!"

Miss Walters clucked her tongue and looked down at her journal. "It's becoming ever clearer that you desperately need one. How much family do you have?"

"What?"

"Family. Sisters, brothers, aunts, uncles, cousins. A mother you might be hiding somewhere."

"My mother has passed on, thank you very much. And I don't have any siblings."

"I should have guessed that."

"You intrusive little beast."

"Yes, you're clearly an only child."

Gideon hauled back on the reins, pulling the conveyance to a sudden and somewhat unpleasant stop. "Let me assure you that you can stop working on this project you've thought to assign to yourself," he hissed, trying to keep their conversation private from the young tiger riding behind the curricle. "If I'm not to marry you, an outcome I assure you that I wish to avoid more with each passing minute, then I am certainly not going to marry some horrid creature from the Marriage Mart no matter how many of them you dream up as possibilities!"

"Well," she said with a resigned sigh. "It's obviously very necessary. You have cousins then?"

Her impassive response to his ire only served to make him more agitated. "Of course I have cousins!"

"Any that you're close to?"

"I have a more than passing acquaintance with one or two. You are the most pigheaded person of my acquaintance."

Her only response to his insult was to raise a brow at him. "You're going to be quite a trial for some poor woman. It will take her two years just to divine whom to invite to Christmas."

"There's no point in inviting anyone for Christmas and I don't want you to find me a wife!"

She patted his arm in a way that was more patronizing than consoling. "You're turning red, Giddy. That can't be good for you."

"Stop calling me Giddy!"

"Did you know that you're easier to rile than a bear? I have my own reasons for calling you Giddy and they have nothing to do with irritating you."

"Fine, then, what are they?"

She smiled, enjoying his irritation. "Perhaps some day I shall tell you."

"If we both live to see that day."

"Perhaps we should move on before we gather too much more notice on this path?"

Gideon took a moment to look around and realized that there were others about during this somewhat fashionable hour. No one had stopped to stare outright that he could see, but surely the earl and his fiancée having what could be politely referred to as a tiff on a public avenue was going to be whispered ear to ear this evening. Taking up the reins again he set the horse off at a smart pace.

Her voice rose over the sound of the wheels to ask, "And then that would be which cousins you are on speaking terms with?"

For the next quarter hour Miss Walters pestered him with more questions than any journalist he had ever come across during his time in politics. She wanted to know about his family, his duties in Parliament, the status of his various homes. To his relief she tucked away her journal when they finally arrived at the park and he was now willing to race anyone if it would make her to hold her tongue. She was an intrusive, irritating busybody and he hoped that she would tire of this supposed project. The only thing worse than marrying Miss Walters herself would be to cope with the endless procession of candidates she was likely to parade in front of him. He would reject them all outright. He didn't want to marry. He wouldn't marry unless he had to. He would grant Miss Walters she was innocent in this whole debacle. While he had been planning a rendezvous with the luscious Lady Spencer, she had been planning to read Thucydides... in the original Greek. She didn't want to marry any more than he did. Perhaps that would be the way to stop her infernal project. Perhaps he should suggest that he find the perfect husband for her! Although who that perfect husband would be he couldn't begin to fathom. Someone with a good deal of patience, he would wager. Enough to weather her stubborn streak and her busybody tendencies. And someone kind. He couldn't say why, but as he studied her profile he thought she would bloom under the influence of a kind man. In fact someone like Quincy Telford, Duke of Beloin. The idea had merit, really. She could make a splendid duchess, if a bit lowborn for the role. Quince had his faults but he was infinitely kind and patient. Perhaps he wouldn't tell her that he knew the perfect man for her but would just get them together and let nature take its course. Now that he had a mission of his own it was much easier to ignore how irritating her little project was going to be until she let the idea go.

CHAPTER SIX

Although he didn't race at quite the speeds she had hoped for, the outing had been a refreshing change to her usual London entertainments. Jack braced her hands on Harrington's shoulders again as he hoisted her out of the curricle. His hands at her waist were warm and firm, even through his gloves and her layers of muslin. She thought that his fingers lingered a bit longer on her ribcage than was absolutely necessary and, come to think of it, she still had her hands resting lightly on his arms. The moment seemed to stretch between them, his dark blue eyes gazing down unblinking into her own. Finally he seemed to come back to himself, clearing his throat and stepping back. He bowed over her hand. "Miss Walters."

"Jacqueline," she replied. "Or Jack if you prefer."

He raised an eyebrow. "Since you say this isn't-"

"A real engagement, I know. But I think we could be friendly at least. And others will expect us to indicate some level of... intimacy."

His hand tightened very briefly on her own, then he released her and stepped back. "Then until we meet again, Jacqueline."

Jack found herself unreasonably disappointed that he chose to use the more formal version of her name even though it made sense that he would do so. She nodded. "The Yancey ball then?"

"Indeed. I shall see you on Friday."

Jack made her way slowly up the steps to her front door, her energy substantially less than it had been before the carriage ride. Once inside, she watched Harrington set off down the street in his curricle. She wasn't sure quite what made her feel dispirited but decided to divert herself with the project of finding him a wife. She pulled the small journal from her reticule and drifted upstairs, flipping through the pages.

Gideon had been brusque and churlish for the last two days, although he wasn't sure why. He was fairly certain that if he didn't finish dressing soon that his valet would bolt in fear and the man was normally unflappable. He had half-expected Quince to put in an appearance again, but perhaps the duke felt Gideon had finally got on with things and didn't require any more nudging. Hopefully he could count on the duke to make an appearance at tonight's ball, however, so that he could put Miss Walters in his path. That was most likely why he had been surly the last two days, impatience on getting the two of them together. The sooner Quince realized Miss Walters was a perfect duchess for him the sooner that Gideon could slip off the marriage noose himself.

It was too bad, really, that he couldn't involve Miss Walters in his scheme to marry her off as she was the type to throw herself into projects with enthusiasm. Honestly, he wasn't sure that anyone else knew as much about him as she now did. He frowned into the mirror and watched his valet uneasily shift back a few steps. Gideon sighed. Had his black moods really been so dire? Black moods had certainly been plaguing him much more often since the beginning of the Walters problem. Not one to torment his employees he schooled his expression into a more benign mask before he turned his mind back to what was bothering him. Certainly he must have someone close to him who knew him as well or better? But he couldn't think of anyone. His servants were probably the closest, having known him from the crib. Some were an encyclopedia of his family relations and knew more about his family than he did himself. His school chums, like Quince, didn't know much about his family and perhaps even less about his properties, other than the ones he used for entertaining. Upon reflection he found it oddly disturbing that his nearest and dearest began and ended with family retainers. One overly inquisitive accidental fiancée was making him think about things he hadn't before, and was fairly certain he'd never wanted to. With one final look at his cravat and a nod to his beleaguered valet, he set off for the

Yancey ball. On time, of course. He was quite done with having to apologize to Miss Walters.

He was here already. Jack wasn't quite sure how she knew as she entered the large townhouse and queued up for the receiving line, but she could feel it like an electric current below her skin. He was here but she couldn't see him yet with her limited view of the ballroom. The front hall was crowded and hot, a welcome change from the frosty night outside. She fanned herself and surreptitiously looked around, both to take in her surroundings and to search for the earl.

The Yancey townhouse was quite grand, easily ten times the size of the Walters' more modest townhome, and had been recently redone in the Egyptian style. Jack thought that all the black lacquer and gold must get tiresome after a time. She was partial to the classic, settled look of their own home. Some of their rugs were threadbare in places but each one had family history, starting with the ancestor who had brought it back personally from Turkey or India. She sincerely doubted that *these* pieces had been brought back from the desert by one of the Yanceys. After making her curtseys to Lord and Lady Yancey she was free to venture onto the ballroom floor. She still hadn't seen Harrington but nearly walked into his friend, the duke, in her distraction.

"Good evening, Miss Walters," he said, bowing over her hand.

She blushed and curtsied. "My apologies, your grace."

"Were you perhaps looking for someone?"

"I was... that is..."

He smiled at her flustered response. "Am I early enough to hope to have a dance with you?"

Jack nearly strangled herself in the effort it took to not laugh in his face. She lifted her wrist to offer her completely blank dance card.

"I have intercepted you upon arrival, I see. Perhaps the second waltz?"

"I would be beyond pleased, your grace."

The duke managed a self-deprecating smile as he scribbled his name on her dance card. "Don't be too pleased. I've chosen a waltz since I think the two of us should talk."

"Oh... I..."

"And here is the man of the hour now. How are you, Giddy?"

The earl bowed to the duke, then over Jack's hand. "I'm passable Quince. I see you have already asked our lovely Miss Walters for a dance."

"Indeed. I predict you should claim yours before she is overtaken by dance partners."

Jack couldn't help the amused smile. "Yes, I can see they will be shoving you out of the way soon."

Harrington took up the pencil and dance card. "The second waltz Quince?"

"Yes, I thought the lady would want to save the first one for you."

"Yes," he said, meeting Jack's eyes for the first time. "She usually does that."

Jack felt herself blushing again. She wasn't used to being fussed over like a tasty treat lain out between two dogs. They weren't fighting over her precisely, but they were circling and more interested than she was used to. She didn't think that the duke was interested in her per se, but more likely investigating what she meant for Harrington. As for the earl, she felt he constantly sent out mixed signals. Denying any interest in marriage, especially with nagging bluestockings, then giving her looks that reminded her of his hands moving over her. Perhaps he was just a thoroughgoing rogue and couldn't help himself from looking at any woman as though she were a flavored ice on a hot summer day. She longed for a library and some Greek or Latin texts to interpret. Something quiet and sane and removed from this world of emotions and unknown motivations.

A new voice interrupted her thoughts. "Miss Walters, if I could beg you for the pleasure of a dance?" She found herself looking at a major, resplendent in his regimentals. He had sandy hair and warm brown eyes.

"Of course," she heard herself responding.

After sending her and Harrington a self-satisfied smile, the duke strolled off towards the card room. Shortly thereafter Jack *did* find herself deluged with men requesting a dance. Harrington stayed nearby, looking grimmer and grimmer as her throng of suitors increased. She lost count of how many glasses of wine he had taken from passing footmen and wondered how he still looked sober as a preacher. The orchestra was beginning the song for the first dance and her partner, the major, appeared to lead her out on the dance floor for a country reel. Looking back she could see that Gideon had an oddly flat and sullen expression but she soon lost sight of him in the swirl of dancers.

Gideon had a mind to find Quince and tell him to go to hell. At first delighted to see that the duke had, of his own volition, shown some attention to Miss Walters, that delight turned sour as he realized Quince had known that his own attention to the girl would guarantee her a list of suitors for the evening. Gideon didn't want just anyone stealing Miss Walters from him. It needed to be someone who deserved her and would treat her as she deserved to be treated. And by that he meant kindly and with consideration, not with the abuse he sometimes thought of heaping on her for her stubborn ways. He didn't have time to vet every baron, military man, and younger son that was dangling over her hand this evening. What if this continued? What if some sot with a pretty face and smooth manners swayed her on a night when he wasn't in attendance? What then? That was just the sort of man that couldn't be trusted. Someone too smooth on the surface, while beneath they were a roiling mass of entitlement and rage. He didn't like the idea of having to face down some idiot to save Miss Walters from herself. Even if she weren't his fiancée he could hardly let her be taken in by a man like that, and he knew much better than she how common those men were in Society.

He stared down into his glass and wondered how many of them he had polished off while waiting for the first waltz to begin. His stomach had soured from the wine and the errant path of his thoughts. It wasn't unreasonable, he didn't think, to want Miss Walters to at least make a practical choice in husband. If she didn't think she wanted to be married at all, then certainly it shouldn't be too hard to keep her away from the reprobates that would sniff around her skirts. He heard the final strains of the dance immediately preceding the waltz and struck out across the ballroom to claim her hand from the obnoxious fop who was still bowing over it.

CHAPTER SEVEN

When Harrington arrived to claim the first waltz Jack was fairly certain she heard him growl at the man who had just led her through an English country-dance. She raised a brow but he merely swept her up into the steps of the waltz as soon as the music started.

"Yes my evening has been splendid, thank you for asking," Jack said tartly.

Harrington looked down at her, furrowing his brow. "What?"

"You're being beastly but I will ignore it for now and pretend that you are the picture of grace."

"Count on you to call me beastly when I haven't said anything yet."

"Your face speaks volumes."

"Why should I enjoy having my fiancée spinning around the floor with every Tom, Dick and Harry of London?"

"I wondered how much wine you drank and I see the answer is quite a bit."

"That doesn't negate the fact that you've been hanging on the arms of a good number of men this evening. Some of dubious character, no doubt."

"You mean like now?"

"Don't try to distract me with your wicked tongue."

"I wouldn't dream of it. I'm sure you realize, of course, that you could have reserved at least a second dance for yourself without causing gossip."

Gideon's expression remained implacably dark and he didn't even recognize her suggestion with a response.

Jack tried a different tack. "Did you hear talk of a dry summer this year?"

"Why are you changing the subject?"

"You weren't going to and the last thing we need to do is end up screaming at each other in the middle of the dance floor."

"At least then you would get to break the engagement like you've been dreaming of since this whole thing started."

Jack frowned. "Is that what you're trying to do? I'd prefer we not make our differences public."

"No, you would rather make your preference for other men public. Although considering the circumstances in which we met I don't see why I should be surprised."

Jack planted her feet and managed to pull Harrington off his balance, causing him to stumble into her.

"That is outside of enough!" she hissed at close quarters to him. *"My* circumstances only included a desire to read rare Greek texts and you well know it."

"You hardly seemed shocked by my attentions."

Jack gasped and looked up at him in outrage. "How dare you! Shocked is exactly what I was." She looked around to see that they had garnered the attention of a good number of the dancers. She grabbed Harrington's arm and dragged him toward the French doors that let out onto the veranda. Once outside she pushed him into the shadows and drilled a finger into his chest. "What exactly is this about?"

"You say you were shocked. You say a lot of things. But your body says something else. And I'm more likely to suspect your words to be lies."

"You are the most outrageous-"

Jack's retort was cut short by Harrington taking her lips in a swift kiss. She started to pull away but he wrapped one arm around her back, his other hand cupping her face as he deepened the kiss. He licked and nibbled the seam of her lips until she surrendered and let him plunder her mouth. She had never felt this before, as though she was floating, all of her nerves tingling in sudden awareness. The sensations were new, novel, wicked. The warm, solid strength of him pressed against her. The band of his arm across her back. The swirl of his tongue in her mouth. The gentle strength of his hand holding her head while his thumb stroked her jaw. As she melted into his embrace he turned and now she was the one hidden in the shadows with her back pressed against the cool stone of the townhouse wall. His mouth moved down to kiss the side of her throat, her ear. His hand caressed one breast, finding and teasing the nipple that had peaked.

"See?" he whispered to her. "Your body welcomes my attentions. I imagine that with very little effort I could have you out of that dress and begging me for more. Why should I trust a woman who can be seduced by a man she doesn't even like?"

With that he pulled away from her and strode back towards the party.

Jack could feel her heart beat with the thunder of a galloping horse, her skin hot from a combination of embarrassment and rage. How dare he? How *dare* he? The man was worse than the devil. She wouldn't marry him if he served himself up on a silver platter. Regardless of how her body betrayed her when he was near, she couldn't imagine a worse man to marry. He was completely without morals or common human decency!

Then she remembered that he had salvaged her reputation with a sham engagement announcement in the library without hesitation. And how oddly vulnerable he had seemed the first time they had danced. How they had stood staring at one another after the curricle ride. She touched her swollen lips and sighed sadly. Hopefully this would all be over soon.

Gideon made his way to the card room, pushing dandies and nabobs out of his way.

Gods, he'd nearly ravished the girl on a public portico. He didn't know what demon had possessed him. It was as though he had been spoiling for a fight with her just to show her how her body would react to him. And Lord, how it reacted. It was like touching a match to gun powder the way she came alive in his arms! No prim bluestocking then but a goddess, all curves and heat and passion. He didn't know why but it made him angry. Because he didn't want her? Because he couldn't have her? Because she shouldn't be able to create a similar reaction in *him?* There would be hell to pay if she ever realized that she could so easily distract him, sway him, with the promise of her attentions. Serious and uncompromising as she was, she would have him begging to kiss her beautifully turned ankle. If she were his mistress she could deplete his accounts in a trice. And if that wasn't the most disturbing thought he'd ever had he didn't know what was.

He joined Lord Whitby as a partner in whist, proving that he was completely distracted because the opposing team featured no other than Lady Spencer. Damn and double damn. To hell with Parliament, he was going out to Cornwall no later than Monday next. It was as though he couldn't turn about in London without stumbling over some aspect of this debacle of an engagement.

"Good evening, Lord Harrington," Lady Spencer greeted with her usual dimpled smile. "I hear congratulations are in order."

"Indeed," he said shortly. "My thanks for your interest."

"Plum girl," said Lord Hartly, Lady Spencer's partner. "Good blood, that Walters. Too bad they didn't marry back into nobility until now."

"Yes," Gideon said drily. "Tragic."

"Oh, don't be such a stuffed shirt, Lord Harrington," Lady Spencer chided. "Certainly just the thought of marriage hasn't dulled your sense of fun."

"Of course not," he said warily, trying not to send any signals that he was inviting the widow to plan a tryst with him again. The last thing he needed was to offend the Walters before he had a chance to make that escape to Cornwall. Much to his chagrin Hartly and Whitby chose that moment to retrieve refreshments, leaving him alone with the beautiful widow.

"Have you set a date?" Lady Spencer inquired.

"Not as of yet."

"Will it be this Season?"

"We feel no reason to rush."

"Nonsense, I have heard all about town that your whirlwind romance is the stuff of Spring fairy tales. Certainly something like that can't be delayed for another year."

Gideon eyed Lady Spencer, wondering how many games she had afoot other than whist tonight. Finally he said, "It will be as my practical, sensible fiancée wishes it. She has not expressed an interest in marrying this season."

"You'd best be careful, Lord Harrington. I've heard it said that she ran off all her other suitors.

If you leave her to her own devices you may lose your beloved fiancée."

"And what would I lose her to, exactly?"

"Fate."

"If she doesn't want to marry that wouldn't be my fault."

Lady Spencer looked at him a bit sadly. "Wouldn't it, though?"

Jack danced almost every dance that night. She danced until her feet hurt and then she danced until she couldn't feel them at all anymore. She suffered all the banal chitchat, the hollow compliments, and the senseless gossip that came with dancing in the *bon ton.* There was only one conversation she would remember from the evening other than the one she had with Harrington and that was from her second waltz, her dance with the duke.

The Duke of Beloin had bowed low to her and taken her hand to sweep her elegantly out onto the dance floor. Once he had secured their spot in the twirling dancers he had smiled at her and asked, "Are you enjoying yourself?"

They were of a height, he only an inch or two taller, and Jack looked almost directly into his eyes if she didn't lower her gaze to his cravat or shoulder. "Of course, your grace."

"You lie abysmally, Miss Walters. As the wife of a politician you will want to work on that."

Jack smiled ruefully and bit her bottom lip.

"As a start," he continued, "you must be enthused about all social occasions. You must love people, even people that you find annoying. And you must never, ever let anyone see how you and Giddy argue."

Jack tried to pull back but she discovered that although of a similar height and build the duke was by far superior in strength. "No," he said. "You won't be stopping this waltz. Unlike Giddy I'm not so easily distracted by you."

"Distracted?"

"Yes, most definitely. Had I known of your powers I would have thrown you in his path four years ago rather than have him focused on Parliament."

"Four years ago I was only fourteen."

His gaze swept over her. "I doubt it would have mattered. Unrequited love could have proven even more distracting."

She distanced herself as much as she was able from him. "I thought you were Harrington's friend."

"I *am* Harrington's friend. Friendship and politics are two different beasts. If that weren't true, Giddy and I would have had it out over pistols one morning long ago."

"I'm not sure what you're trying to tell me, your grace."

Beloin sighed. "Quince, if you please. I am trying to tell you to stop fighting with Gideon. At least publicly. Your engagement couldn't bear much scrutiny, I would think. And when I originally asked you to dance it was to tell you one simple thing."

"What is that, your grace? I mean… Quince."

The duke gave her a remarkably boyish smile when she used his nickname. "I think you will make Giddy a splendid wife."

"Once I learn to lie," she said solemnly.

After a moment of surprise the duke threw his head back in a loud guffaw. She had never seen the debonair aristocrat do such a thing and she giggled nervously. "Yes," he finally agreed. "Once you learn to lie."

CHAPTER EIGHT

When Jack awoke early in the morning it was to a front hallway full of flowers. Flowers thanking her for a dance, flowers with poems attached, and flowers with notes begging for a carriage ride or trip to the theater. And then two special arrangements. One small arrangement of Cantebury Bells from the Duke of Beloin with the note "*Thank you for the laughter - Q.*" And a very large arrangement of yellow roses from Harrington. A letter was attached, which Jack took to the front window in order to catch the early morning light for reading.

"Dear Jacqueline, It seems that I am always doing something that requires apology and last night was no exception - which occurred to me only after all those glasses of wine wore off. The florist assures me that a yellow rose represents an apology so with this bouquet I hope to apologize for every transgression thus far and perhaps have a bit of payment towards the future.
- Gideon."

Jack was holding the letter to her chest and staring out the window wistfully when she heard her mother scream in the dining room. Knowing it could be anything from a mouse to a pirate, because her mother would have the exact same reaction to either threat, Jack ran to the room. She found her mother sitting at the table, newspaper clutched in hand and tears streaming down her face. Her father was trying to pull the paper from his wife's grasp while consoling her, a bit at sea about what was so upsetting. Seeing Jack, Mrs. Walters thrust the paper towards her. It was open to the society pages.

Jack turned the paper towards the light.

"It has come to this reporter's attention that Miss W and Lord H were on the outs last night. This can hardly be a surprise since I have it from a Very Good Source that the 'fairy tale romance' is exactly that - a fairy tale. According to the VGS Miss W and Lord H were found in an illicit embrace in Lord W's library less than a fortnight ago. Miss W may be smart, but not smart enough to remember that you should stay out of the kitchen, or rather library, if you don't want to get burned."

Jack threw the paper down on the table. "I'm going to kill him."

Mr. Walters jumped up out of his chair. "Jacqueline, what is it?"

"I'm going to kill him," she said once more before running from the room towards the stables.

Gideon had already started on his second cup of tea. Wine usually didn't give him this much of a headache but then again, he usually didn't try to drink a whole vinyard's worth in a single night. He had risen early and had a productive morning, however. Going through his correspondence he had a letter from his steward at Kellington reassuring him that the rumors in Parliament about smuggling along the shores of Kent were not on his lands. Now Dibbs was packing for Cornwall because Gideon had decided there was no time like the present to escape London. And three footmen had been dispatched on early morning errands, including the delivery of flowers and a letter to Miss Walters. That had been a difficult letter to write since he didn't like apologizing in general, but nearly mauling an innocent, especially while in such a temper, was far beyond the pale. Honestly he should just be glad that he wasn't spending the morning on the dueling fields, or already married this morning. Soon he could leave for Cornwall to inspect his new investment and this mess would stay behind in London. Miss Walters could do what she wanted to maintain the story of their engagement, their Spring fairy tale as Lady Spencer had called it. Or not. He wouldn't counter her, but he certainly wouldn't be adding to the story himself either.

That was when he heard the crash in the front hall.

"Tell me where he is *now* or by God I will tear down every brick of this house until I find him!"

Gideon closed his eyes briefly. If this was a fairy tale then the troll had just arrived in the guise of his very enraged fiancée. Either the wrong letter had been delivered to her or she sincerely did *not* like yellow roses.

He arose from the breakfast table and she was in the doorway before him. She was breathing hard, her hair pulled from its pins in loose wisps around her face, her dress rumpled. She looked like she had just ridden pell-mell across the city to his door. Or, gods help him, like she had just been tumbled. Her cheeks were flushed and those magnificent breasts strained against the fabric of her morning dress from her gasping breaths. It wasn't just the wine after all. He desperately wanted to press her against the wall and start back where they had left off last night.

"You!" she said viciously. He realized she was pointing a riding crop at him and backed up a bit.

"Yes, me. Can I hope you haven't abused my staff terribly?"

"How dare you," she said, advancing on him. Retreat seemed the best option until he knew what she was about.

"Care about my staff? Yes, it is daring."

"Why couldn't you just leave well enough alone? Why did you have to do this? Roses? You sent roses as a salve? There is *nothing* that you can ever do to apologize for this!"

She was glorious in her fury but Gideon was at a loss to understand its source. "Perhaps you'd best tell me what it is you think I've done."

"You've ruined me, you bastard!" With that she sprang to attack, landing one solid blow to his shoulder before moving close enough that he could trap her wrists and try to contain her. After a bit more struggle, wherein she managed to land some less significant blows, she finally dropped the riding crop and began to weep. Giant, heart-rending sobs that sounded like her entire world had been destroyed.

Gideon pulled her to his chest, cradling her in his arms while she cried. He rested his cheek on the top of her head and just held on to her. They were still in that embrace when Mr. Walters came into the room, tight lipped and silent. Gideon raised his brows in question to the older man and Mr. Walters handed him the paper.

Gideon stared, the words refusing to make sense at first. Once they did he nodded dumbly to the girl's father. The story was out and their options were narrowed to one. He had expected to feel enraged if trapped like this but he only felt numb. The inside of his chest felt cold and brittle, like the top of a pond in winter. Even breathing hurt.

"I'll go get the special license," Mr. Walters said. Gideon nodded again.

Walters began gently prying his daughter away. "You need to come with me, Jackie."

"Papa, I'm sorry. I'm so sorry."

"Don't worry about that right now. Let's get you home. Harrington, do you have a carriage we can borrow?"

"Of course," Gideon managed to say.

With that the Walters withdrew far more quietly than Miss Walters had arrived. Gideon found that his arms seemed oddly empty without the warmth of Miss Walters in them. He frowned. He had never wanted to marry. Didn't want to marry. Not Miss Walters, not any woman. Women were difficult, sly, and vindictive in his experience. Manipulative. Downright evil by his estimation. Unless he missed his guess Lady Spencer as an excellent example of the species and had provided that tidbit to the newspaper. To what end he had no idea. But that was a common failing for him, not understanding the subtle manipulations of the feminine mind. He couldn't count the number of times he had failed to anticipate his mother's plots.

He rubbed his bruised shoulder. As difficult as Miss Walters might be she perhaps wasn't exactly sly. In fact she might be more direct than most men of his acquaintance. But no matter her temperament, there was to be a marriage.

"Dibbs!"

"Yes, my Lord."

"I'm not going to Cornwall."

"No, my Lord."

CHAPTER NINE

Jack spent the carriage ride home staring listlessly out the window at the passing town homes. Although still in a fashionable district, the Walters lived fairly distant from the grand London address where the earl resided. When she and Sam had toured Mayfair to gawk at the homes of aristocrats last summer, she had never guessed that she might use the knowledge of where the Earl of Harrington lived in just such a way. She had been furious this morning and had wrested Tyche's reins from the groom before he'd had a chance to saddle the creature, then rode barebacked across town like the hellion she was out in the country and had been careful to hide while in town. How could he do this to her? She felt the fat tears start to roll down her cheeks again, helpless to stop them.

If he wasn't the one to give the story to the paper, then why would the Wynders or Lady Spencer do so after all this time? Seven days had passed. It didn't make any sense. Besides, even if he wasn't the one to talk to that spiteful gossip at the newspaper, all the trouble had started with him.

And with her, she admitted to herself with a gusty sigh that fogged the carriage window. She always went her own way. She just *had* to sneak into Lord Wynder's library to read some of his Greek texts and now her family would suffer for it. She knew they couldn't leave London to escape the censure since father had leased out the country house to help pay for both her and Sam's seasons. It wasn't something that was talked about, but Jack knew. She knew they were living close to the fine, every inch the impoverished genteel. She knew that both her and Sam's dowry's had been gifts held in trust from Grandfather, their mother's father, and it had been the shiny hook that was hoped to raise the girls above their current station in life.

Now Jack had compromised everything, and her lone possible path was marrying the earl. Immediately. Even then there would be talk and speculation. Sam's prospects would be slim until the vicious gossip blew over, provided that it did. Her mother, never quite accepted for her bourgeois background, would be entirely snubbed. Her father was the sole one who could hope to continue his life without significant change, but she knew that wasn't his way. He would worry about them all and stay close to home, because if they weren't accepted in society then he would have no interest in engaging in it himself.

She looked across the carriage at her dear father, tight-lipped, pale, with arms crossed and a rigid posture. He also studied the passing town homes as though they were vastly interesting.

Feeling her gaze he glanced over to her. Her damp cheeks and woebegone expression pulled him from his own thoughts and he offered her a wan smile.

"I thought you were going to kill him and save me all this trouble."

Jack gave a watery laugh that turned into a sob. "Oh papa. I'm so sorry."

With a sad sigh he opened his arms to her. "Come here, pumpkin."

She went into his arms like the child she had once been, who had needed comfort after a skinned knee or broken teacup. He smelled like pipe tobacco and bay rum. He smelled like Papa, like home. A place she knew she wouldn't be much longer. No more tears, she promised herself. No more tears over things that couldn't be changed.

Gideon sat at his writing desk and stared at his quill absently. He knew he ought to finish this letter. His future father-in-law would return presently, but that didn't seem to motivate any action. After reading the gossip column he'd been a bit surprised, really, that Walters hadn't finally called him out over this stain to his daughter's reputation. But he supposed that a dead earl couldn't marry anyone and right now the best way to reduce the damage was a quick marriage followed by a retreat to the country in order to ride out the storm of censure sure to follow. Not to Cornwall, though, but to his seat in Kent. His business in Cornwall would have to wait until after this fiasco was appropriately handled. Though it was hard to imagine a time when Jacqueline Walters wouldn't be causing him trouble. She was headstrong, smart, independent, and volatile. Honestly if he had written a list of the characteristics that he didn't want in a wife, those attributes would have all been on it. Nor did she want him, another item that would have made the list now that he thought of it. No, if he had to have a wife at all he would want a gentle creature. Compliant. Sweet and lovely. Not that he believed such a creature existed.

He sighed. Perhaps she would be content if he gifted her with one of his smaller estates where she could live as she pleased. Perhaps he had something near where her parents lived. If he didn't, then perhaps he could acquire something. Hearing voices in the hall, most likely Walters returning, finally spurred him to dash a few lines on the parchment in front of him.

"Quince - After this morning's society page I must say the good news is that I am not calling on you to be my second. The bad news is that I must prevail upon you for something else. Could you be the best man at my wedding in the morning? Sorry for the short notice, old man, but I'm sure you can find something to wear.
- G"

He could only hope that Quince would grant an old friend the advantage of what amounted to a ducal blessing of the wedding. It would take much more than that to counteract the damage of this morning's society article, but it would be a start.

Jack packed her trunks with a numb, automated efficiency. Sam and mother tried to help but mostly they fluttered at the edges of the room and behaved as though they were afraid of upsetting her further. Since the family had leased out the country house this year, most of her valued possessions were here in London. Some of them were packed up at Sabre's house and she supposed she should send for them. She wondered where they would live. Or at least where she would live. She had no illusions that Harrington would want to keep her at his side in all things. She would most likely be sent to rusticate while he came back to London to perform his duties in Parliament. Perhaps she shouldn't complain. Being free to ride when she wanted, read when she wanted, and generally keep to herself were among the things she liked best. Whatever manor house he took her to was likely to be grander than the small estate where she had grown up, perhaps even grander than the Biddlesworth's.

As a child, she had thought of Sabre's house as being the most amazing castle but had since learned that larger, better-appointed homes were spread throughout England. Undoubtedly a good number of the earl's fourteen estates featured just such houses. And now she was to be their mistress. A sobering thought, that.

She didn't care much for decorating, managing staff, or entertaining. She would make a horrible countess and be miserable doing it. She briefly wondered if running off to Scotland or throwing herself in the Thames might not more easily solve everyone's problems. But no. She was, if nothing else, a Haberdasher. That meant that, as their pledge went, she could not "run from a fight, back down from a foe, ignore someone in plight, or bring another Haberdasher woe." She smiled, remembering the old rhyme that Sabre had coined as their pledge of duties. She wondered if her hasty marriage would bring woe to her beloved friends. She hadn't received letters back from either of them yet, but it was no surprise, what with George being up in the wilds of Scotland and Sabre touring Italy. But she missed them desperately, so desperately, and wished that they could be here.

The flowers had been brought up from the front hall and decorated her room. She very carefully pressed the duke's Canterbury Bells between clean sheets of parchment and tucked them into one of her larger books. She gave the yellow roses to her sister. One bright yellow petal had fallen to the floor. After a moment's hesitation she picked it up and pressed that in one of her books as well. Looking around she saw that in less than four hours every essential bit of her had been packed into three trunks. All that remained out was the dress that she planned to wear tomorrow. It was going on less than two o'clock and she had nothing useful left to do. As her mother took her downstairs for an early tea she was sure that the afternoon would be interminable. But it was better than having the morning come too quickly.

Her father was waiting in the front parlor when they arrived, looking solemn but not as pale and tense as he had that morning. "All is prepared then?" he asked.

Jack nodded, keeping her eyes downcast.

"After I procured the license the earl arranged for the service to be at St. Mary's first thing in the morning. He will send a carriage around for your trunks to be loaded before the ceremony. After the wedding you will be repairing to Kent."

Jack nodded again, feeling even more desolate. Kent, south of London. She had grown up in Derbyshire, which was leagues away. She had never been to Kent. Had never been south of London.

The tea service was brought in and the family talk turned to inconsequential things. Jack sat with her teacup and cake, feeling as though she were already separated from them. She wasn't listening to the conversation but finally cleared her throat and looked at her little sister Samantha.

"Would you... would you do me the kindness of attending me in the morning as my maid of honor?"

Sam's large blue eyes welled with unshed tears and she gripped Jack's hand tightly. "Of course I will, Jackie. Of course."

Later that evening the family sat at dinner, their last dinner together as a family, Jack couldn't help but think morosely, as a footman came to her father with a message. He raised his eyebrows at the note, and then looked over at her.

"Jacqueline, there is a package and letter for you from the earl." He turned to the footman. "Have them brought in here."

"And ask the lady to wait in the hall, sir?" the footman replied.

"Yes, tell her it will only be a moment."

Jack felt curiosity drawing her from her lassitude, and no small amount of irritation. Why did the earl have to intrude on their last evening together as a family? She supposed she had best get used to it. Harrington was domineering, temperamental, intractable, and rude. He personified the worst qualities she could think of in a man, proving in their very first encounter to be a rogue and a rake. At the moment she couldn't recall why she had ever found herself starting to soften toward him at all. The footman returned with a large box and a letter, setting them both near her on the large dining table. She decided to read the letter first, to keep whatever was in the box from being too rude of a surprise.

"Jacqueline - Every bride should have something new and beautiful to wear on her wedding. Your father was kind enough to tell me the name of your modiste and although her selection of ready-made gowns was sparse I am

*hopeful that this one will be to your liking.
Madame Lacress said the fit would be fair, but I
have sent a seamstress for any last minute
alterations.*

- G"

Jack set the letter aside and began prying
open the box. It was large and heavy enough
that she stood up to better pull off the top. There
was a cloud of white tissue paper to be pawed
through but at last she was able to get to the
dress. Forest green velvet trimmed with olive
green water-shot silk. She raised the bodice up
and heard Sam gasp.

"Oh Jackie," her sister crooned. "It is *just* the
color of your eyes."

Her mother came closer. "And it is the stare
of fashion, my love."

She looked over at her father. "You know the
name of our *modiste*?"

He smiled wryly. "I pay the bills, don't I?"

Jack looked at the gown again. It was
remarkable. And probably cost more than the
rest of her wardrobe combined. This was what it
meant to be an earl. To be able to carelessly
distribute kindnesses because the expense was
inconsequential and others were available to do
whatever was required.

Her mother began settling the dress back into
the box. "Let's go upstairs and try this on."

"I don't want to wear it," Jack said quietly.

Her mother looked aghast. "What?"

"I don't want to wear it. I'll have to wear what
he requires me to soon enough." Even Jack

could tell that her chin had set in that mulish expression that drove her mother to distraction.

Before his wife could begin to get upset Mr. Walters spoke very calmly from his place at the head of the table. "Do you remember when you were eight years old?"

Jack narrowed her eyes at her father. He wouldn't dare.

"I remember clearly," he continued. "You were eight years old and absolutely dying to pony race with Sabrina. When I explained that it wasn't safe you got that same expression on your face that you have now. Do you remember what I said?"

Jack continued to stare at him.

"I said that if I let you race ponies with Sabrina that you had to promise me something. You had to promise me that you would allow me three times that I could give you an order that you would obey without question. I've only had to redeem that promise once before, do you remember? That summer when you were twelve and your mother and I were both away to see Grandmother. You weren't to swim in the lake while we were away. That had to be a hard thing for a young active girl such as yourself, but you stuck by your word then and I've always been proud of you for it."

Jack looked down at her hands, indeed remembering the summer. She had spent an entire hot month avoiding the lake. She had been deviled by temptation but remained stolid and the pride of it had made her strong.

"Wear the dress, Jacqueline," her father said. "It's a little thing to do."

Jack nodded quietly and, picking up the box, led her mother and sister upstairs for the fitting.

CHAPTER TEN

The clock was chiming nine when Gideon heard footsteps in the hall. He was still in his office, sorting papers and deciding what to take with him and what to leave with his man of business in town. A new steward in London was what he needed. The last man had made more mess than anything, which was why Gideon now preferred to do it himself, but he had to admit that having one would be far preferable to the state of his papers at this juncture. A steward, and perhaps a clerk for his Parliamentary papers. Those were at least half of what was on his desk, the rest being reports from his various properties and financial holdings. It was tempting to just leave it all here and see what if anything was truly necessary once he reached Kent. The footsteps came closer.

"His grace," Dibbs announced.

Quince strolled in, looking freshly turned out as always, and came up to place a bottle of brandy on the middle of the papers on Gideon's desk. "I've been saving this for a special occasion, Giddy. As your best man I take it as my solemn duty to get you absolutely smashed tonight so that even if you have cold feet you won't have the ability to find the door and try to run."

Gideon raised one eyebrow.

"Don't give me that look. I've seen you run from far less scary things than marriage."

Gideon continued sorting papers around the brandy bottle. "Marriage doesn't scare me, Quince."

The duke dropped into the chair angled in front of Gideon's desk. "You're right, you don't sound scared. You sound dead inside."

"No need for the dramatic. We're getting married in the morning. It's not the end of the world."

"It's the end of life as you know it. No more running around with loose women, staying out late in dens of drunken debauchery. Because doing those things would make you... what is the word I'm looking for?"

"Don't do this, Quince. This isn't about politics."

"Oh yes, that's right, that would make you a hypocrite. And no, this isn't about politics at all. Certainly Miss Walters is delighted to know that she is marrying a pillar of the community, a husband who will never stray nor engage in unseemly behavior."

"That's enough, Quince."

"I don't see why you're getting upset, Giddy. I'm complimenting you on your value system. Or at least how that value system will play out for that charming girl you're marrying tomorrow."

Gideon narrowed his eyes at his friend. It was easy to write off Quincy Telford as a dandy and a snob if you didn't know better. But Gideon did know better and he could see the truth in Quince's eyes. Jacqueline had somehow enlisted another defender that would likely call him to account if he so much as offended her delicate sensibilities. Fabulous. Perhaps he would have that drink after all. He rose to retrieve two glasses from the sideboard and poured generous servings for each of them.

"To your health and happiness," Quince toasted him.

"It's too bad this turned out like it has," Gideon said. "Because I thought you'd like to marry her."

The duke had unfortunately been mid-swallow as Gideon said that, the consequence of which was brandy sprayed on both the desk and Gideon himself, followed up by two minutes of coughing. "Good Lord, man," the duke finally managed, his voice rough, "what made you think that?"

"I thought you would be a good match and you seem to like her."

"Of course I like her. She's likeable." That comment received a snort from Gideon but Quince continued. "I especially like her as a wife for you. Trust me, I do not fancy her as a wife for myself."

Gideon looked down into his glass. "Neither do I, but," he shrugged, "that's how it's working out."

Quince retrieved the bottle. "We obviously need more brandy."

"Indeed."

The carriage had arrived shortly after dawn to load Jack's trunks. It seemed that the earl's trunks were already stowed onboard as they would be leaving immediately for the countryside. Jack declined the offer to use the rather plush conveyance to the church, opting instead to ride with her parents and sister in their more modest carriage. It would be their last morning together. She might not see them for months or years after this. The quiet of their ride seemed to honor this time together as a family. Father and mother held hands while across from them the two sisters also held hands. As they drew near the church Jack stretched her other hand out across the aisle and Sam, seeing her, did the same. For a few moments they were a complete circle. Then the carriage stopped and it was time to disembark.

Father went to check in the church to make sure all was ready while mother and Sam fluffed and fiddled and smoothed her dress out. Sam had made a lovely bouquet from the flowers they had received the previous morning, insisting on incorporating the yellow roses that Harrington had sent. Jack suffered through all the fussing and primping, then father was ushering her forward and she entered the church on his arm, mother and Sam preceding them.

At the front of the small church Gideon stood with the vicar and the Duke of Beloin. The earl was fitted with black breeches, a snowy white shirt, and a coat of bright blue superfine. He looked roguishly handsome, although as Jack approached she could see that both he and the duke looked a bit green. Well, she might have been drinking last night if she'd thought of it. She took a deep breath, handed her bouquet to her sister, and took her place beside Harrington at the altar. After that the proceedings became a blur. Even the vows that she recited didn't register in her conscious mind, she just repeated them by rote while staring at the earl's cravat. Finally the clergyman called for the ring and Gideon took her cold, stiff hand in his own.

Jack finally looked up into his face but he was concentrating on his task. His expression was the same picture of focus that a little boy had when building his first castle out of sticks. One lock of his unruly hair had broken free from restraint to curl over his temple and she wanted to brush it back, to hold her hand against his face until he looked at her. She stopped breathing and tried to shake some sense into herself. Being near him was weaving a spell over her again.

Perhaps sensing her gaze he did look into her eyes, his face earnest and solemn. It was then that Jack realized that this morning she wasn't marrying Gideon Wolfe, Earl of Harrington, but Giddy, the serious man that she had enjoyed teasing during the curricle ride. She smiled as a tiny flicker of hope came alive in her breast.

"Do you like the ring?" he whispered to her.

She looked down, realizing she hadn't seen it yet. It was heavy, a band of gold with a large blue sapphire, the style made more delicate by the intricate gold filigree decorating it. It was a lovely ring that looked like a treasured family piece with a long history. It fit a bit loosely on her finger.

"You could choose another," he said. "Or I could replace the stone."

Jack smiled up at him and whispered. "You're right. I should have one in every color."

He raised a brow, clearly not sure if she was joking or not. The clergyman continued the ceremony and was now called for the groom to kiss the bride. Gideon leaned down to take her lips in a brief, sweet kiss. And then it was over. Her family and the duke wished them well, signing as witnesses to the nuptials. There was to be no wedding breakfast, no additional well-wishers. They entered the coach that was to bear them to Kent and Harrington handed her onto the forward facing seat before taking the one opposite himself. She scooted to the window to let it down and wave to her family until they were out of sight. When she closed the window again she looked over to see that Harrington had sunk low into his seat, arms crossed and eyes closed, legs stretched out, from all indications asleep. She opened the small bag she had packed for the trip and pulled out a book.

Apparently today was not the day they were going to discuss how they would proceed.

Gideon watched his wife from under his nearly closed eyelids. His wife. It seemed a very strange term, meaning that he possessed her. Was in turn possessed by her. He was a husband. It wasn't something he had ever aspired to be or expected to be. But here they were, husband and wife. It had merely taken some influence and a tiny bit of cash in order to have a wedding in less than a day. He had expected the event to feel angry or rushed, but it had been sedate and almost unearthly. When he had seen her entering the church she had been backlit by the early morning sun, creating a halo around the soft waves of her hair. Once the door had closed he could see her more clearly. The dress he had hoped would suit her had done much more than that. Her skin glowed like the finest pearl against the deep green. Her figure was shown to its best advantage, all lush curves and slender grace in silk and velvet. Even sitting here reading in the mid-morning light she looked like a feast he wanted to indulge in. Marrying a woman who could ignite his lust after he'd polished off half a bottle the night before was either a very good or a very, very bad idea. Knowing that she wasn't ready for him to press her on that point he closed his eyes and tried to sleep off the horrible hangover that Quince's brandy had given him.

He jolted awake some time later to find that she had put her book away and was herself dozing while sitting up. She didn't look terribly comfortable with her head nodding to the side. He crossed the carriage and settled himself into the corner, pulling her gently down onto his chest. She wriggled once while settling in and his body responded with alacrity, but then she was in a deep sleep again. He contented himself with settling one hand on her hip and using the other to smooth her hair back from her face. She was a pretty girl and looked much sweeter in sleep than he had suspected she could. Knowing that he was driving himself to distraction he closed his own eyes again and slowly faded to sleep.

Jack awoke to the feel of the carriage rocking to a stop. She was lying against a warm, rumbling surface that her fogged brain finally deciphered was her snoring husband. When had he crossed the carriage? And what had he been doing? His arms were wrapped loosely around her but tightened as she tried to sit up. His snore changed to a low growl as he tried to make her lie back down against him.

"Gideon," she whispered. "I think we've arrived somewhere."

"We're always somewhere, darling."

She poked his ribs. "Aren't you clever. I was thinking perhaps a carriage house."

He finally released her and sat up himself, rubbing his face and looking at the light seeping around the curtains on the window. "We have most likely arrived at home since it is already late afternoon."

"Well, just so long as we have arrived somewhere."

"Undoubtedly."

There was a knock on the carriage door. Gideon seemed amused that his retainers thought it necessary to give the newlyweds privacy.

"Come," he called. A footman opened the door and bowed.

Gideon looked out and then quirked a smile at Jack. "We are better than somewhere. We have arrived at Kellington." He stepped down from the carriage and held his hand up for her to take. Emerging from the carriage, her first impression of her new home was of wind-swept fields and tangy salt air. There were grasses and gorse growing wild in the fields as far as the eye could see, as well as the largest manor home that Jack had ever seen, with an impossible number of staff assembled in the front circle to greet them. She stood for a moment on the steps of the carriage, struck dumb by the size of her new home. She could easily imagine her family's country manor fitting inside six times over, with room to spare. She was to be mistress of this? And other properties as well? It was difficult not to retreat back into the carriage and demand to be taken home. But now this was home. She gripped Gideon's hand tightly to steady herself and stepped down to face her new life.

CHAPTER ELEVEN

When Jacqueline stepped out of the carriage Gideon could tell she was overwhelmed. Her hand tightened convulsively in his and her expression went blank and wide-eyed. The softly waving hairstyle that had been fetching at the wedding had been mussed by travel and sleeping, giving the impression they had been doing far more interesting things on the carriage ride. It was better, he thought, for the staff to assume it truly had been a love match that had prompted the hasty wedding. She kept hold of him even after stepping down and he didn't try to move her hand to rest more appropriately on the crook of his arm, so they moved forward to greet the staff looking more like lovers than earl and countess.

Gideon nodded to the butler. "Dibbs." This was not the Dibbs of London but instead that butler's father.

Dibbs bowed deeply. "We are glad to see you return, my Lord."

Gideon then nodded to the housekeeper. "Mrs. Gladstone."

She curtsied. "My Lord."

"Let me introduce to you my wife, Jacqueline Wolfe, Countess of Harrington."

The servants both greeted her deferentially, then began the process of introducing the countess to the one hundred and thirty-three staff required to maintain the house and grounds. Gideon knew the number by heart since he reviewed the payroll monthly. He could also name almost all of them on sight except for the few that Mrs. Gladstone had hired most recently. As they made their way he asked after children, pets and health as matched each retainer. He also assessed the staff that his steward Philip Gladstone had suggested might be interested in pensioning in the next year or so. Philip was the last staff member to be introduced and Gideon saw he was carrying his satchel in case there should be any immediate questions about the household or finances.

Gideon turned to his wife. "Would you like to rest before dinner, my love?"

She still looked a bit pale and shocked but answered him steadily enough. "That would be lovely."

He gave her into the care of Mrs. Gladstone and watched her walk up the steps. It occurred to him that they hadn't argued all day. Perhaps this wouldn't be the disaster that it at first seemed, but time would tell.

Jack followed Mrs. Gladstone upstairs and through a wide, sunny hallway. The housekeeper chatted amicably about the furniture and paintings in the hall while Jack tried to take in her surroundings.

"And these are your quarters, my Lady," the housekeeper said, opening double doors. The room beyond was devastatingly beautiful. The tall wooden doors opened into a sitting room decorated in light blue, gold, and pale yellow. It gave the overall effect of sunshine on a beautiful summer day. Stepping inside, Jack could tell that the room had been rather hastily cleaned and aired out. Dust motes still hung in the air, and the scent was stale from disuse. But oh, the soaring ceilings, delicate furniture, and soothing colors. She ran her hand over the silk covering on the tiny settee. The room was exquisite.

"Happy we are to have you here, my Lady," Mrs. Gladstone said. The matronly woman had tears welling in her eyes. "We had given up on his Lord choosing a bride. But we always knew that if he did you would be quite the perfect lady. Sensible his Lord is. Not like his father, God rest his soul."

It wouldn't do to explain to the housekeeper what a horrible accident the marriage had been. Instead Jack smiled and said, "Why don't you tell me about the room? It's quite beautiful."

Mrs. Gladstone proceeded to do just that, describing both the history and significance of all the paintings and furniture. The last countess had redone the entire suite, except her husband had put his foot down and not let her replace the bed that had been in their family for generations. His reasoning, said Mrs. Gladstone, was that "every Earl of Harrington has been born in that bed and if I have any say every one of us shall." His last will and testament had even dictated that the bed could not be removed. As a consequence the bedroom was dominated by the huge dark wood piece, almost medieval in style, that the previous countess had attempted to disguise under pale blue and yellow drapes.

Jack thanked Mrs. Gladstone for her time, agreed that yes she would need to have a lady's maid assigned to her. She closed the door and, once alone, sank down on the bed and stared at the ceiling. My, how things had changed. Still exhausted from the stress of the last two days she drifted off to sleep again.

Gideon knocked on the connecting door that led to his wife's suite. Not hearing a response he pushed the door open and paused. Looking at the pale blue and gold panels brought memories of his mother flooding back. The airy, innocent look of the room was in stark contrast to the woman she had been. High-strung. Demanding. Neglectful. When he was a child it could be weeks, sometimes months between times he would see her. Every once in a long while his nanny would bring him here, where his mother would fuss over him until he no longer entertained her. Or until a servant displeased her, perhaps snagging her hair with a brush or knocking over one of her perfume bottles. Her shifts from mawkish sweetness to vengeful harridan could happen so swiftly as to be terrifying.

"Jacqueline?" he called out, hesitant to walk in any further. Silence greeted him. He became annoyed that memories of his mother had stopped him and took a deep breath. Weakness was something he could not abide in himself.

Entering the room he could see her feet poking beyond the bed hangings. As he approached he saw that she was asleep again, stretched out cross-wise on the coverlet with her arms flung to the side. Watching her, the memories of his mother dissipated. The lamplight from his room spilled across the pale bedding. Her chest rose and fell with the even breathing of sleep. He felt an impulse to join her, to awaken her with kisses and gentle strokes. Would she come alive in his arms again? Would she welcome him, as a wife should, pull him to her body and encourage a joining? Temptation made him lightheaded. They could both enjoy it. He was confident that he could fan her naturally passionate nature into a blaze of need that he could satisfy. But his Jacqueline was primarily a creature of the mind. As long as she had doubts she would feel betrayed by her own desires. He knew she had doubts because he had put some of them there himself out of anger and frustration. But the temptation was so strong he could nearly taste what it would be like to kiss and nibble at her throat. Could nearly feel the softness of stroking her hip, her breast. Before he could be swayed by his own desires he touched her foot to wake her. She jolted and then drew back when she saw him. He watched as she sat up and rubbed at her eyes. He had indeed made the right decision not to bed her at this juncture.

"What time is it?" she asked, sounding sleepy and disoriented.

He pulled his watch from its pocket and tilted it toward the light. "Nearly seven. Would you like to have dinner brought to your room or eat in the dining room downstairs? My apologies that I didn't think to ask you that earlier."

She looked at him strangely then answered. "I think the dining room would be more appropriate. The staff will want to know more about me and how we will all get on together."

"You have a point. But if they think we are in here being inappropriate it will fuel the gossip of our love match."

She seemed to think for a moment. "Clever. And I would certainly appreciate more time to consider what I've gotten myself into."

"Do you mind if I dine with you?"

"Of course not. Besides, it is important for maintaining the ruse."

He moved to the window to look out on the gardens in the pale light of the rising moon. "You can redecorate your rooms, of course. We can discuss budgets tomorrow if you like."

"Redecorate? There's no need."

"It is customary for the countess to change her suite to her taste."

She had joined him at the window, looking up at him with a furrowed brow. "But this is lovely. Blue is my favorite color." He saw that she was twisting her wedding ring on her finger.

"So I don't need to buy you one of those in every color?"

She smiled down on the ring. "No, indeed you don't."

"Is it uncomfortable? There was no time to consider a fitting."

"Perhaps a bit loose, but mostly just different. I don't usually wear jewelry. I'm sure I'll become accustomed to it in time." She looked at him more keenly. "Does the room bother you?"

"It reminds me of my mother."

"I take it that's not a good thing?"

"Not in the least."

"Very well then, we can redecorate. Perhaps I can take inspiration from this ring and the bed, something more in a medieval mode with a darker blue and gold."

Gideon clenched his jaw. No weakness. "No, if you like it we can leave it as it is for now. Perhaps later you will decide on something you want."

She smiled up at him. "Well, bookcases certainly. I could use some bookcases."

"I'll have to show you the library soon."

He watched her brighten at the suggestion. "Yes, soon."

"Not tonight, though," he cautioned. More lightly he added, "The staff wouldn't understand that it would be part of a seduction for you."

She laughed. "Nor should we tell them it could be a reenactment."

Gideon saw that she realized what she'd said because she began to blush. "Perhaps we can dine in my suite?" he suggested. "No memories of my mother in there."

"Of course," she agreed.

"And for our... ruse, I suggest you change into a nightgown and robe to dine."

She blushed again but nodded.

He pointed to the door he had entered through. "When you are ready just come through there. I will send for our dinner shortly."

CHAPTER TWELVE

Jack found that her clothing had been arranged in her dressing room while she slept. Of the three trunks she had brought one had contained clothing, the other two being mostly filled with books and mementos. Her maid had been at a loss with what to do with those and had just left the trunks propped open. Having familiarized herself with where things were she couldn't think of anything else to delay going to Harrington's rooms. She pulled the sash on her robe tighter and then tied it with a double knot. She had decided to wear her hair down considering the picture they were trying to paint, but as a result of that and the scant clothing, she felt very vulnerable. Taking a deep breath she walked across to the open door he had indicated earlier and knocked lightly.

"Come in," he said.

She ducked around the door and found the earl standing at the door to what must be his own sitting room. He was also dressed in a robe, his of silk in a deep ruby color. Just seeing him also in such a state of undress made her cheeks heat again. Glancing around the room she saw that it was done in warm autumnal colors, very subtle and masculine, with an emphasis on polished wood. Her gaze skipped nervously over the bed and her fingers started worrying the end of her sash. Gideon walked over to her and cupped his warm hands gently on her shoulders.

"Do you trust me?" he asked.

"I... yes?"

He smiled. "So dubious."

She tried to smile but was afraid she was failing miserably at it. Gideon leaned close to her ear and whispered, "Trust me." She shuddered as his breath caressed her neck. He had leaned close enough to her that she could feel the heat from his body and found herself leaning into it like a chilly traveler drawn towards a hearthfire. She feared that he made her wanton, but feared more that he would step back from her. He nuzzled her neck and she released her pent-up breath in a sigh. His kisses and nibbles made their way to her jaw, then the side of her mouth. She was beginning to feel boneless and her entire being focused on the pleasure his lips were bringing to her. At long last he took her lips with his own, pulling her body tightly against him. He thrust his tongue into her mouth to caress and swirl against her own and she felt her reaction move from surrender to something more primal and demanding. Her hands clutched at his shoulders then went to his hair, his face. The rough texture of his day's growth of beard excited her and she could hear herself making a mewling sound in her throat. His hands moved down to her hips and he pulled her even more intimately against himself. She felt a hard ridge against her belly but was too caught in the moment to be shocked. Her breasts felt swollen and there was a needy ache pulsing from where her body pressed against his. She wanted to wriggle and rub against him like a cat. He tore his mouth from hers and then stood there with his forehead against hers, his eyes closed and his breathing labored.

"We need to stop."

"Why?"

He laughed. "I said you could trust me."

"I do trust you." She gave in to her need and wriggled against him. His hands clamped more securely against her hips to make her stop.

"Jacqueline."

"Jackie."

He kissed her forehead, her temple. "Jackie."

"Yes, Gideon?"

"We need to stop."

"Yes, Gideon," she said. But she moved her lips to his and the kiss began again. One of his hands slid up from her hip until it was cupping her breast, the thumb tracing lazy circles around her puckered nipple. The pleasure was so intense that it was agony. She didn't know what she wanted but she knew there was something more, something with far fewer clothes and more intimate touching. He was pulling away from her again and she clutched at him desperately.

"Dinner has arrived," he said.

She growled and kissed his throat.

"Jackie," he said again. "You need to eat. I'm not sure you've eaten at all today."

He had successfully distracted her from her intense desire and she sighed. "No, I was too nervous before the wedding."

Stepping back he held out his arm to her. "Let me take you to dinner, countess."

She slipped her hand in the crook of his elbow and allowed him to lead her out to his sitting room where his footmen had laid out a meal on a round table near the window. One footman remained and stood at attention as they entered. Gideon held out Jack's chair for her and she settled into it with as much decorum as a half-naked woman who had just been thoroughly kissed could muster. The footman held out the earl's chair and then asked, "Would you like for me to serve, my lord?"

"No," Gideon said. "I think we would like to be... alone."

The footman nodded and slipped out the door to the hallway.

Now that her ardor had cooled, Jack was feeling self-conscious again. Gideon was busily filling her plate with choice tidbits, seemingly unconcerned with her murmured answers and shy nods as he tried to discern which items she wanted to eat. After he had filled his own plate and made sure they both had wine he said, "We gave the footman something to talk about. And I suppose it goes without saying, but just in case it doesn't, if you ever do that," he waved his fork to indicate the doorway to his bedroom, "with another man, I will kill him."

Jack set her wine down with a thump. The shock of the whole situation was wearing off and she felt prickles of irritation. "And if you ever do that with another woman I will kill you," she announced, stabbing at her beef tenderloin with her fork. She didn't even look at her husband for fear of what his face might betray at her statement. Amusement? Pity?

After a few moments he said, "Aren't we a pair?"

She continued to chase the food around her plate with violent little stabs of her fork. She should have remembered that he was at heart an arrogant, overbearing clout. And it was not to be forgotten exactly how they had met as a consequence of his planning a liaison with another woman. Which reminded her of another thing.

"I should still like to know who talked to the nosy popinjay at the paper. There were too many details for it not to be someone very familiar with the evening."

"You didn't give your parents the details?" Gideon asked.

Jack did look up then, to see Gideon lounged back in his chair studying her with a lazy scrutiny. "No, but why would that matter?"

"Your mother was obviously in favor of the match."

"You're impugning my mother?"

He shrugged. "Some women will do almost anything in order to secure a good marriage for their daughters. What is a little scandal in comparison to having your daughter marry an earl? Or it could have been your father determined to see me do the right thing by you, especially if he suspected we were planning to call off the engagement."

She began tearing apart her dinner roll into tiny pieces. "My parents did not know the details of the evening, or if they did they didn't hear those details from me. And I also didn't talk to them about our agreement, that we could call off the engagement if the details didn't emerge."

"I don't remember that being an agreement. I remember that being a plan that you continued to advocate."

"You were the first one to complain that you never wanted to marry!"

Gideon set his jaw. "I was also the one to offer marriage and seemed most willing to do the right thing."

"Because of your pride."

"It's a matter of honor," he said cooly.

"Which you are undoubtedly very proud of."

"Why are we even arguing about this?"

"You treat me like I'm a doxy and that isn't very gentlemanly of you." She started to feel tears burn the corners of her eyes but she willed them away. No more tears. Not over this.

Gideon set down his wine and began rubbing his forehead, looking very much like a man trying not to lose his temper. He finally sighed, his hands folded in front of him in an almost prayerful position. He nodded. "You're right, I apologize."

Jack was shocked enough she thought she had misheard him. "You what?" she asked before she could stop herself.

He raised a brow at her but repeated it. "I apologize, Jacqueline. You have not done anything in particular to make me question your loyalty. At least not yet. It's just easy to imagine that a young woman of your beauty and temperament who hasn't had a great number of suitors could be swayed by a handsome rake bent on seducing her."

She raised her own eyebrows. "You think I'm daft."

He started to look irritated again. "No, I don't think you're daft."

"You think that some pretty face spouting poetry will make me compromise my own honor."

He gazed down into his nearly empty wineglass. "As I recall it didn't require poetry and you hadn't even seen my face."

She had thrown her own glass of wine at him before she even realized her hand had moved. She lurched from her chair, fury burning in her chest. "How dare you!"

He also rose, wiping wine from his eyes and looking equally furious. "How dare I? In what way am I speaking anything other than the truth of the matter?"

Jack fled the room before she could start throwing cutlery. She slammed the door that divided their rooms but discovered there was no lock on her side. How typical of their entire relationship that seemed. She dragged one of her trunks full of books across the room and lodged it firmly against the door. She didn't dig out one of the fancy knives that Sabre had sent her from Spain as she knew she would be too tempted to use it on him. Instead she searched through the trunks until she found her copy of the *Iliad* and then read in her sitting room until she dozed off in her chair in the early morning hours.

Gideon was cutting his breakfast ham with a good deal more force than necessary. He was still irritated with the final confrontation between himself and his wife the night before. He hadn't been unreasonable, he didn't think, pointing out that she had been quite receptive to his advances. First, before she knew him at all. The second time when she had been bent on calling off their unwise engagement. Even last night it could be reasoned that she would have had reservations but instead she had been like a cat in heat, all sensual movement and hot demand. He hardened at the memory of those occasions which served to make him more irate.

He saw his footman move to hold out the chair on the other end of the table and realized she had entered the room. She was wearing a morning gown the color of freshly churned butter and the soft fabric glided over her figure to float in a small flare around her feet. She had paused at the door and was looking over the table.

"Couldn't I sit closer to my husband?" she inquired softly. The footman immediately gathered up the place setting and almost stumbled in his haste to do his new countess's bidding. She settled into the chair at Gideon's right elbow with the delicacy and grace of a butterfly alighting on a bush. She appeared ready to resume their campaign of convincing the staff that theirs was a love match, but he wasn't sure he had the stomach for it just now.

"Good morning, Gideon."

"Good morning, Jacqueline."

She was selecting items from the trays that the footmen offered to her. Her eyes looked shadowed this morning as though she hadn't slept. Gideon would have expected her to have enjoyed the sleep of the righteous after her magnificent show of temper followed by dragging some heavy piece of furniture in front of her door. He had considered shoving it out of the way just to prove that he could, but continuing a screaming match didn't seem like the best way to cap off their first day together as a married couple.

He would do best to remember that he thought, looking at her more carefully. She was his wife. No matter what else they might think, they were now together. Forever. Even beyond death if the vicars were to be believed. She was his responsibility and this morning she looked tired. But she was trying her best to be cheerful and gracious.

"You could have had your breakfast in bed," he offered.

"Oh, no. I've always come down to breakfast. It's one of my favorite meals. It's the best family meal."

Gideon felt a small lurch in his heart. A family meal. His family had rarely all taken meals together and when they did it was always a formal dinner. The idea of having a new family where everyone wanted to have breakfast together seemed odd but strangely uplifting.

"Also," she said softly while buttering her toast, leaning in as though she were sharing a confidence. "I accept your apology."

"You what?"

She looked up at him and smiled, seemingly tickled by his surprised tone. "I accept your apology. We are both in the habit of making horrible assumptions about each other."

He frowned, not sure he was ready to easily let go of their confrontation from the night before.

"And thus I must apologize myself for making assumptions," she continued. "In addition to apologizing about the wine."

She went back to her breakfast, apparently content. What a riddle his wife was. But he supposed he had the rest of their lives to figure her out. Provided they didn't kill each other first.

CHAPTER THIRTEEN

Gideon gave her a tour of the house and grounds that day and within a week they settled into a routine. Riding together early in the morning, breakfast, then Gideon went to his office to work on his accounts while Jack worked with Mrs. Gladstone on menus and other household chores. Lunch together followed by each of them going off in individual pursuits, a time that Jack usually spent in the library. Afternoon tea. Dinner. They remained warily polite to each other, rarely talking about more than the weather or mundane household topics.

Jack used that time to study her new husband. His staff adored him and he was a kind and considerate employer. He was diligent, usually using his afternoons to visit his tenants with Phillip Gladstone in tow like an obedient puppy. Phillip was, she learned, Mrs. Gladstone's son. It seemed the Wolfes had a tradition of keeping as many members of a family in their employ as possible. She also noted that Gideon received a steady stream of mail from London, many of the packages looking like weighty documents she assumed were from the sessions of Parliament. He churned through his correspondence relentlessly, sending out almost as many items per day as he received.

She didn't receive nearly as many letters, just notes from her mother and sister until finally one of her mother's envelopes held a forwarded letter from Sabre. Letting out a small whoop of surprised delight she raced from the front hallway all the way up to her sitting room in order to read it.

My dearest Jack,

You don't need to tell me what he's done. Just tell me where he is so that I can kill him for you. We should be back from Italy before March is out. Send his direction by way of Robert's address and I will take care of it.

Love, Sabre

Jack was still laughing over Sabre's staunch and pithy support when she heard a knock at her open door. She looked up to see Gideon leaning on the doorframe.

"Is everything all right?" he asked. "Dibbs said you shrieked in the hallway and ran upstairs."

She bounced off the settee and sashayed towards him, holding out the letter. "I have you now. My friends will be here soon."

He read the short letter and handed it back to her with a laugh. "Your friends are assassins?"

She laughed again. "Not assassins exactly, but we are all quite deadly."

He stepped forward and hooked his arms around her waist, holding her to him. "Really? You're deadly are you?"

"Quite."

"Perhaps I should give you a reason to defend yourself in order to test your skills."

"You have a gun or a knife on you?"

"You aren't threatened by an assault on your chastity?"

"That's hardly deadly, I shouldn't think."

Gideon kissed the side of her neck and she could already feel her resistance to him melting away.

"You make a good point, though," she said.

"I do?" he asked, moving to the other side of her neck. "What's that?"

"I should defend against this simply because you think I can't."

"Can you?" he murmured.

She quickly ducked out from under his arms and danced away. "Yes, I can. And don't test me, it will make us argue again."

"Why argue when we can do something much more... interesting."

"Stop it," she scolded. "You always start this and you never finish it, apparently distracted by your need to lecture me on my wanton ways."

"I've never called you wanton."

"You've implied it. I'm not stupid."

"Nor have I called your stupid, although you seem bent on assuming so."

"Again, you have implied it. I don't want to argue about this. I'm happy that my friend is coming home in another month so just go away." She made a shooing motion. "Go away. Go back to whatever you were doing before Dibbs told you that your wife was screeching in the hallway. Go."

With a shake of his head and a lopsided smile he finally left and Jack sat down to write some more letters to her friends.

Gideon sat at his desk idly tapping his pen on his blotter as he had been doing for the last ten minutes. He had sent Phillip on a break to have time to think. Seeing Jacqueline with that letter in her hand made him realize he had never seen her happy before. She had vibrated with it and it had drawn him in like a bee to a flower. He wanted to taste that joy, feel it under his hands. But she had been right to push him away. He could still sense that moving too quickly on the physical side of their relationship would be a mistake. An intensely satisfying mistake, no doubt, but a mistake nonetheless. Since he now dreamt about her nightly it was hard not to join her in her bed and try the acts his mind had come up with. Every day began and ended with thoughts of her long, silky legs wrapped around him as he pleasured her until she called out his name in ecstasy. Fabulous. Now those thoughts intruded on the middle of his day. He wondered how much longer he was going to have to wait, but when he weighed his current frustration against whether they could have a satisfying long-term marriage it really wasn't a contest. He had always been one to believe in long-term investments. For good or for ill, they were married now and that meant at least attempting to make a good marriage of it. His Jacqueline had to make sense of their relationship in her own mind and that would take time. He wasn't sure what it would look like when she had made up her mind but he was confident he would recognize it. Until then he would just do his best not to think about her in the middle of the day.

Buoyed by Sabre's note Jack spent the rest of the morning reading her own journals from their childhood together. Many of the stories were familiar from constant retelling, but others had been forgotten over the years. She had chosen to tuck herself into the charming window seat in her bedroom that looked out over the side garden. With the delicate embroidered pillows and yards of gauzy drapes it was the sort of spot that the three girls would have hidden in to giggle over these stories when they were young. She heard the maids enter to straighten her room and didn't think much of it. She supposed they did that every morning when she was most often downstairs with Mrs. Gladstone or doing other errands. The two girls chatted without her notice as they worked, until one sentence caught her attention.

"My sister says as he turned off his mistress without even so much as a by-the-by."

"Don't see why he did that as it's certain he's not getting any attentions from her ladyship."

"Gull, I think they're quite sweet together."

"Tidiest beds I've ever seen slept in. You're not going to keep a man inside his marriage that way."

"But when they arrived they certainly looked, well, you know."

"Some women go cold quick. Especially the blue bloods, my mama says."

"I adore milady," the first girl defended. "She's always kind."

"A man doesn't want a kind woman in his bed, that's all I'm saying duck."

Jack's cheeks were burning. She had drawn her feet up tight against herself to ensure that she was fully hidden behind the curtain unless the girls decided to clean the window seat. Once they had left she crept out of the window and put her journals away in the trunk again. Then she took to her bed for the rest of the day, sending word that she wouldn't be down for dinner due to a headache.

Late that evening she heard a light tap on the door between her sitting room and bedroom followed by Gideon's voice. "Jacqueline?"

She couldn't talk to him, not yet, and pretended to be asleep. He came over to the bed and felt her forehead then smoothed her hair back from her cheek. He stood there over her for long minutes and it almost made her open her eyes and ask him why he was lingering. Finally he straightened the coverlet over her and walked to the door that connected their rooms. After moving her trunk out of the way, something he was able to accomplish far more quietly than she had the night she had dragged it there, he went through to his own room and left the door open. She could hear him moving around and preparing for bed. Even after the sounds in his room quieted she continued to stare at their open connecting door. She finally fell into an exhausted sleep in the middle of the night.

Jacqueline was already at the breakfast table when Gideon came down the next morning. She looked wan and tired but not much worse for wear. He had been concerned that it might be a fever, but at least that hadn't been the case. Perhaps it had been something she ate the day before. This morning she seemed to be eating lightly, buttered toast and some clotted cream on her plate. Following an impulse to touch her and reassure himself that she was all right, he leaned down to kiss the top of her head.

"Feeling better?" he asked.

She smiled a bit morosely and nodded. "Yes. A touch of the ague I suppose."

As he seated himself beside her, his mind became crowded with the things he wanted to say, the primary one being that he had missed her yesterday. Abruptly he was appalled at the direction of his own thoughts. When on earth had she suddenly become important? And why? He'd had a full and satisfying life before she had come into it, and he certainly hadn't been tied to any woman's apron strings. What would be next, an inability to leave her on business? That would be ridiculous. The more he thought about it the more irritated he became. What made her any more exceptional than any other woman he had bedded? He looked at her with a critical eye. She was certainly lovely. When she wasn't being waspish she was actually quite pleasant, but there was nothing special about that. There were dozens of lovely, pleasant women throughout England. Perhaps the issue was precisely that he hadn't bedded her. It was the combination of his unquenched desire and their constant companionship, that was all. After they had consummated their marriage and got past this excruciatingly polite interaction he wouldn't feel as drawn to her.

"May I ask you a question, Gideon?" Something in the tone of her voice put him on alert.

"Of course," he said a bit hesitantly.

She glanced around to make sure none of the footmen were close by and asked in a low voice, "Why haven't we consummated our marriage?"

That her mind had been thinking along the same lines as his own stunned him for a few moments. "I wanted to give you time to become... acclimated. Since we didn't have a long courtship."

She looked over at him with a sardonic smile. "We had *no* courtship."

"That's not true," he said. "I took you riding in my curricle."

"That was after we were officially engaged."

"Picky little thing, aren't you? Next you'll be saying that you really do want rings in every color."

She looked down at her wedding ring a little sadly. "No, I like this one."

Something in her morose expression began to irritate him. "Well then, shall we? I don't have anything on my calendar for the next two hours."

Her attitude became wary and that served to infuriated him further. "You don't have to be brusque about it," she said.

"I said that I was being considerate and you said it wasn't necessary."

"I didn't say that."

He arched a brow at her. "You implied it."

She withdrew into the kind of huffy silence he hadn't seen since that day in her parent's garden.

"Meet me upstairs in a half hour," he said.

She gave him a baleful look but excused herself from her chair. He stood when she did, as a gentleman should, and then resumed his meal after she left. Perhaps he had been wrong, he thought. Perhaps it was best for both of them if they just got this over with. It didn't mean anything in the grand scheme of things, they were both giving the act more significance than it deserved. He wished, for the first time, that he kept brandy at the breakfast table.

CHAPTER FOURTEEN

Jack sat at her vanity brushing out her hair. She had changed into her nightgown and robe, not sure how else to prepare. Her husband became distant and prickly at the strangest times. She was given to understand that men enjoyed the marriage act, and he had on a number of occasions complimented her looks. And when they had kissed before... Well, she had no reason to believe that he was indifferent to her in that way. She saw movement in her mirror and turned to see that he had entered through the open door connecting their rooms. He had also donned his robe and stood near the doorway watching her. She couldn't decipher the look on his face. It seemed a mix of concern, anger, and even grief. She was cold and could barely feel her feet, but rose and moved across the room toward him. She didn't want to lose her chance at whatever happiness or contentment they could have in their marriage. If this was the path to securing it, then so be it. Before she could join him at the door he motioned, "The bed, then?"

She nodded mutely, moving to the side of the bed. As she stood there, untying her robe, she heard his footsteps behind her. He helped her slide the robe off her shoulders, tossing it aside once it was free of her arms. Settling his hands on her shoulders, his thumbs circled on her back as he began kissing her neck. His nibbling kisses where her throat met her shoulder made her shudder, and he ran his hands down her arms.

"You're cold," he said.

"I'm fine." She knew that she was still tense but trusted that he would distract her shortly.

He pulled her against his chest and settled his cheek on her head, sighing. "We don't have to do this."

"It's fine, if you want to."

"I rarely think about anything else."

Jack didn't know what to say to that. She hadn't considered how interested he might be in marital relations but it lent credence to the second maid's opinion. She turned towards him, tipping her head back to look at his face. "Then show me what to do."

He cupped her chin in his hand and brushed his lips gently over hers, stroking the corner of her mouth with his thumb. Keeping his kisses lighter than butterfly wings he touched her cheeks, her eyelids, and then made his way back to her lips again. The sweetness of it made her want to weep. She clutched at the lapels of his robe, her fingers sinking into the slick softness of the silk. His grip on her jaw strengthened and the kiss deepened bit by bit. His other hand slid her nightgown off one shoulder and he moved his mouth to follow it down her arm. When he bared her breast she heard him moan deep in his throat, his hand cupping the globe while his tongue laved the nipple. When he sucked her nipple into his mouth she gave a gasp of surprise. He drew back to look down at her, concern clear on his face. His hand stroked her face, running his fingers through her hair to cup the back of her head.

"It will be all right," he said.

"I know," she said, nodding and bringing her gaze down to where her hands clutched at his chest. "I'm just afraid that I don't know... know what to do."

He pulled to his chest again, where she nestled in the comforting warmth of him.

"I'm sorry, Gideon."

"Shh, it's all right."

He continued to stroke the nape of her neck until she began to relax.

"Stay here," he said, drawing her nightgown back up to her shoulder and kissing the top of her head again.

Jack nodded, feeling miserable and out of place. And truly cold now that his body didn't warm hers. It was odd to feel so despondent with the sun was shining cheerfully through her windows. This time hadn't been like the others. She hadn't lost her fears to the rush of desire and longing that he could stir in her. Her mind had raced with questions and anxiety about what she should be doing. She leaned on the bedpost for support and watched the door between their rooms. Shortly he came back in, holding a small book in his hands.

"You read French, I trust?"

She nodded and he handed the book to her.

"Don't leave it out where the servants can see it or someone will likely take it. Tell me if you have any questions." He rubbed her arms and kissed her forehead. "Stop worrying, Jacqueline. Now I'll leave your to your studies."

She looked up into his face and he was smiling wryly at her. He tapped the tip of her nose with his finger and turned to go. When he reached the door she called out, "Gideon?"

He turned towards her. "Yes?"

"I... Thank you for the book."

He nodded and slipped through the door.

Why couldn't she tell him that what she really wanted was him, not the book? She was still chilled and unhappy, wanting to be held in his arms. He was probably still in his room, changing back into his day clothes. She could go to him and he would hold her like he did that morning of the society article. Then he might kiss her like he had that first night in the library. Or at the party. Or even their first night at Kellington. Her skin warmed and tingled at the direction of her thoughts. And then he might... Well, she didn't know what came next really. She opened the book in her hands and almost immediately discovered that it was illustrated in a most shocking manner. She didn't even know that such books existed! She withdrew to the window seat to start from the beginning. This was *definitely* a book she didn't want the maids to see her reading.

Gideon jogged down the front steps of Kellington on the way to ride to one of the more distant farms on his estate. He was intensely frustrated and honestly wondered how he managed to function on a daily basis. But he felt good about giving Jack the book and waiting for her to read it. Of course his studious, educated wife would want a book to study on the subject and he should have thought of it earlier. A blindingly simple solution, really. But sometimes the obvious things were the hardest to see. Right now all he wanted to see was the most beautiful breast he had ever encountered in his life. Ripe, succulent, and soft. The dusty rose color and upturned tip begging for his ministrations had made him think that mid-morning sex on a sunny day had much to recommend it. He wondered what she was doing now. Had she dressed or was she still in her nightgown? The thought that she might have already discovered guidance on pleasuring herself, could be doing it even now, almost sent him straight back into the house. He wrestled with his impulse and finally forced duty to win out over desire. An estate didn't run itself and he had responsibilities to attend to. There were a limited number of hours in a day, and days in a year. If he didn't stay on schedule he would have no hope of covering all the territory he had planned. Visiting Cornwall in the first quarter had already fallen through. No more delays.

Since her husband had still been out riding the estate at lunch, Jack had eaten quickly and gone back to her room. She left instructions with the staff that she was to be informed when Gideon returned. By mid-afternoon she had read the book three times, and studied the illustrations even though many of them seemed impossible or at least unlikely to her. She hid the small book underneath other less interesting tomes in her trunk, on the theory that no one would dig past a large botany book written in Latin and two Greek texts on astronomy. She chose a French novel to while away her time in her sitting room.

Shortly before dinner was usually served, her maid Lara entered the room and curtsied. "The earl has returned, my lady."

"Where is he?"

"I believe he was returning to his room, my lady, in order to change for dinner."

"Thank you, Lara. That will be all."

Jack set aside her novel and went through her bedroom to the connecting door. It was slightly open as seemed to be their new habit, and she could hear someone moving in the room beyond. She knocked.

"Come," he said briefly.

When she entered she could see that he had already removed his jacket and was taking off his ring to set on the bureau while he washed. He appeared dusty, tired, and forlorn.

"What's wrong?" she asked.

He looked over at her and after a moment shook his head. "It's nothing."

She walked over to him and wrapped her arms around his waist, her head resting on his chest. After a moment he put his arms around her back.

"I need to get dressed for dinner," he murmured into her hair.

"Why don't we eat up here?"

She felt some of the tension leave his body at the suggestion. "Hmm, that sounds nice. You aren't going to throw your wine at me, are you?"

"Has anyone ever told you that you have a tendency to hold a grudge?"

He laughed at that and his arms tightened around her.

"If you don't let me go," she protested, "then I can't talk Dibbs into having dinner sent up."

"Starvation seems a small price to pay."

"You would let me starve?"

"Manipulative minx. No I wouldn't let you starve." He pulled back to look down at her. "How was your day?"

"It was..." she thought for a moment. "Educational."

He laughed again. "Perhaps at dinner we can talk about your further instruction."

"That sounds promising. Now you wash up while I go sweet talk Dibbs."

"Dibbs doesn't require sweet talk."

"No, but he likes it."

"Now I have to worry about my wife with the butler," he said with an exaggerated sigh.

She laughed as she walked out to arrange dinner in their rooms. Upon her return she saw that after Gideon had washed he had stretched out on his bed and was now sound asleep. She was loathe to wake him since he'd seemed terribly tired. After she ate her fill she made up a plate for him of items that wouldn't spoil and, covering it with a napkin, left it on his bedside table. Although she was tempted to crawl into the bed next to him she still found herself too shy to do such a thing. She pulled the free half of his coverlet over him and gently kissed his forehead before going to her own bed.

When Gideon awoke he swore he could smell roast. Once he had his eyes open and could focus he saw that a lamp was burning low on his bedside table and a covered plate was near at hand. He was absolutely starving and made short work of the cold food. He went out to the sitting room to see if there were any more leftovers, but his footmen had been diligent and already cleaned up after the meal. He prowled his rooms, briefly considering going down to the kitchens for something more to eat. But he knew what he really wanted. His eyes kept straying to the door leading into her room. He decided he was tired of waiting. It had been a fortnight since their wedding. She had all but told him that she was ready for marital relations. No, he thought to himself with a smile, she had *implied* it. He went through the door before he could second-guess himself again. Her room was bathed in moonlight, and as he approached her bed he saw that she slept on her side with one hand curled under her chin. She had plaited her hair into one long braid, which he hadn't seen before, and the simple hairstyle made her even sweeter, more innocent. Moving to the other side of the bed he drew off his robe and pulled back the covers to join her. When he settled against the pillows she mumbled and rolled over toward him. He put an arm around her and pulled her closer, so that her head rested on his shoulder and one of her legs was thrown over his own. It was both arousing and oddly comforting. Stroking his hand up and down her back he decided he didn't want to wake her and that waiting was for the best. He fell asleep again, inhaling the scent of her hair and feeling her soft breaths on his chest.

He awoke before dawn with her still pressed against his side. His body had already reacted to that soft warmth and he realized his thumb was gently stroking the side of her breast. She murmured and nuzzled closer to his throat bringing him to a nearly painful state of arousal. He turned to face her, fully cupping one breast and testing the weight in his hand. Beautiful. Perfect.

Gideon wanted to push her down into the feather bedding, cover her body with his own, and thrust into her until they were both crying out. His need for her had become so great that his hand trembled as he stroked her. She sighed and stretched under his touch, pushing her nipple against his palm and his body flamed even hotter. What was this need to claim her, possess her? It felt like he was bordering on madness. Would this pass with their joining, or become even more pronounced? Raising himself up on his elbow he looked down into her sweet, young face softly outlined in the dim light and his heart twisted in his chest. He felt raging need, cloying panic, and something else he dare not name. He carefully and silently withdrew from her bed and escaped to his dressing room to put on his riding clothes. A vigorous ride across the countryside would certainly ease both his panic and desire. As the sun rose he was hurrying down to the stables.

CHAPTER FIFTEEN

Jack awoke slowly, feeling languid. She stretched and curled up on her side to doze for a few minutes longer, slowly realizing she was on her left side, when her habit since coming to Kellington had been to sleep on her right. She sat up and saw the mussed bed clothing on the left side of her bed. Pulling the pillow to her nose she confirmed her suspicion. Mint, cloves, and man. Gideon. He had slept here for some portion of the night, undoubtedly coming for some bed sport and she hadn't awakened.

Her capacity to sleep through almost anything during the dead of the night had provided years of entertainment to Sabre and George. Whenever the girls stayed together she could count on them attempting to do something to her while she slept. Pose her, re-braid her hair in an amusing way. One time they had carried her outside on a blanket and left her in the rose garden, where she had awakened to the gardener's gasp of surprise. Over time she learned that her sole defense against their shenanigans was staying up later and rising earlier than the two of them could manage.

Rising early was something that came naturally to her, and since she had been here she had enjoyed exploring Kellington's grounds on morning rides with Gideon. He was most affable in the morning, perhaps because it was before he began reviewing the financial and Parliamentary papers that flowed unceasingly into the house.

She dressed in her riding habit and hoped that he hadn't risen much earlier than she. She suspected that he now waited for her at the stables some mornings when he had awakened early, and the idea that he looked forward to their quiet morning rides together as much as she did warmed her. It was interesting that what had just seemed polite and perfunctory in the beginning was taking on the significance of sweetness and companionship. And now... now there was something more. Or perhaps there always had been.

She looked out the window and, assessing that she had overslept, hurried down the steps and out towards the stables. Before she could enter the spacious building she heard the clop of hooves trotting over gravel. Shielding her eyes against the early morning sun she saw Gideon riding in from the fields. His horse Falcon was lathered and winded. Gideon had an oddly severe expression when he saw her. Trotting Falcon into the stableyard he pulled up in front of her.

"Take a groom with you if you plan to ride," he said shortly. At Kellington she had just ridden with him. Which was unusual now that she came to think of it. At her family's country house she had ridden whenever the mood had struck her, which was quite often.

"I prefer to ride alone," she said softly, wondering why her husband's attitude had shifted dramatically from the night before. Had he taken her not waking as a rejection?

"Well, you won't be doing so anymore." A groom had come up to take Falcon. Gideon jumped down from the large horse with his usual grace.

Jack felt a prickle of annoyance. "I always did at home."

Gideon spun on her with an expression that almost made her back up a step. Pride had her raise her chin instead. "By home," he said acidly, "I assume you mean your father's house. Well, you weren't a countess at your father's house. Now this is home and you are a countess and you will not ride alone."

She could feel her heart pounding in reaction but something her mother used to say came back to her. She said the best advice that her successful merchanting father had ever given her was that when someone provoked you don't get angry, get curious. What do they hope to gain? What are they afraid to lose? She realized now that Gideon had been provoking her at almost every stage in their relationship and she began to wonder why. Some of her speculation and curiosity must have shown on her face as his expression became fierce.

"I can see those wheels turning in your brain. Don't think that you will find a way around my command. Within the hour every groom at Kellington will know of it. Within the week every groom on my estates will know it."

It was extraordinarily difficult not to react to his autocratic approach but Jack clung to her curiosity. Surely her marriage would be the most important business transaction of her life, and if there was ever a time to follow her clever grandfather's advice it was now. What did he hope to gain? What was he afraid to lose? Those questions would most likely preoccupy her for the rest of the day, and she and her husband couldn't spend it out in the stable yard staring at each other.

"Have you had breakfast yet?" she asked.

It wasn't the response he was expecting and his expression became wary. "No."

"Then let's go in to eat, shall we? You must be starving after little to no dinner last night." She wrapped her hand around his elbow and, although stiff with irritation, he behaved as the gentleman he was and led her back toward the manor.

"I ate the plate of food left in my room last night," he admitted.

"Good, I'm glad," she said. "I was concerned that you hadn't had lunch."

"Just a bit of it at the tenant farm."

She felt him stiffen even more at the memory. "What happened yesterday?" she asked. "You never did say."

He looked down at her, appearing very grave, then looked away again as though considering whether to tell her. He finally blew out a long breath. "I had to evict a family."

"Oh Gideon!"

"I didn't want to." He looked grave and a bit forlorn. "But it was necessary. The Hobbes. Mr. Hobbes passed away after an accident last year. His wife and two eldest sons have tried to keep the farm up but they haven't been able to without him."

"That doesn't seem fair, not giving them time to put the farm to rights."

"They've had this year, Jacqueline, and it looked that they were falling further and further behind. It's one of the larger steads on our land."

"This is over profit? You would turn them out because they made one of the larger farms unprofitable?"

"It's not that. Or not just that. Certainly at some point you need to think of the business of it. But they couldn't hope to keep up with such a large plot of land and with the low yield... The family was near to starving and the boys, Jacqueline, the boys are fourteen and twelve. They would spend all day in the field to come home to a meal of gruel unless a neighbor took pity and dropped by with something more substantial. Mrs. Hobbes was beside herself feeling that she owed her neighbors more than she could ever repay."

"Where will the family go?"

"Right now they are at the vicarage. I'm hopeful to find positions for at least Mrs. Hobbes and the boys so that the family can afford housing. Then the eldest girl will have to take care of the five younger children."

"How old is she?"

"Eleven."

Now she understood why he had seemed bleak and withdrawn when he had returned last night. She remembered very clearly the year she was eleven. The Haberdashers had held their own contest that summer to test which of them was best at various weapons. It had been a secret contest, of course. But looking back she knew that year had been silly, innocent, and free of responsibility. She tried to imagine her eleven-year-old self responsible for five younger siblings and couldn't picture it. At that age she could barely stand it when Sam had tried to tag along on Haberdasher outings. Since then she had met more children and knew that Sam was as sweet as anyone's little sister could be. No, an eleven-year-old Jacqueline Walters would have been a miserable nanny to five younger children. This girl might be better suited to it, but was it even a fair task to ask of such a child?

"Isn't there anything else we can do?" Jack asked.

Gideon handed Jack into her seat at the dining table and took his customary place. "Not that I can think of. Even a poor struggling mother and her eight children have their pride. She insisted on preparing that lunch. Poor fare as it was, it probably represented a week's worth of food for her and the children. And she kept a stiff upper lip as Phillip and I explained what we needed to do. The only time she came close to crying was when she told me about the charity of her neighbors and her inability to do them a good turn."

"I should like to visit them in the vicarage."

Gideon nodded. "I can take you tomorrow."

"Not today?"

"I have some other business to attend to today that will keep me from being able to make the trip." He stopped in the midst of cutting his meat to eye her. "And if you should decide to make the trip on your own you will take the carriage with at least two attendants."

"Did you presume that after breakfast I would leap on my steed and dash off to the vicarage on my mission of mercy?"

"Let's just say that I wouldn't consider it to be beyond you."

"How very challenged the Earl of Harrington must be with his headstrong new wife."

"I shall pretend to ignore that. But your instincts are good. Visiting the Hobbes at the vicarage is very much the correct thing for a countess to do. And I'm sure Mrs. Hobbes would appreciate it," he added. "Speaking of the correct thing, that reminds me that we have been at Kellington for over a fortnight and will be expected to join the local society soon."

"I thought it was a honeymoon," Jack said, "not a honey fortnight."

Her tart reply managed to thaw Gideon enough that he smiled. "We can make it a honeymoon if you like, but we should begin planning now for a ball."

"A ball? You mean we should hold a ball? Here? Soon?" She felt stunned.

"Yes, that would be the customary thing. A ball to celebrate our new marriage."

"I'm sorry, sir, but you have the wrong Walters sister."

He placed his hand over hers on the table.

"I don't have a Walters sister, I have Jacqueline Wolfe, Countess of Harrington. We must have a ball. It is expected." She must have looked as shocked as she felt because he squeezed her cold, tense hand and then leaned closer to whisper in her ear. "Perhaps after the first waltz we can rendezvous in the library."

As he pulled back, Jack looked up into his eyes. "Last night did I... sleep through something important? My friends can tell you that I'm famous for sleeping through everything."

Gideon's expression became guarded again. "If you sleep through that then I have sincerely done something wrong."

"One time they put me on the roof."

"They what?" Gideon asked, startled.

"Sabre and George. They considered it a challenge to find out how many things they could do without waking me."

"These are your friends? They could have killed you if you had rolled off."

"Oh, they tied me up there," Jack said. "In my blanket. Snug as a bug in a rug. When I woke up I couldn't get out and started screaming for someone to help me. That was one of the times Mama found out so they got in some real trouble."

"The other times you didn't tell on them?"

"Of course not, they're my friends."

"Darling, I don't know how to tell you this," he said, "but those aren't friends."

Jack raised a brow. "You're telling me that you and the duke wouldn't have tested such a weakness if you had found it in the other?"

Gideon laughed as he considered it. "Oh, Quince would have woken up tied at the top of a church steeple. Naked. Honestly I shudder to think what his fertile imagination might have come up with if the tables had been turned."

"Exactly. Friends can't help but to tease one another."

"Well, but you're..."

"Girls?"

Gideon shrugged. "Exactly."

"We may be women but we were never girls. Not the way you mean it."

"I knew there would be dangers in marrying a free-thinking bluestocking."

"I offered to break the engagement," she said with mock sweetness.

He looked at her speculatively. "Yes. Yes you did."

After breakfast the earl withdrew to his study and Jack decided to take a walk as she had much to think over. The book for one, the contents of which still made her blush just to think about. She couldn't imagine discussing it with Gideon but there was certainly no one else to talk to about it. Her husband's moods for another, how

he seemed to alternate between drawing her
closer and pushing her away. And last but not
least how she was going to handle the social
obligations of being the Countess of Harrington.
She realized now that this fortnight had indeed
been a honeymoon period and that she would
not be allowed to continue on with as few
responsibilities.

CHAPTER SIXTEEN

Gideon had not enjoyed the emotional tumult of the last few days and was relieved to be back in his study dealing with problems he could solve. Financial decisions, business decisions, agricultural decisions, governance decisions. He was finishing off a letter to Liverpool and staring out the tall windows that afforded him a magnificent view of the front lawn when he noticed a wagon coming up his drive. It was a bit unusual to receive a delivery at this time of the day, especially as the driver seemed to come towards the front of the house rather than go around to the side entrance, but he thought little of it and merely watched the wagon idly as he considered his words to the Prime Minister. Idly, that was, until he saw his wife running up the driveway. And saw the driver break the wagon and jump down to catch her as she flew at him with the joy of a child. The man spun her around while she laughed and they looked for all the world like reunited lovers. Gideon was out of his chair and pounding down the hallway to the front door before he had put together a coherent thought.

Jack stepped back, still laughing. "Look at you, Justin! I can't believe how much you've grown. I have to look up at you now."

The young man blushed and looked at the ground. "I suppose I should be bowing and calling you milady."

She grabbed his hands. "Don't be silly. We shall always be friends, regardless of anything else."

Still staring at the ground, he said, "It's alright Miss Jack-ma'am-milady. I know my place."

"Poppycock. You are Sabre's brother and that makes you my brother as well, just like Robert and Charles. But why are you here?"

"Sam wrote and said you would probably like to have your trunks when it was convenient."

Looking at the wagon Jack almost melted. "Oh Justin. You brought my trunks? From the attic? That couldn't have been convenient."

"Anything for you, Jack."

The earl's voice cut through their conversation like a steel blade through soft flesh. "Take your hands off my wife."

Justin jerked away from Jack's hands like he had been burned and immediately started bowing to the earl. "Begging your pardon my lord."

"Gideon!" Jack admonished. "Justin is one of my oldest and dearest friends."

The earl continued advancing on the young man who was now cowering back towards the wagon. "And how dear a friend is he?"

Jack grabbed Gideon's arm and began tugging him back before he had Justin pinned completely against the wagon. When she gave one particularly vicious tug Gideon turned his gaze on her and she decided his expression was most likely the one the devil wore when you showed up in perdition. It made her realize that this wasn't just an irritating situation but one that was rapidly becoming dangerous for her young friend.

"Gideon!" she said. "That is Sabrina Bittlesworth's little brother and if you hurt so much as one hair on his head I swear to you that I will open up those boxes he brought down here and I will have at you."

When he looked at her this time he at least wore a more rational expression than before. "The Bittlesworths only have two sons and I know both of them."

"Justin is their half-brother."

"I see. And what is Justin to you?"

"Family," Jack said staunchly.

Gideon had been propelled out onto the lawn with a fury greater than any he had ever known. It was a miracle beyond reckoning that the young man in front of him wasn't lying as a bloody mess at his feet.

"Stand up," he said to the boy who was cowering against the wagon as though he knew exactly what kind of violence Gideon had been capable of. Justin very slowly stood to his full height, looking like a wary fox ready to bolt at the first howl of the hounds. Tall. Taller than Robert and Charles and younger than Gideon had first guessed. He could see some of the Bittlesworth features in the boy's face and that at least bore out Jack's claim about his parentage. "What is your business here?"

"De-delivering items to Jack, er, the countess. Milady."

"What items?"

At that the young man seemed to bristle. "Her property."

Jack sighed. "It's alright Justin. My weapons, Gideon. He brought my weapons."

Gideon felt his world tilt slightly. "He brought your what?"

"My weapons." She was at the edge of the wagon peering in with the expression most women used when gazing at babies. "Bows, swords, knives, staves, chains. And guns, of course."

"You have chains?"

"Have you ever seen chain fighting? It's quite spectacular. I'm not nearly as good at it as George but I could at least give you a passable demonstration."

"Why do you have weapons?" he asked, still feeling dumbfounded.

She smiled up at him as though he were daft. "Why do *you* have weapons, Gideon?" Turning her attention to Justin she said. "Let's get these in the house and then we can settle you in."

As the young man moved the wagon away to the front door of Kellington, Gideon held Jacqueline where they stood. "He is not staying here."

Rather than arguing with him as usual his young wife slipped her arms around his waist, leaned into him until their bodies were aligned from chest to thigh, and looked up beseechingly into his eyes. "Please?"

Oh bloody hell. He'd known this day was coming from the beginning but he hadn't thought she would figure it out this fast. Brilliant woman, his wife. Brilliant, warm, soft, beautiful... He felt his cock twitch and harden as he looked down into her forest green eyes.

"Kiss me, Gideon," she said. As his lips descended to hers, he admitted to himself that the bloody bastard was staying.

Jack was so excited that she could barely contain herself. Her weapons had arrived! She thought she would at least need to wait until the Bittlesworths got home from tour and then politely ask Sabre in a letter if she wouldn't mind terribly sending someone whenever it was convenient. But her adorable little sister had cut through all of that by appealing to the one person who could execute the plan without anyone else's approval. And although he said he would do anything for Jack, she knew it was really that he would do anything for Sam. Justin was a full year younger than her little sister and had worshipped the ground Sam walked on for as long as anyone could remember. It was sad in a way since it was unrequited love, and even if it weren't, it wasn't as though their father would let Sam marry the bastard son of a viscount.

When Gideon started kissing her she had put all of her joy from this unexpected delivery into her kiss and he had responded to her enthusiasm with a searing intensity. Within moments Jack had forgotten all else in the world other than Gideon's taste, his heat. She wanted to crawl inside him, crawl all over him. Her body pressed itself even more flush to his of its own accord. One of his arms wrapped around her and his hand stroked her bottom, then pressed her closer still where they joined.

He finally tore his lips away, panting. "We need to stop."

"Why?"

"Otherwise I'm going to make love to my wife on the gravel of the front drive. As well as being uncomfortable it is likely to generate a great deal of talk."

"Let them talk."

"We can do this later, Jack."

She gave a frustrated growl. "Whenever later comes we either argue or find some other reason to avoid it.'"

He rubbed his nose against hers. "Try not to be impatient."

When she looked up at him she assessed that he was the good Gideon again, not the arrogant, autocratic, moody Gideon. She decided to tell him the truth. "I don't want to lose you."

He looked surprised. "I'm a bit large to be misplaced."

She snuggled into his chest and said irritably. "You know what I mean."

He kissed the top of her head. "Yes I do know what you mean, but what I don't know is what put that thought in your head."

She paused, not sure if she should tell him all but decided that it was usually best to be forthright. "I heard some of the servants talking. They said that you had dismissed your mistress but they didn't know why since it was obvious we weren't... having relations."

Gideon had gone very still. "What else did they say?"

"One of them was of the opinion that... relations were very important to a man and that any woman who hoped to keep her husband in a marriage had best please him in bed."

"I see."

"I'm sorry Gideon, did I make you angry?"

"No. In fact, would you like to hear something amusing?"

Jack pulled back and looked up into his face. "What's that?"

"The morning you rode hell for leather across Mayfair to face me down? I assumed the footmen had mixed up the letters and you had received the one intended for my mistress. It was her dismissal but still, what fiancée wants to hear about her future husband's mistress at all?"

"You dismissed her with a letter?"

"Which included a diamond bracelet."

"Still, that seems rather cold."

"You're defending her? How interesting. Typically I wouldn't do something like that by letter but... it didn't seem right to see her in person again since I was engaged. I wouldn't have wanted a story to get back to you about me seeing my mistress."

Jack looked up at this considerate, complicated man who was her husband.

"And another thing," she said, furrowing her brow. "You sent your mistress diamonds and I received yellow roses?"

Gideon laughed and gave her a quick kiss on the lips. "You can have all the diamond bracelets you want."

"I can run them up and down both arms?"

"If that is your desire. Perhaps you will start a fashion."

"A fashion that would bankrupt half the *ton*."

Gideon laughed and kissed the top of her head. "Since I think I can walk again, shall we go investigate your boxes?"

"And Justin can stay?"

"Yes, Justin can stay. But if he grabs you again like he did this morning I won't make any promises about his continuing health."

Jack pulled his head down for one more kiss. "Thank you, Gideon."

By the time they entered Kellington the footmen had already taken his wife's boxes up the stairs to her room. The young man who had brought them was nowhere to be seen. Gideon summoned Dibbs over to him.

"The boy is to be a favored guest, as he is a friend of the countess. Ready a room for him in the east wing. Have the grooms see to his horse and wagon."

"As it pleases you, my lord."

It didn't please Gideon at all but Jack was holding his hand and smiling up at him as though he had set the moon. Hopefully keeping the boy on the opposite end of the house would forestall any untoward behavior. He would hate to have to kill the lad.

CHAPTER SEVENTEEN

Once in her sitting room Jack immediately fell to opening one of the crates on the floor. Seeing her struggle Gideon helped her to pry off the lid. Pushing aside the packing she reverently pulled out a long, cloth wrapped bundle. The cloth was quickly unwound and tossed aside, revealing a wooden bow. She sat on the floor running her fingers over it, and then sighting up and down the length of it.

"No warping," she said with a sigh of relief. "I had oiled it as best I could before packing it away, but you can never be sure."

"How long was it in storage?"

"Twenty-six months."

"That's a rather exact number."

She arched a brow at him. "Send something you hold dear to Quince's house for safekeeping and we'll see how closely you track the passage of time."

"*Touché.*"

"You don't have to stay if this bores you."

"On the contrary," he said, lounging on the settee and watching her sitting on the floor with her boxes. "I find myself intrigued."

Over the next half hour Jack continued unpacking and unwrapping her collection. That seemed like the only potentially accurate term. She had three short bows, including a recurve that she described in detail before even having it out of its wrapping, two crossbows, two staves, four swords, he wasn't sure how many knives, two tightly wound chains with a purpose he couldn't divine, two sets of dueling pistols, a hunting rifle, and two large pistols that looked to have come from the military. He was, honestly, floored.

"What on earth do you plan to do with all this?"

"Get back into practice, as a start. I should probably think about having some cabinets built," she added while looking around the room. She had talked about building shelves for her books, but he realized that had been an idle comment compared to the light of purpose he saw in her eyes regarding what to do with all this. He had assumed that her passion was books but it was now apparent that those were a hobby.

"I find it confusing that you didn't express your interest in weapons before now."

"You don't talk about weapons," she said haughtily, "and you use them."

"But you didn't even have weapons with you when you came here."

She looked at him for a moment and then disappeared into her dressing room. He heard her moving items in her trunks and when she reemerged she was wearing a belt over her dress that held five sheathed knives. She was also carrying a small wooden box that she set it down on the table in front of him and opened, pulling back the fabric cover inside. "Blowgun and darts," she said.

Gideon leaned back and looked at his wife. She was smiling and flushed with delight over her collection the way most women might be over their wardrobe. He realized that he really didn't know her that well.

"I stand corrected," he said, not sure if he was amused or terrified. "If you don't mind I will go back to my study and finish my work."

"It's almost time for luncheon," she said. "Won't you join us?"

Gideon flinched at the thought of his wife lingering over lunch with the lad who had brought her beloved collection. "Sadly, I cannot. The Prime Minister isn't known for his patience and I must get this letter en route to London within the hour." He bowed over her hand and turned to go.

"I'll have them send a tray in to you," she called after him.

He stopped to look back at her. "My thanks."

And so he left her standing in her bedroom with weapons belted over her pale peach morning dress and more weapons strewn on the floor around her. His new wife was beyond unusual. Had her parents noticed her martial tendencies? How had she managed to procure such things? Surely her father wouldn't have purchased them for her, and she had no brothers. Archery was an acceptable hobby for a woman, but did she actually practice with the swords and guns? He shuddered to think it.

Jack rang for her maid and sent instructions to Mrs. Gladstone that all of them would have luncheon in their rooms. She didn't want to completely curtail her friendship with Justin but she had seen the look on Gideon's face when she had suggested that they would be lunching together. Hurt and fear that he had quickly covered over with a polite mask. Although she still had more to think about in regard to Gideon she knew she didn't want to ruin what progress they had made by being insensitive. Now with free time, she began organizing her weapons in her dressing room. Mary would, no doubt, be convinced that her mistress was crazy.

After an hour had passed she ventured downstairs to Gideon's study. She had been inside once, very briefly, as part of Mrs. Gladstone's tour of the household and discussion of cleaning regimens. This would be the first time she had approached him at his work, or at any time really. She knocked on the door before she could lose her nerve.

"Enter," she heard him say abruptly. He was either angry or deep in his work as some could be. She slipped inside.

Her husband was sitting at the large desk in the middle of the room. His chair was light brown leather and the entire room had a lighter, more golden color than her father's study. Tall windows looked out on the front and side of the house, framed with drapes made of an intricate golden pattern. Gideon was like a solemn dark spot in the room with his black jacket and dark brown hair. Much of his hair had worked loose of its queue again to fall over his forehead and against his cheek. He seemed focused on his work, head still down, scratching a pen rapidly over paper. She was able to study him unobserved, taking in his broad shoulders and handsome profile.

"Yes?" he asked shortly without looking up.

She leaned against the door she had entered and said, "I thought I should check to make sure you had eaten your lunch. Which I can see that you haven't."

His head had come up at her voice and he stood immediately, as propriety dictated. She waved her hand at him. "Don't trouble yourself. Do you mind if I look around?"

"Of course not."

She pushed away from the door and started browsing through the room much more leisurely than she had when following in Mrs. Gladstone's wake. It seemed her husband liked to collect things. Or perhaps his father had. A tiny reproduction of a Grecian statue here, a lacquered Oriental box there. As she continued to explore he finally sat down again.

"How was your lunch?" he asked.

She looked over her shoulder. "You could find out yourself if you ate yours. Did you get your letter to the Prime Minister done?"

"Yes. After that I sent Philip to eat."

"Yet you can't find time to eat your own food."

"I'm not hungry. How is your... friend?"

"Doing well enough, I assume. We can find out at dinner. I had Mrs. Gladstone send trays to all of us since you couldn't join us in the dining room for luncheon."

From the corner of her eye Jack could see him relax a bit. As she continued her slow perusal he eventually turned his attention back to his work and she was able to study him more openly. She had been thinking about his behavior, trying to use her curiosity instead of being irritated by his capricious changes in mood. The first thing she concluded was that he was intensely jealous. That was flattering in a way, but spoke more of possessiveness than any particular affection for his wife. The other thing she noted was that he tended to be most irritating when she had made headway on getting to know him better. He didn't like letting people becoming close to him. He had no siblings and never spoke of his parents. It was possible he just wasn't used to being close to anyone. Although his staff adored him there was a barrier between them and himself. He was the earl and acted every inch the nobleman.

Jack had made her way around the entire room. As she looked at Gideon, still bowed over his desk, she thought of her parents. When Papa stayed too long at his work Mama would always come into his study and wrap her arms around him from behind, teasing him that days had passed since the family had last seen him last. Jack wondered how Gideon would react to such a display of affection. Although it made her heart beat rapidly to consider he might not take it well, she was drawn to do it. She at least had some affection for her husband and he did work too hard. As she slipped her hands over his shoulders and across his chest to hug him she felt him tense in surprise. With her mouth now close to his ear she whispered, "Am I going to have to feed you that lunch from my hand?"

His voice was warm and soft as he replied, "Are you afraid I'm going to waste away?"

"I would hate for you to lose any of your strength or vigor."

He leaned back, his shoulders pressing against her breasts. "You're concerned about my vigor?"

"I would certainly hate for you to lose it," she whispered.

His hand reached back to cup her head and he turned to capture her lips with his own. The kiss was exquisite, drugging. Jack could feel her body begin to tingle as his tongue teased her own. He drew back from her and asked, "Have you read the book yet?"

"Oh yes, many times."

"Do you have questions?"

"Hmm..." she said speculatively. "Only...when do we start?"

Gideon shifted and Jack suddenly found herself in his lap. This kiss was hungry, almost brutal, but after a moment of surprise she strained toward him. There was no thought of duty, or fear of losing him to another woman. This was pure, driving need. After some moments of deep, soul-drenching kisses he pulled back and rested his forehead to hers. "Philip will be here soon."

"Lock the door."

He laughed breathlessly. "Would you join me upstairs?"

"Yes."

"I'm going to take a bath before joining you."

"I'll order it now. And one for myself as well."

He began to kiss her again and then there was a perfunctory knock at the door followed by the sound of the door creaking open.

"Just a moment!" Gideon called out brusquely. He said more softly to Jack while kissing her jaw, "Phillip is used to being able to walk in and out at will."

"I told you we should have locked the door."

Gideon set her on her feet with a laugh. "Get on with you."

She passed Phillip at the doorway, giving the steward an embarrassed smile. She called for her maid and ran up the steps to her bedroom. What to wear? What should she do with her hair? Should she retrieve the book in case they were going to discuss it? She stopped on a landing and nearly laughed at herself. Surely they weren't going to do a recitation session on it. But still, perhaps she should have it close at hand. Would they be in her room? His room? He had said her suites reminded him of his mother and there couldn't be anything good in that, surely. Oh gods she was doing it again. Thinking. Worrying. She took a deep breath and slowed her pace.

CHAPTER EIGHTEEN

In her suite, Jack concentrated on bathing, applying lotions and scents, then brushing her pale brown hair until it shone. Covered in a dressing gown, she went through the adjoining door to his room. He wasn't there yet. After considering her options she decided to sit in the chair near the bed. She set the book on his bedside table and immediately regretted not having brought something else to read. It was impossible to know how long he would be gone since he tended to obsess about his work. Shortly, however, she heard a sound from his dressing room and he was at the doorway, wearing a robe that fell open above the sash and toweling off his hair. She hadn't seen a man's naked torso before, and found that his book had not done him justice. He was a magnificent stallion, all thick muscle that bunched and rippled as he moved, with curling hair spread across his chest and tapering down to a point that disappeared below the loosely tied sash. She felt her mouth go dry as she stared. He pulled the towel off his head and saw her, going very still. Then a grin spread on his face. "Couldn't wait?"

Without thought she rose from the chair and went to him. He stepped forward as well and they came together in a kiss of melting heat. His skin was warm and damp from his bath, scented with the faint lemongrass of his soap. She ran her hands over the damp hair on his chest, intrigued by it. With a soft growl he lifted her up and carried her to the bed. He followed her down onto the soft surface, his weight pressing her into the mattress. He was kissing her jaw, her throat, while his fingers worked the ties on her robe. Once the ties were loose, he looked down on her as he brushed the silk aside.

"So beautiful," he whispered, running his fingers over the sides of her breast, her ribs, her waist, in a soft touch that both tickled and inflamed. His hand tightened possessively on her hip, his thumb stroking her side.

She ran her hands over his chest, feeling the solid muscles quiver under her fingers. He moved down to kiss her belly and she threaded her fingers in his soft, damp hair. He moved lower still, kissing her thighs and nudging them apart. She relaxed and opened to him with a soft sigh. Although the book had given her information on the mechanics, it had been woefully short on insight into how this would feel. She was floating in a drugged haze, both reveling in what Gideon was doing to her body and somehow strangely detached from it. Then he ran his thumb along that private spot between her legs and she hissed in a quick breath, his carnal touch bringing her crashing back into the reality of her body. His tongue followed his thumb and the rush of sensation made her scramble back towards the headboard. His hands anchored her hips, and when she stopped squirming away from him he used one hand to open her more fully to his mouth. She dug her fingers into the wood over her head and tried not to scream but the heat and pleasure that bordered on pain built and built until she couldn't think, could only feel Gideon licking, kissing, stroking. He began suckling on the nub that seemed to be at the core of sensation and she felt herself bow up from the bed as waves of pleasure thundered through her. She realized she was calling his name in a desperate chant.

He moved up her body, kissing her hip, her belly. She was still panting and now her body was quivering in new reactions. When he reached her breasts he settled in to lick and nibble and kiss, molding the delicate flesh in his hands. His weight on her was strangely invigorating and as his lips and fingers played over her sensitive bosom she felt heat, dampness, and pressure building. She squirmed under him, running her fingers through his hair, over his shoulders. His weight on her, his touch, felt right but she knew she wanted something more. The pictures from the book played through her mind and made her think she knew what that 'more' was. Once she started squirming his mouth became more avid, his touch more intense, and that made her more desperate.

"Gideon, please," she gasped.

He moved up to kiss her throat, her ear, while still tweaking her peaked nipple with his fingers. "Please what?"

"Please make love to me."

He chuckled, "Now?"

"Yes, now!"

He kissed her with a powerful tenderness that had her melting into the pillows. He whispered into her ear, "This can hurt the first time."

She whispered back, "I know."

He smoothed his hand down her body until it found the sensitive spot between her legs again. He kissed her, keeping the rhythm of his tongue in time with the sweep of his fingers and she thought she would go mad with wanting. She pulled away from him, breathless. "Gideon!"

He smiled and sat up on his knees, removing his robe. He was so magnificent that she couldn't breathe. She'd never thought to find a man beautiful, but he was to her. His skin was darker than her own, and covered in dark, curling hairs. His shoulders were broad and muscled, his trim belly adorned with that intriguing arrow of hair. Her eyes traveled to below his waist and she gasped.

"This isn't going to work," she announced.

"I assure you that it is," he said solemnly. "You can trust me."

She looked back into his eyes and his confidence calmed her fears.

Taking the towel he'd used earlier, he folded it and slid it under her hips, spreading her thighs open with gentle hands. "I haven't made it a habit to deflower virgins but my understanding is there can be a bit of blood." He paused, "That is provided, of course, that you are a virgin..." There was that vulnerability again that he rarely showed. A hope that she was his, that he was special to her.

She ruthlessly suppressed any remaining fear and reached toward him. "Yes, but only because I can't seem to lure my husband to my bed."

He smiled and lay down on her, his weight pressing her into the soft mattress again and the hardness of his cock pulsing against her inner thigh. He kissed her cheek and then stared down into her eyes as he guided himself into her. As he entered her she felt him shudder. He felt impossibly large and she almost told him again that he wasn't going to fit, but as he slid shallowly in and out of her she felt the tightness relax and the excitement low in her belly began to intensify. With each thrust he went slightly deeper until finally he gripped her hips and thrust fully into her. She felt a tearing pinch and squeaked in protest. He lay still on top of her and smoothed hairs back from her cheek. "Are you alright?"

She nodded, knowing that there were tears in the corner of her eyes. "Yes, I'm fine."

He kissed her again. The gentle, drugging kiss that made her forget everything else. After a few moments he started to move in her again and there was no pain. When she relaxed he quickened his pace and she felt a new aspect to the pleasures her body had experienced earlier. She instinctively tilted her pelvis and met his rhythm with her own, feeling a wild abandon beyond curricle racing or fighting. Her body began to pulse and she dug her nails into his skin from the intensity of the shuddering contractions that made her body quake. As she began to call his name he shouted hoarsely and after a final thrust he slumped forward, taking his weight onto his elbows above her and breathing heavily. His face was mostly covered by his dark, wild hair and she brushed it back to see his eyes. She didn't recognize his expression but decided that it was good. He leaned down to kiss her mouth and forehead before pulling rolling onto his back and pulling her on top of him. She tucked her head into the crook between his neck and shoulder while he ran his hands down her back and over her bottom. This aspect of marriage to him was, as she had suspected, quite pleasing.

Gideon squeezed his beautiful, passionate wife's bottom and tried to get his breathing and galloping heart under control. Entering her tight, wet body had been one of the most amazing experiences of his life. When he had driven fully into her he had almost forgotten his concern about hurting her, as the whole of his being had sighed with relief and joy at finally joining. That first deep thrust had been accompanied by the thought "Oh, thank God." Then she had yipped in pain and it had felt like he himself had been stabbed. She had recovered quickly, once again a lush, demanding goddess. Just thinking about what it was like to be in her, he could feel himself hardening again, but it wouldn't do to cause her pain. He set her back on the towel and stood up to get the water bowl and assess how much blood there was. Seeing it smeared on his cock cooled his ardor for entering her again tonight. He cleaned himself off and then came to the bed to clean her as well. There was a small amount of blood on the towel and a bit more on her inner thighs and the lips of her cleft. He washed her silently while she watched him and the circumstance, which could have seemed awkward, was intimate and slightly erotic instead. Through her relaxation she signaled that he had full access to her body, and it was difficult not to start arousing them both again. After he set the bowl and towels aside she reached out for him, and he lay down next to her on the bed but she gripped him on his sides and pulled.

"On top," she said.

"You want me on top of you? I'm heavy."

"I like it."

As he liked it, too, he complied. She had spread her thighs and he settled into the intimate connection, his cock hardening and throbbing against her. She was running her hands through his hair again, then over his face and shoulders. It was both arousing and relaxing, and he thought it would be the better part of valor to sink into a nap rather than slide into her again as he intensely wanted to do.

"Gideon."

"Yes, love?"

"Are you falling asleep?"

He kissed her shoulder. "Perhaps, if you'll be quiet."

"Then am I doing it wrong?"

He rose up on his elbows to look down at her. She was worried now, he could see it in the tiny crease between her brows and the troubled look in her eyes. He kissed her on that tiny crease and smiled. "If you were doing it any more right I would probably burst into flames."

"Then why aren't we... I can tell that you're...interested."

His cock pulsed again. "Oh yes, I'm very...interested. But I don't want to hurt you." He stroked her cheek. "We have plenty of time."

She gazed up at him, looking oddly serious. "Do we?"

"Tomorrow isn't soon enough?"

She seemed to give it serious thought. "Tomorrow is an abstract concept. All we really have is today."

"Very well, you clever little vixen. I suppose this is what I get for marrying a woman who can read Greek. Philosophy in the bedroom." He rolled onto his back and pulled her on top of him. "If we're going to do this then I want you to be able to stop if it hurts too much. Do you remember this from the book?"

She gave him a triumphant smile. "Oh yes."

He helped her to place her knees to the side of his hips and sink down onto his throbbing erection. She tilted her head back with a soft moan and began to move over him. As she found her rhythm he saw the flush bloom over her heavy, rounded breasts, bouncing with her movements. He thought it was very possible he would die from the pleasure of his new wife. His thumb found and stroked the pearl between her thighs to make sure she experienced her climax before he gripped her hips and drove up into her until he found his own release.

CHAPTER NINETEEN

As Jack entered the drawing room on Gideon's arm before dinner, she felt herself flush as she spotted her childhood friend. She wondered how long it would be until she stopped feeling like she had just been discovered doing something naughty. But that brought thoughts of exactly what they had been doing upstairs, which made her face burn even hotter.

Justin had changed into dinner clothes, which meant that either he had packed some, which she doubted, or her husband had ordered his staff to produce some for him from somewhere. They actually fit rather well, if a few years out of style. He bowed politely to them both and it made her smile, remembering how Sabre would lecture him on his manners. *'Even as a bastard you may have occasion to move in Society one day and it will reflect very poorly on me, indeed, if you cannot do so with aplomb.'* Jack knew that Sabre had put in that extra twist about how it would reflect on her because Justin would do almost anything to help his half-siblings, and would be appalled to have his own behavior reflect poorly on them.

How prescient Sabre had proven to be, now that Justin was here, making his bow to an earl and countess, preparing to eat at their table. Even the viscount had never allowed Justin to eat at table with the family. From what Jack had seen the viscount tried very hard to ignore that Justin even existed, which had been both boon and bane to the boy. On the one hand, it meant that Justin could do almost anything as long as he didn't run afoul of the viscount. On the other hand, it meant he didn't have the attention and affection of the person who meant the most to him. It was, Jack thought, a very strange and sad life to lead. And it was evident that without his half-siblings and the rest of the Haberdashers around, Justin had settled into less than what he had the potential to be.

When entertaining, it was customary to chat in the drawing room until dinner was announced, and as the two friends hadn't uttered a word, Gideon started the conversation. "Have you found your room satisfactory?"

Justin nodded, "Yes, thank you, my lord. The view of the gardens is stunning and the room is quite comfortable."

Jack suppressed the impulse to applaud him, as she used to do when he gave a particularly good answer as they played what Sabre called "Lord and Lady." It had been a game designed to prepare all of them for precisely this circumstance. And, as Jack recalled, she had always been abysmal at it. She had preferred to watch the others play. Justin with his earnestness, George with her sly wit, Sabre with her haughty arrogance, and Sam with her sweetness. On the rare occasions that they could press Robert and Charlie into playing with them, she had enjoyed Robert's smooth authority and Charlie's silly playfulness as well. Just then she had a terrible wave of nostalgia and missed her friends all the more acutely. She missed those innocent games with her friends and now, as she realized she still hadn't participated in the conversation, she also wished she had been more diligent in using them to improve upon the flaw in her character that made her silent in social situations. She searched her mind for something to say and blurted out the first thing she found, "We're having a ball. Next month. I do hope you can come."

She realized that both of them seemed stunned. The first person she was going to invite to this nebulous idea of a ball was the nearly unacknowledged bastard of a peer? She had made the mistake of letting her genuine feelings run her mouth again, rather than putting a Society gloss over all her true thoughts and emotions. But if she were to choose who would be at her ball then of course Justin would be on her list. If she had her druthers it would be completely confined to her "Lord and Lady" playmates, save she supposed she had to add Gideon. Perhaps she should go back to the silence that had formerly seemed like such a bad idea.

Justin flushed and looked at the earl, then back to Jack. "If I am able, then of course I would be most honored."

Fortunately Dibbs saved them by announcing dinner.

Their places had been set at Gideon's end of the table as Jack had requested, placing her in her usual seat and Justin across from her at Gideon's left. She remained quiet through the first course and fortunately her friend and her husband found an accord in conversation almost immediately. Their topics ranged from regional agriculture, including the proposed Importation Act, to the latest news from the Congress of Vienna. After pushing her peas around her plate while listening she finally said, "It's nice to hear the latest news after being out here without the newspaper."

Gideon stopped and looked at her. "We take the paper. It's a day late from London, but we get it."

"We do? Since we never read it at breakfast I assumed we didn't."

He reached out to take her hand. "Yes, we do. I take it in my study. You may come by any morning you like to read it."

She smiled at him, thinking this would be something else they could share.

"Well," Justin said, spooning up some potatoes. "I'm glad to see that what they say is true."

"What's true?" Gideon asked, turning his attention to his young guest.

Justin looked from the earl to Jack as though not sure he needed to say anything. "That it's a love match."

Gideon withdrew his hand stiffly from Jack's and picked up his fork again. "Yes, well, if you can't trust London gossip what can you trust?"

Jack raised a brow at Justin and said tartly, "And what else did Samantha put in her letter?"

Justin smiled down into his fish course and shrugged. "Some other things."

"Gideon, I have to apologize for my sister. She is immature and intrusive."

"Jack!" Justin exclaimed, ready to defend his ladylove.

Gideon leaned forward slightly to catch the young man's eye. "Are you shouting at my wife?"

Justin slinked down in his seat a bit. "My apologies, my lord."

"So," Jack said briskly to divert them, "what were you saying about the Corn Laws?"

That set them off into another fifteen minutes of debating agricultural issues while Jack wondered what other things Sam had mentioned that had made Justin smile.

Gideon considered it lucky that Jacqueline's young friend was a rather well informed and intelligent conversationalist, otherwise there would be nothing stopping him from taking his wife back upstairs for another round of lovemaking, and it was too soon for that, certainly. He found that he couldn't stop touching her, although he tried to make it less obvious after Justin's comment. Just a tap on the arm or sliding his foot to intercept hers under the table. It began to feel like a game. The "how many times can I touch Jacqueline without anyone noticing?" game. He knew that she had entered into the spirit of it when she leaned forward to ask Justin a question and used that opportunity to set her hand on her husband's knee. Being just as surreptitious, he took her fingers in his own and they spent all of the dessert course holding hands under the edge of the table. Fortunately the berry compote chef had served was easily eaten one-handed.

After dinner Jacqueline insisted on withdrawing to leave them to their port, something Gideon resented both because it meant there would be a stall in his game, and he didn't fancy taking port with a wet behind the ears bastard pup. The more he chatted with the lad, the younger he assumed the boy to be. Not that there was anything wrong with being young per se, but undoubtedly they would run out of agreeable topics before long. And besides that, he didn't particularly care for port and he wanted his wife and really there wasn't anything wrong with either of those things, and what was the point of being an earl if you couldn't avoid what you disliked and have what you liked? His mind was clicking along on that track while his mouth was talking about agriculture when the young pup in question threw out an unexpected observation.

"I think the most important thing in marriage is what you bring out in each other."

"Pardon me?"

The boy had slouched down in his chair as befitted the coze of after dinner drinks, and now stared down into the port glass he had barely sipped from. "What you bring out in each other." When the earl remained silent the boy looked up again. "I don't know you, my lord, I can't say as to what effect Jack has had on you. But I can certainly see the effect you've had on Jack."

"I've.. had an effect?" Gideon looked into his own glass and realized he was already on his second serving and well on his way to claiming a third.

"You confuse her. Fluster her."

"And is that... good?"

"It remains to be seen, my lord."

Gideon decided that he would stop at two glasses and set to swirling the liquid at the bottom of his glass as he contemplated the boy's words. It took a great deal of guts to tell a peer that you weren't sure you thought much of how he was treating your friend. Provided it was just friendship and not something more fueling the boy's courage.

"How long have you known Jacqueline?"

"All my life."

"And how would you describe the nature of your relationship?"

At that the boy looked up and smiled at him. "She's one of my sisters."

"One of?"

"All the Haberdashers are my sisters."

"Haberdashers?"

The boy looked confused. "The Haberdashers. Sabre, Jack, and George."

"Not Samantha?"

That made a laugh bubble up out of him. "Of course not."

"What's funny about that?"

"Have you ever seen Samantha try to shoot a gun?"

"Of course not."

"If you do I suggest you take cover behind something."

"The Haberdashers is a shooting club?"

The boy tilted his head to one side as though considering Gideon's limited knowledge of the Haberdashers. "I suggest you ask Jack about it."

Gideon began to feel out of sorts over this Haberdashers business. "Why do they all use boy's names?"

Justin shrugged. "Ask Jack."

"Do you never call her Jacqueline?"

"No one does. Except you. Sam calls her Jackie."

After a moment Gideon said, "Well, that's all very interesting but I think it's time to rejoin my lovely wife."

Justin nodded and set his barely touched glass of port aside. Well, at least they had a distaste of port in common.

Jack lingered in the drawing room reading a book of Greek plays that Lara had been kind enough to fetch for her. She had been so proud of how Justin comported himself at table that she knew just how a mama bird felt the first time her baby bird flew. Later she would write letters to Sabre and George to tell them all about it, knowing they would be jealous that they hadn't been here to witness it. But meanwhile it was her lot to wait and see if the men rejoined her for after-dinner entertainments. It wasn't terribly long before they did, seeming perhaps a bit more out of sorts than they had been before she left them. Sadly they didn't have a fourth for whist and after a short discussion of potential entertainments the group broke up to make an early evening of it. She insisted that Justin take the book of plays up to his room with him since she knew he wouldn't trouble anyone with a request. And besides, it couldn't hurt for him to practice his Greek.

CHAPTER TWENTY

Once they were upstairs she and Gideon went to their separate dressing rooms to ready themselves for bed. They hadn't discussed what the sleeping arrangements would be and Jack was a bit nervous of what she would do if he seemed to avoid her, but he reappeared while she was brushing out her hair and sat on the bed watching her.

"What is this young man's last name, anyway?" he asked. "I assume it isn't Bittlesworth."

Jack laughed. "Oh my goodness, I didn't introduce you."

Gideon shrugged. "By the time it seemed I wasn't going to thrash him I'm sure the moment had passed."

"Well, my apologies that I let your bad manners inspire my own. His name is Justin Miller."

"And his mother?"

Jack paused. "Sibyl Miller. She was a maid at the Bittlesworth's estate."

"Where is she now?"

"She died of a fever within a week of when Justin was born."

"And he was raised by the viscount?"

Jack set her brush down and went over to stand in front of Gideon. "Not exactly."

He pulled her forward so that she stood between his knees with his arms hooked over her hips. "Do I sense a story to be told?"

She smiled and threaded her fingers through his hair. "I'm sure you would rather do something else than be told a story."

He was diligently inspecting the bows, ties and ruffles on her diaphanous nightgown and robe. "On the contrary, I love stories."

Jack thought that if marriage consisted only of moments like these, sweet intimate moments, then it was something that everyone should aspire to. "Sometimes, if both his Lord and Ladyship are out, you can still get the servants to tell the story of the day poor Justin's mother died. Sibyl was shunned by her family, you see, for becoming pregnant. She had also been turned off from employment at the estate. But our local midwife, Old Madge, took sympathy when it was time for the birth and let Sibyl stay at her home. When Sibyl sickened, Old Madge went to the family, and Sibyl's brother Bert finally consented to see her. They say she admitted to Bert who the father of the boy was and, on the day she died, Bert confronted the viscount." She paused which drew his attention from where he was untying one of the bows securing her robe. "Bert worked in the Viscount's stables, you see. A veritable mountain of a man, the servants always say, although I assume over the years tales of his size have become exaggerated. I was three when it happened and don't remember him. But they say the death of his baby sister had pushed him too far, and on that day he confronted the viscount who was fresh back from his morning ride. Pulled him off the horse and threw him up against the stable door. Told the viscount to take on the responsibility for his son or Bert himself would send the man to final judgment, which with Sibyl's death and only God knew what other sins on his soul would undoubtedly send him straight to the Devil."

"That should have earned him a thrashing at least, if not outright execution."

"After he extracted that promise, which according to Courtland required him to finally allow the viscount to breathe, and more the pity that, he left and was never heard from again."

"Courtland sounds a bit bloodthirsty."

"Most butlers are."

Gideon choked. "Are you saying I need fear Dibbs?"

She smiled. "No more than you need fear me."

He pulled her down onto the bed. "That, my dear, was a politician's answer. And it leaves me quaking, I assure you."

She ran her hands down his back. "Yes, I can tell."

"You've quite taken to this like a duck to water, but I think it would be best if we didn't have another joining tonight."

Jack felt a bit petulant, but admitted as she plucked at her husband's silk sleeve. "I am a bit sore."

"Instead perhaps we can try some of the more exotic pleasures from the book."

Jack smiled. "Oh yes. That sounds delightful."

Although exhausted from bed play, Gideon slept fitfully and was awake before dawn again. He slipped away from the soft, warm body of his wife, making sure that she was covered and snug. True to her stories, she hardly seemed disturbed by his efforts to disentangle himself and pull up her covers. It was tempting to carry her somewhere unusual to wake up, but as she was naked it limited the number of places he would want to put her. His thoughts brought him up short. When was the last time that he had teased someone or been playful? He honestly couldn't remember. There were some stories from school, mostly he and Quince when they were in shorts. Before Gideon's father had died. Not pleased with the direction his mind had wandered, Gideon went to the escritoire in his bedroom to write Jack a short note and leave it on her pillow.

Once downstairs he said to the footman on duty, "Please ask our guest Mr. Miller if he would like to join me on my ride. I shall be taking coffee in the morning room when he comes down."

"Yes, my lord."

A mere ten minutes later the young Mr. Miller made his appearance, once again dressed in what Gideon knew to be his own clothes from his youth. He indicated that the boy should take the seat next to him at the small round table. As a footman poured coffee and offered milk and sugar, which the boy politely refused, Gideon assessed him.

"It's clear that you're younger than my wife, but how old are you?"

"Fifteen, sir. I mean, my lord."

Gideon raised a brow, knowing that the clothes the boy wore had been from his own twentieth year and he had not been small, even then. The lad would most likely turn out to be a mountain of a man himself.

"You can ride, I assume?"

"Oh yes sir, I mean my lord. Charlie taught me."

Charlie Bittlesworth, known to be as horse mad as any Englishman had a right to be, had taken the time to teach the boy to ride, which meant the young man could be a fine rider indeed. Neither Robert nor Charlie had ever mentioned having a bastard half-brother. Not that it was something that would come up in polite conversation, but if Justin were truly as doted upon as his and Jack's comments seemed to suggest it was odd that the brothers hadn't let something slip after all these years. Then again they hadn't mentioned that they let their little sister and her friends race curricles at home either. Perhaps there was just a great deal he didn't know about the Bittlesworths.

Gideon signaled the footman over. "Have them saddle Brier as well as Falcon. She could do with some exercise."

Justin seemed to deflate a bit at the thought that he was being assigned a mare.

"Oh, don't let her sex fool you. I live in fear that my wife will take a fancy to her. She is one of the most headstrong and spirited animals I've known."

The boy smiled, amused. "Jack or the mare?"

Gideon nearly choked on his sip of coffee. "I see your point, but I was referring to Brier."

After finishing his second cup and allowing Justin time to sip at his own brew, Gideon rose and led the way out to the stables. Although polite and deferential, Justin didn't quite have the puppy dog quality of Philip, which was a bit of a relief. As much as he liked Philip and thought the young man was maturing into an effective steward, it was tiresome to always have him underfoot while at Kellington. As Gideon took up the reins for his own dark bay, Falcon, he observed Justin approaching the massive and stomping dapple-gray mare. The boy had not only been taught well but also appeared to have some of Charlie's affinity for animals, greeting and calming the horse before attempting to mount her. If they continued to get along well perhaps he would gift the mare to the young man, both removing it from his stable before his wife could decide to ride her and gaining his wife's approval for indulging her young friend. The desire to both protect and delight his young wife didn't bear close scrutiny so he urged Falcon into a gallop along the open field with the young Mr. Miller in close pursuit.

When Jack awoke she found her husband's note almost immediately, having reached out a hand for him on the bed.

"Good morning wife - I think I shall take your young friend riding since you and I will be going to the Vicarage later and I don't want you to become overtired of my company. Will ask Dibbs to place the newspaper at breakfast table. Hopefully this change to protocol will not inspire him to choke off my air as you say butlers are wont to do.
Yours, Gideon"

She lay on the bed laughing quite helplessly and thinking that oh yes, there was definitely much to be said for the state of marriage. Before she left the bedroom she tucked the note into the same book that held a pressed yellow rose petal.

Not wanting to tear apart his paper before he had a chance to read it, Jack was pushing a bite of egg around her plate and considering whether she should redecorate her suite when she heard them return. There was laughter in the hallway, which was a relief. Honestly she was more than a little afraid that Gideon had taken Justin on a ride simply to terrorize the boy. Not that he was a boy any longer, she corrected herself. He was a young man. It had amazed her to see how much he had grown in the two years she had been gone. Sabre, who had seen him more recently, had said as much in one of her letters, but it was still difficult to believe. He had always been the little boy following them around. Beloved and indulged. No, the viscount had not raised his son. Other than allowing the boy to live on the property, he had had as little to do with him as possible. The Bittlesworth boys and the Haberdashers had raised him, with no little help from the servants that adored him and reveled in the memory of how his Uncle Bert had secured his future.

CHAPTER TWENTY-ONE

The men entered discussing politics again. Justin said, "But what if the entire purpose of Rutledge's vote is to call out Lexington's opinion since Rutledge has two years before his reelection while Lexington has to explain his actions to his voters now?"

Seeing Jack sitting at the table Gideon came over to kiss her cheek before sitting. "It seems your young Mr. Miller is quite well educated for a man who hasn't ever gone to school."

Justin flushed at the odd combination of compliment and set-down that the earl's comment embodied and took his own seat. Jack tried not to let her hackles rise at Gideon upsetting her friend and said mildly, "Yes, we always tried to make sure he received the best of our instruction."

"That might explain it, then. I always felt that at least half of our instructors were drawn to the profession due to their sadistic intent towards boys. However, why is it that the viscount never sent Mr. Miller to school? It seems oddly remiss of him."

Jack crumbled some toast in her fingers and flitted her gaze past Justin, who seemed diligently absorbed in cutting his ham.

"I already asked Mr. Miller himself," Gideon pressed, "and he seemed quite uninformed on the topic. Perhaps you have some insight?"

"I'm sure it never occurred to him to do so."

"How can it not occur to you do to so? The list of duties to one's... other children is quite short but I'm fairly certain that the list includes preparing them for a livelihood."

Jack looked at her husband speculatively, wondering if he had any by-blows she would come to learn about. "To the best of my knowledge, the viscount has never spoken to Justin nor, perhaps, even thought about him. Justin hasn't as much been recognized as ignored and allowed to live at the estate. Perhaps we could find something else to talk about?"

"He spoke to me once," Justin said softly, still focused rather intently on his plate.

"When?" Jack blurted before she could stop herself. It didn't seem a memory that Justin treasured.

"Before they left for Charlie's tour. Sabre had..." Justin gave a deep sigh, distressed by the memory. "Sabre had asked that I be allowed to join them. The viscount came to me to see if I had asked her to do that, which I hadn't."

"Of course not," Jack said loyally, "you would never presume."

Justin nodded, now absorbed in pushing small bits of ham with his fork. "He said that...

he said that I was nothing and should learn to be content with such a lot in life. That I was lucky he allowed me to be a servant in his home and I was old enough to put myself to better use in the stables. You see, my lord," Justin gave the earl a wry smile, "the viscount undoubtedly believes he has prepared me for my livelihood."

Jack's heart broke, both at the words the viscount had said and the brave face that this young man put on about a scene that must have pulled his own heart out by the roots. "Oh Justin!" she cried, jumping up and racing around the table to throw her arms around his shoulders. The sympathy was his undoing and, covering his face with his hands, he sobbed under her embrace.

Gideon realized he was sitting with a forkful of egg halfway to his mouth and finally set it down. He was not used to outbursts of emotion at his breakfast table, certainly, but it was also the shock of what the viscount had said. The boy was intelligent, well educated, and well mannered, yet Bittlesworth expected him to work in the stable? And be glad of it? More shocking still was that the lad seemed to accept it.

He also, he noticed, wasn't as irritated by his wife's affection for the boy as he had been. She truly did seem sisterly, and sometimes even motherly, when it came to Mr. Miller. As the boy's sobs subsided she patted his shoulder, kissed him on the head, and pushed a linen napkin into his hands. She took her own seat with a brisk efficiency, looking a bit red-eyed herself but wanting to move them past this episode with the minimum of fuss. Justin wiped his face and set to cutting more of the food on his plate although nothing seemed to be going into his mouth.

"How do you like London, Mr. Miller?" Gideon asked.

"I've never been there, my lord," he said, still staring at his place setting.

"Well, there may be something better than the stables for you there. I'm in need of a clerk."

The young man looked up at him with such a surge of hope and gratitude that Gideon almost backed away from him.

"I'm at your service, my lord," the young man said quickly.

Blast it all, this *was* another puppy dog. To change the subject Gideon gestured to the paper lying folded on the table. "You haven't read the newspaper yet this morning, my dear?"

"I usually enjoy our morning conversations. We can read it in your study afterwards. Besides... I wouldn't want to risk your respiration," she added with a surreptitious nod to Dibbs.

Gideon had to suppress a chuckle as the butler tried to assess whether the countess had been signaling for him.

As of this moment Jack was completely and totally in love with her husband. He would do something later to irritate her, she had no doubt, but as of this moment he was the most wonderful, amazing man of her acquaintance. Offering Justin a clerkship as though it were completely natural to do so! She understood the quiet and reverent devotion of his servants now. Somehow he always knew the thing to do to put everything to rights.

Gideon checked his watch and addressed Justin. "Perhaps you can come to my study at ten o'clock to begin reviewing papers you will need to understand. That will give the countess and I time to read our newspaper."

Jack jumped up from the table and handed the newspaper to her husband. "I'll be to the study in just a moment," she said. "If you gentlemen will excuse me?"

They both stood and bowed as she dashed out of the dining room and up the stairs. She wanted to write a quick note to Sabre and George about Justin's turn of fortune. Since Sabre had instructed her to send correspondence by way of Robert now anyway instead of the viscount's London address, which as she thought about it seemed odd, she wrote a short cover letter to Robert as well. "Am delighted to inform you that Justin Miller has accepted a clerkship with my husband, Earl of Harrington." Although it felt odd and gave her pause, she signed the letter "Lady Harrington." Then below that she scribbled "Jack."

She was back downstairs and entering her husband's study in less than ten minutes, carrying the letters that he would need to frank for delivery. He was seated at his desk and had already pulled the newspaper apart, his head buried in the foreign news section. Seeing her he stood but she waved him back to his seat.

"The society pages are right there," he said, nodding to a section he had set on the edge of his desk.

Jack wrinkled her nose. "I don't read the society pages."

He looked over his paper and raised a brow at her. "Then how did we come to be married?" he teased.

"My mother reads the society pages, if you must know. And in our case even if both of us were blithely ignorant of the pages our fate would have become clear in short enough time."

"True enough. What section do you want, then?"

She rifled through the stack in front of him. "The financials, if you don't mind. Ah, here they are."

She pulled out the thin section with tiny columns of numbers and went over to the couch.

"What on earth do you do with the financials?"

"Check on my investments, dear. What do you do with them?"

"You have investments?"

"Technically they are my father's investments."

"Your father allows you to invest his money?"

Jack set down the paper in her lap. "Since this is apparently very difficult for you, I will assure you that I don't invest *all* of father's money. Although I do think he follows my investments fairly closely now."

"How much does he allow you to invest?"

"I started with fifty pounds when I was twelve and have it up over two hundred now. Well, at least as of three weeks ago. I haven't checked my investments since we left London."

"How old are you?"

"You don't know? I'll be nineteen this year."

"But that's... the average rate of return must be..."

"Over twenty percent per year, yes."

"That's remarkable."

"Thank you. Although it's become much easier in the last two years."

"Oh, and how is that?"

"Now I primarily follow the company W.T. Investments," she murmured, becoming distracted by the information in the paper in front of her.

"Indeed?"

"Yes. This time I've tried to anticipate them and made a gamble that they are going to acquire the Jones-Berry mining concern in Cornwall but haven't seen yet if I was correct."

"You were correct."

Jack looked up in interest. "Oh, you follow them as well?"

"They have been very successful."

"Yes they have," she said, smiling in satisfaction, "and by anticipating this acquisition I have positioned myself to make an even tidier sum than usual."

"If I may ask, how did you surmise they would make this purchase?"

She set the paper down for a moment, warming to a favorite topic that few people wanted to talk to her about. "It was about three years ago that I began to notice W.T. Investments. At first I thought that they were merely excellent investors but it soon became clear that they purchased majority interest in companies that were in need of management improvement. Based on the results I assume they use their majority position to force specific remedies."

"But how did you know they would purchase this mine?"

"I ran across an article on the mine and thought that it fit the profile of previous W.T. acquisitions." She counted the items off with her fingers. "In a cash poor position, running losses for more than three years, likely to be quite profitable with proper management since the vein seems far from played out, and, the clincher as far as I was concerned, reported abuses of the workers."

Gideon sat back in his chair. "You arrived at this by reading one article?"

She shrugged. "Or perhaps by reading many articles and noticing a particular pattern. I've become more interested in both speculation and long-term investments. Since it has worked out, this prediction allowed me to do both. It will be at least two years before the stocks turn a profit."

"When your father gave you those fifty pounds he created a monster, didn't he?"

She laughed. "Perhaps. It's diverting and probably something he wanted me to do instead of racing curricles. He gave Sam fifty pounds to invest when she turned twelve but I think she's lost it all now. I'm not sure as she won't talk to me about it."

"If she were wise she would have had you invest it as her financial advisor."

Jack looked at her husband in surprise at his compliment. He seemed at ease behind his desk, not aware that he had said something at all unusual. She searched her mind to pick the thread of the conversation back up. "My little sister can be surprisingly stubborn when it comes to certain things. She wanted to follow her heart, not the advice of her analytical older sister."

"And her heart proved fallible?"

"Don't they all?" Jack asked.

Gideon laughed. "My wife seems cynical for one so young."

Jack set her paper down again. "I'm observant. When you observe the human condition you can't help but to notice patterns."

"And what other patterns have you seen?"

"Some men engage their wives in conversation just to stare at their bosoms," she said tartly, snapping the paper back up in front of her. Hiding behind the columns of numbers she smiled in delight that her husband was looking at her with such interest.

"In my defense," he said, his voice lowering, "that's a very fetching dress."

"I'm glad you like it," she said from behind the paper.

"And you were breathing."

She peeked over the top of the paper. "I'm likely to do that for the rest of my life so you had best get used to it, or you'll find yourself ogling me at dinner parties."

"I thought you didn't like dinner parties."

She laughed. "Beside the point."

"And what happened to your fear of losing me?" he said, his voice plaintive.

At that she laughed even more. Setting his paper aside, he crossed to join her on the couch. "I see, it's funny now is it? I'll give you something to laugh about." He carried out his threat by tickling her sides until she shrieked and squirmed completely off the furniture and onto the floor. He followed her down, stretching his length atop hers and brushing her hair back from her flushed cheeks. "See what comes of laughing at me?"

"Yes, Giddy," she said, breathless from her giggling, "I see very well."

His brows knit together in irritation. "You know I hate that nickname."

She hooked one arm over his neck and stroked his cheek with her other hand. "I can't help it, sometimes you make me feel giddy."

He looked at her dubiously and she sighed, raising her lips to his own. "I love you, Giddy."

CHAPTER TWENTY-TWO

At Jack's words her husband became almost rigidly still. She teased his lips but it was a moment before he started to respond and when he did it was tentative at best. She knew that he would need time to become accustomed to this thought so she applied herself to distracting him with her body. At long last he sank into the kiss, palming one of the breasts he had been ogling, proving that the dress was indeed cut low by slipping two fingers under the fabric to tease her nipple. She moaned deep in her throat and spread her thighs under her husband's weight, hoping that he would accept her wordless invitation. He thrust once against her clothed body, enough for her to feel the bulge of his erection against her dampening center, then he pulled the bodice of her dress off her right breast and set himself to laving and nibbling at the globe. His other hand was making its way under her skirts when there was a brief knock at the door and it opened, only to be closed after a brief gasp.

Jack laughed. "We really need to learn to lock the door."

Gideon pushed himself up on his elbows to look down at her with a wry grin. "I doubt we need to worry about Mr. Gladstone entering unannounced anymore."

"He couldn't really see anything from the door."

"You're saying we need to be even more concerned about Mr. Gladstone since he hasn't see anything yet?"

She laughed. "Of course not!"

"I worry about you, Lady Harrington."

"As well you should."

He gave her breast one last kiss before pulling her bodice to rights. "I suppose we should save this for tonight in our bedroom instead of mid-morning in the study."

She twirled his hair in her fingers. "I suppose."

They lay there for a moment, forest green eyes to sapphire blue ones, contemplating this new plateau in their relationship. Then Gideon stood and offered his wife a hand up. Once standing she smoothed her dress and he moved back to his desk. Stopping at the corner, he picked up the letters she had brought. He looked over his shoulder at her with his brow raised again. "Robert Bittlesworth?"

"Sabre asked me to send her mail to her brother's address, as you might recall."

"But it's not to Sabrina Bittlesworth by way of Robert Bittlesworth."

Jack sauntered over to his desk, slit open the letter, and handed it to him.

"That's not necessary," he said.

She shrugged. "Read it."

He tried to hand it to her and she pushed it back at him. "Read it," she insisted. He unfolded the sheet and Sabre's letter, which was the bulk of the packet, fell into his palm. He read the brief missive to Robert, giving a lopsided smile at her signature line.

"Satisfied?" she asked sweetly.

He tapped the bundle in his hand. "If you discovered that I'd written a letter to a lady, say perhaps Lady Spencer from the Wynder's Ball, wouldn't you be curious to know what was in it?"

Jack felt herself flush. "I think I'd have a good deal more reason to wonder."

"Do you really? You know almost the entirety of my acquaintance with Lady Spencer. I know almost nothing of yours with Robert Bittlesworth."

She crossed her arms and tapped her foot. "Very well, I'll grant you that. But I'm not known to be a-a gadabout, spending all my time charming men."

He set the letters aside and, putting his hands on her hips, drew her closer. "I have a good deal of reason to wonder about that. Almost every man at my club wanted to tell me how charming you are."

She braced her hands on his chest, keeping him from pulling her completely to him. "Don't be ridiculous."

"That's very similar to what you said the last time I brought it up. Your lack of acceptance doesn't make the circumstance any less true."

He leaned forward and kissed the inside of her elbow.

"You're being difficult," she said.

"Difficult? How could I possibly be difficult for my wife who charms dukes and butlers with equal aplomb?"

"No I don't," she said with a laugh, allowing herself to be pulled closer.

"Oh yes you do," he whispered. "I can't upset you for fear of either a ducal summons or too much starch in my collars."

"Don't be silly," she whispered back, now almost nose to nose with him.

He leaned forward to whisper into her ear. "Only for you, Jack. I'm only silly for you."

She giggled at that but then he was kissing her again. An aggressive mating of tongues that made her body reawaken to the possibilities of the morning. There was another knock at the door, this one sharper and more authoritative than Phillip's had been. Gideon set her aside with a curse followed by a muttered apology, then seated himself behind the desk before calling, "Come."

Jack smothered a smile at how frustrated he sounded and took a seat in a chair near the desk.

Dibbs entered to announce, "Mr. Miller, my lord."

Gideon nodded and the young man came into the room.

Jack rose. "Perhaps I should leave you to your work."

Gideon nodded again, then picked up her letter for Robert. "Can I add a note to this before sending it?"

"Of course," she said.

So, thought Gideon, this was what it meant to be married. Constantly frustrated either by his wife or by not being able to be with his wife. Perhaps it was petty and jealous to be concerned about what she might be writing to Robert Bittlesworth. But Robert certainly wasn't a bad looking man and had more self assurance than he should at twenty-four, a trait that tended to draw young women like flies whenever they would carouse together. And that might be part of it. He knew Robert and Charlie as friends to carouse with and Jacqueline knew them as friends of the family. Certainly neither of the Bittlesworths would do something untoward with their little sister's friend. Especially now that she was the Countess of Harrington. And he knew that she had been untouched coming to their marriage bed and... He was driving himself mad and he knew it. Shaking off his circling thoughts he turned his attention to his new clerk.

Fortunately Gideon knew his Parliamentary papers well enough to take Mr. Miller on a cursory tour of them without having to think about it. Listings of the various bills in progress, tallies of the voting records and reports on anticipated voting. He explained that among the duties he expected of Miller was to act as his aide in assessing potential votes. He also had two drafts of bills that he would like to take up either at the end of this Session or the beginning of the Little Session, and suggested that Miller familiarize himself with the issues. The boy took no notes but appeared to be absorbing the information. Other things might prove frustrating, but this at least seemed to be a good decision on many fronts. If the boy proved himself competent then Gideon might even consider sending him for his letters at Oxford, something that would undoubtedly make his wife look at him as though he had conquered the Continent on his own.

And thinking of how she might react reminded him, what did she mean saying she loved him? That was, well, it was absurd. Especially after she herself had said that hearts are always fallible. It was almost an insult to him or herself to admit to foolish feelings after making such a statement. How was he supposed to take her seriously when she contradicted herself like that? If she had been hoping to engender soft feelings in him for herself it had been a horrible tactic. What he felt was irritated and flummoxed. Hopefully she wouldn't do that again. It just muddled things that hadn't been terribly clear to begin with.

He realized that Miller was looking at him expectantly and he hadn't said anything in awhile. In fact, he couldn't really remember the last thing that he had said. To recover he scooped up the pending bills and handed the heavy stack over.

"There is a desk in your room, as I recall?"

"Yes, my lord."

"Review these in detail. We shall meet here each morning at ten o'clock throughout the week and if your progress seems adequate I will send you to London after that."

"Preceding you, my lord?"

"Yes, Miller. You'll do fine. Now take yourself off, I have estate business to discuss with Phillip before I take my wife to the Vicarage."

"Of course, my lord."

Due, perhaps, to the late start on their morning Gideon found himself working well into the lunch hour as Phillip furiously scribbled to keep up with his directives. A footman arrived with a note on a silver salver. "From the Countess, my lord."

Furrowing his brow Gideon picked up the small envelope and tore it open.

"Since you are working through lunch again have decided to take my meal in my room. Where I will be all alone. Naked."

Gideon stood, crumpling the note in his hand. "Take lunch, Phillip."

"Yes, my lord."

He took the stairs two at a time. Entering her suite he locked the outer door and was already stripping off his jacket as he walked into her bedroom. She was tucked in the bed with the covers pulled up, hair down, arms and shoulders bare as she spooned up some of chef's berry compote. Seeing him she lounged back against the pillows and held up her hand.

"Ah! No further. Your tray is over there by the door."

Gideon looked to his left where she indicated and saw that another tray had been set out.

"For each bite you take you can come closer or have me lower the sheets a bit more."

Infernal witch. He narrowed his eyes at her. Two could play at this game. Since she hadn't said anything about his own clothing he started by stripping himself. He could tell by her widened eyes that she hadn't considered he might start there. Once naked he picked up his plate and said, "Pull down the sheet until I tell you otherwise." As he made his way through chef's goose pie which, honestly, could have been sawdust for all he noticed the flavor, he watched his wife inch the sheet down her body with each bite he took. She revealed that her chest was already flushing, her nipples already puckered with want of his attentions. Her soft belly quivered as she drew the sheet over it. He wondered if she would be too shy to pull the sheets all the way down but she didn't hesitate as he made short work of the pie and then picked up a dinner roll.

"Stop," he said, and used small bites of roll to come across the room, stalking her like a wolf scenting a doe. He pushed aside her dinner tray and tossed the remainder of the roll onto it. Crawling over her he braced his body above her own so that they were barely touching and whispered into her ear. "Did you think to torture me?"

Laughing she reached for him but he pulled away. "Ah," he said. "If you want to touch me there will have to be payment."

She giggled. "I've already eaten my lunch."

"That wasn't the payment I had in mind. I want to see you touch yourself."

Now she looked flushed and embarrassed. "Gideon."

He leaned closer, using his breath as a caress on her skin. "Do you want me to touch you? To be inside you?"

She squirmed and reached for him again, but he again drew away from her.

"You remember, don't you? From the book?"

"Yes, I remember. Though it might be easier if you showed me."

"No, you little minx. Show me what you remember."

Keeping her eyes on his she ran her hands up her sides to her breasts. Watching her elegant hands play over the milky white skin and dusky pink aureoles made Gideon's stomach clench with raging lust. She plucked at her nipples and rolled them between her fingers then ran one hand down the center of her body to the curls at the apex of her thighs. God, he was torturing himself much more than he tortured her. Her delicate fingers lightly explored her own folds, rubbing the lips and skimming over her nub. She gasped in surprise, eyes widening, and set to rubbing her index finger over that magic little button. He wanted to see if she could bring herself to completion, but his body was burning with the need to be inside her. She held out the hand that had still been teasing her nipple and said, "Please, Gideon, be with me." Oh gods, he would swim oceans to be with this woman. He came into her and she was so wet and hot and tight that his world narrowed down to their joining, the surging pleasure of body to body, sex to sex. He wasn't thinking about her pleasure or even his own. He wasn't thinking at all. As he cried out and emptied his seed into her he knew that it wasn't just sexual completion. He had given all of himself to her. Everything he was and everything he would ever be. Even though they were both gasping from the exertion he fused his mouth to hers. He needed to distract himself. He couldn't think about it, couldn't face it, whatever this was between them. He kissed her passionately, gently, erotically, in all the ways he knew until they were both distracted into a haze of sensual pleasure again.

CHAPTER TWENTY-THREE

Jack finally recovered enough to say his name. "Gideon."

He looked down at her, his face still flushed and damp from their bed sport. He seemed afraid of what she was going to say. Vulnerable. Her strong, domineering husband looked terribly, terribly vulnerable.

She wriggled under him. "We should get dressed soon if we hope to make tea at the vicar's."

That hadn't been what he was afraid of her saying because he laughed and kissed her shoulder. "We can't show up to tea naked at the vicar's?"

"No, I'm thinking that would court the wrong image for me as your new countess."

"I don't know, I like my naked countess."

"But you don't like to share your naked countess with other men."

That stopped him short in his teasing. "No, I don't."

She wriggled again. "Then let me out of this bed so that I can dress."

"In a moment." He smoothed her hair back from her face with an earnest concentration that reminded her of the expression he'd had at the wedding when sliding the ring onto her finger. Serious, yet somehow sweet. He cupped her face in his hands and studied her as though memorizing all the lines and curves of her features. At long last he kissed the tip of her nose and rolled off of her to begin gathering his clothing from the floor.

"An earl that picks up after himself? What a novel concept."

He smiled at her a bit sheepishly, as though she had caught him doing something vaguely naughty. How interesting that her husband could stand in that spot shamelessly naked with the confidence of Ares, but question why he was cleaning up after himself and he looked embarrassed.

"I thought you wanted to get dressed," he complained.

"I do," she said, stretching languidly on the bed. "But I'll need to ring for Lara and assumed you wouldn't want her to see you parading naked around the room."

"Indeed." With that he departed and Jack summoned her maid to prepare for the trip to the vicarage. Checking her mantle clock she realized they would need to hurry.

As Gideon guided their phaeton he looked over at his wife. She had been quiet for most of the trip, absorbed in the landscape. Kent was much different from where she grew up in

Derbyshire. Kellington's lands ran to cliffs facing the Channel on the east side and to marshlands at the north. He had mostly taken her through the rolling Downs on their morning rides. This trip to the vicar's had taken them along the marsh with its oddly fetid yet sweet smell and milling sheep. Wildflowers grew along the roadway and throughout the marsh grasses, bobbing in the sea breeze. She glanced over at him and seeing him watch her she smiled. It caught at him, how dazzling she was in her pale blue dress and straw bonnet in the sunshine. He leaned down to kiss her and she laughed.

He gave her a mock frown. "That strikes you as funny somehow?"

She wrapped her hands around his arm and leaned into him. "You're just making me giddy again, Giddy."

He realized he was indulging in a self-satisfied smile and decided it didn't matter with no one here to see it. Marriage was proving to be nothing at all what he had expected. Although much of that, he knew, was due to how unique his wife happened to be. If he had been trapped in marriage with one of the brainless twits that made up the majority of the Marriage Mart he would have already packed her off to the estate of her choosing. Worse yet, what if it had been one of those scheming materialistic girls who ran through pin money like water and charged outrageous clothing bills to their husbands. Which reminded him that his wife had something of a limited wardrobe and hadn't requested any clothing allowance.

"I should take you shopping," he said.

She sat up at that. "Whatever for?"

"Clothing, for one. I'm sure you didn't have time to assemble a trousseau and I should have seen to that before now."

"It's a small matter. We can wait until we're back in London."

Neither brainless nor materialistic, his wife.

"There is one thing, though," she said, plucking at his sleeve absently.

"What's that?"

"I was hoping... That is to say, if it wouldn't be too expensive."

"Out with it. Are we back to the rings and diamond bracelets again?"

She laughed. "No. I was hoping that perhaps we could buy Tyche, my horse, from my father."

"He won't just give it to you?"

Her brows furrowed. "He wants to, but I've told him to sell her."

"Well if you want her then why did –" He broke off as he realized what her words hinted at. The Walters were not in a position to carelessly give away something as precious as prime horseflesh. And their daughter knew it.

"How long have you had Tyche?"

That question relaxed her. "Oh, forever. She was out of Charlie's Black Bitterroot and Dancing Fool, one of his early breeding attempts. He gave her to me for my tenth birthday but she had to grow up and be trained. I didn't ride her until I was twelve."

Having his daughter insist on selling her beloved horse to help fill the family coffers was probably causing Walters no small amount of shame and disappointment. "I'll talk to your father," Gideon said. "I'm sure we can arrive at an agreement."

She hugged on his arm. "Thank you, Giddy, that would mean the world to me."

His wife was oddly easy to please. To have her horse, to help her family, to have breakfast together with him in the morning. Perhaps if someone had explained what marriage could truly be like he wouldn't have avoided it all this time. Although it couldn't have been like this with anyone other than the woman beside him.

For the rest of the ride to the vicarage Gideon told her stories about the swampy lands around them. About the dangers that lurked in the murky waters of the marsh, and the smugglers known as owlers who had run in roughshod gangs over the lands in past centuries. That made him think again about the rumors he had heard in London. Perhaps he would have Philip make some inquiries while they were here, just to ensure that no one on his lands was involved in the smuggling.

He found they arrived at the vicarage much more quickly than he might have hoped. He would have been happy if the afternoon of sunshine, old stories, and his adoring wife could have lasted forever.

Jack's first impression of the stately old vicarage was that it certainly looked too small to house a family of nine in addition to the vicar's family. They were expected and the vicar himself came out to greet them. She assumed her considerate husband had sent a footman over to give the families time to prepare.

The vicar was a spare man, a few inches short of Jack's own height, with sparse blonde hair and a ready smile. He greeted his new countess with the proper mix of enthusiasm and decorum and bowed them into his home where his matronly wife greeted them at the door. They repaired to the sitting room where the Hobbes were waiting, all scrubbed clean and in what was probably the finest of their poor clothes. The youngest was still a babe in arms and Mrs. Hobbes clutched the child to her bosom as she made her awkward curtsy. The woman was thin to the point of sharpness, no doubt from skipping meals to feed the young ones. All of the children aside from the babe curtsied and bowed, looking quite overwhelmed to be in the presence of both an earl and his countess. The seating was limited and the youngest children sat on the floor at their mother's feet, clutching at her skirts.

As the vicar's wife, Mrs. Bycroft, served tea to everyone, Jack began to feel the stirrings of panic. The simple pleasantries were at an end and soon, as the highest-ranking female in the room, she would be expected to direct the conversation. She wished fervently that she were someone other than herself. Either of the other Haberdashers would do splendidly in this situation, although it failed her imagination to guess exactly what they would do. If she knew then she could at least try to emulate them. As the last little child was handed a plate with a cake, which was of course quite pleasing to the tyke, Jack knew that her opportunities for stalling were at an end.

"Thank you for hosting us, Vicar and Mrs. Bycroft. And eversomuch for opening your home to the Hobbes during this difficult time."

"It's the Lord's work," Vicar Bycroft volunteered cheerfully, "we're happy to do it."

Mrs. Hobbes flushed and rocked the baby on her shoulder, obviously embarrassed to be in this situation. Jack turned her attention to the woman. "Mrs. Hobbes, I'm sorry to hear of the loss of your husband last year. You must be very proud of the efforts your sons put into keeping the farm going all this time."

"And me," the oldest girl said.

"Keep civil, Emmy," her mother admonished, flushing an almost alarming shade of scarlet.

"Oh," said Jack to the rebellious looking Emmy, "you also worked the fields?"

The girl nodded, not wanting to test the stern eye her mother had bent on her by speaking again.

"Hm," Jack said. "With such a large farm I'm sure that everyone had chores to do. Perhaps you could each tell me one thing you did on the farm."

Between the cake and opportunity to speak the children were well entertained. Each child did indeed have at least one chore to report, down to the seventh, who at no more than three years old was responsible for the sweeping.

"Well, your mother must be proud of all of you then," Jack said, which prompted Mrs. Hobbes to speak.

"Indeed I am," the thin mother replied and for a moment Jack glimpsed the woman as she must have been before her husband died. Proud, confident, and by the sound of her voice a bit more educated than most country folk. Her four oldest children sat quietly on the settee next to her, hands folded in laps. The three youngest other than the babe sat at her feet with a bit less decorum and sucked on fingers or twiddled hair. Jack knew with a certainty that it would be a mistake to make this mother work and have the oldest daughter care for the children. The heart would go out of this family as sure as anything.

As Travis, the oldest boy, had spoken of caring for the draft horses Jack asked him, "Do you like horses, then?"

"Yes, my lady, more than anything."

His brother Gordon, next to him, rolled his eyes a bit. Since Gordon had spoken about how he planned the planting schedule Jack asked him, "Why did they look to you to plan out the planting?"

He blinked and answered as though it were obvious, "I'm the only one who understands it."

"Oh? What does one need to understand?"

He furrowed his young brow as though she were trying to ask him a trick question. "Crop rotations, weather patterns, and potential sales returns in the market for the crops that can be grown."

Jack could scarce believe the child talking to her was twelve years old. His grasp of the complexities of a farming life obviously far exceeded her own.

"My only regret," he admitted, "was not knowing how much work a hundred acres of grain could be."

"And you couldn't predict the insects," Emmy said loyally. Travis nodded sad agreement.

After another fifteen minutes of pleasantries the earl and countess took their leave of the Bycrofts and Hobbes.

CHAPTER TWENTY-FOUR

Once the phaeton had drawn away from the vicarage some distance Jack turned to Gideon. "Is there a cottage somewhere on our lands where Mrs. Hobbes could live?"

"Even if there were she couldn't afford the rents."

"She can if we take her four oldest into service at Kellington."

Gideon raised a brow at her. "Oh? And what do you suggest they can do?"

"Travis for the stables and perhaps as a tiger. Mary for the kitchens. Did you see how proud she was of cooking for the family?"

"And the other two?"

"Well, you've been complaining that Philip's greatest weakness is not understanding farming and he can't help the farmers learn the latest agricultural innovations. Gordon seems like he would be a natural to learn and share changes that could make the land more productive."

Gideon mulled this over. "His father was well-respected among the men so his name could go a long way in this part of the country. But he's only a twelve year old boy so it would be a considerable investment of time and education."

"And meanwhile he can serve as Philip's assistant, traveling to the farms and assessing how the land is currently used. Certainly his observations would be superior to Philip's who grew up inside the walls of Kellington."

"And for the oldest daughter?"

Jack smiled. "She will be my companion."

"Your companion?"

"Indeed. Do you have any idea how difficult it would be finding a companion for an eccentric countess who prefers riding, archery, and swordplay to shopping and gossip?"

"You need a companion?"

"Will you practice swords with me?"

"Of course not."

"As well I guessed. If Emmy Hobbes doesn't take to martial hobbies I'll eat my hat."

"You trust an eleven year old girl to control a sword safely?"

"Well, she is getting a bit of a late start but we can begin with wood sabres and tipped foils. It will be safe enough."

"How old were you when you started practicing?"

"Eight," she said. "That was the summer we formed our club."

"A sword club?"

Jack grinned. "No, a boys club."

"A boys club?" Gideon asked, raising a brow. "Why did you form a boys club?"

"Because boys always get to do the really fun things. Like climb trees, race horses, and fight."

Gideon thought about it for a moment. "Madam, I think I find you disturbing."

Jack chuckled.

"So that's why you all have boy's names? Because you are a boys club?"

"Exactly. It was easy for Georgianna and I since our families gave us feminine versions of male names, but Sabre was quite clever in her nickname."

"Indeed. So, who is the leader of your boys club?"

"Sabre."

"Not even a hesitation."

"Of course not. She's like a tiny, beautiful Wellington."

"Not Napoleon?"

"Do not insult my friend by comparing her to Old Boney," she said with a sniff.

"Regardless of how we English feel about him he is a brilliant leader." Gideon quirked a grin. "And tiny."

Jack snorted. "Well, I'll leave it to you if you want to tell Sabre that comparison."

"I think that Mr. Miller said your club had a name?"

"The Haberdashers."

"Odd name, isn't it?"

"Oddly appropriate. How did it come up?"

"He said that all of you were his sisters. Thought that as your husband I must have heard of it."

"Yes, well, we've hardly had time to become acquainted have we?"

"So it would seem. Should I search my brain for trivia and salacious secrets in the hopes of telling you before one of my friends does?"

"Do I even know any of your friends other than the duke?"

"I've spent more than a fair share of my time with Robert and Charlie Bittlesworth."

Jack laughed. "Oh, that's funny. Have you? I don't remember them mentioning you at all. Have you known them long?"

"Oh, perhaps six years or so now."

"Six years? Then perhaps you are that reprobate Lord Lucifer!" she exclaimed with a laugh.

"Guilty as charged," Gideon agreed with a grin.

Jack felt her heart tumble in her chest. Lord Lucifer was the nickname Robert and Charlie used for the gentleman who had introduced them to some of the seedier aspects of London. When questioned by their father over their conduct, which had included at least one arrest each and numerous other scrapes requiring intervention, Charlie would quip "the devil made us do it." The only name they used to refer to the man was Lord Lucifer, a moniker that they had apparently shared with him. And a nickname that didn't seem to bother him in the least as he still sat as relaxed and happy guiding the team as he had been before the revelation. Swallowing her shock Jack sat back against the cushions and stared straight ahead. Perhaps she really didn't know her husband. This revelation was most unwelcome. "Is it true that you would sometimes take them to up to three whorehouses in a single night?"

At that Gideon's brow drew down into a severe line. "Why did they tell you that?"

"There were a lot of things that they didn't tell us directly but we found out anyway."

"Why on earth would you want to spy on the Biddlesworth brothers?"

"Because they were our heroes. We wanted to be them. Until Lord Lucifer."

"Well, if it makes you feel any better there isn't a mean bone in either of their bodies. It's hard to say which of them is the better chap."

Jack glanced over at her husband. His hair had become unruly again in the breeze and he had turned back his sleeves in the heat, the casual *dishabille* making him look the pirate. What had just an hour ago been attractive now made her apprehensive. It seemed he *was* the rogue and reprobate that she had accused him of being when first they met. "Then why did you drag them all over the darker side of London? And why did they go with you?"

"Sometimes a good man likes to test himself to see if he has a darker side."

She wasn't sure if he was referring to himself, the Bittlesworths, or all of them. The rest of the ride home was spent in quiet contemplation of the scenery. And trying to reconcile the man she was coming to know with the dark shadow known by the name Lord Lucifer.

As Gideon prepared for dinner he considered his wife's reaction to his role in the Bittlesworth brothers' lives. She didn't seem to approve of his influence, although in his defense they had all grown up quite a bit over the last six years. He was now both a staunch ally and trusted advisor to the younger men. They weren't as close now as they had once been since they no longer caroused so much. It was at least two years ago when they had last all gone to a gaming hell. Gideon had become more serious about his role in Parliament, Robert in his work with the Foreign Office, and Charlie had focused on his horses. But Robert knew that Gideon would support any of his requests that might come to the House of Lords. And Charlie knew that Gideon could always be counted on for a referral at Tattersall's. Gideon had even purchased two of Charlie's colts himself to encourage bidding. Honestly, he refused to feel guilty about his role in their lives. They were free to do what they liked, regardless of how they had blamed Lord Lucifer. At the time it had seemed an amusing lark to be the "cause" of their mischief. He hadn't expected in his wildest dreams that one of the people who would think ill of it would become his wife. He had, after all, only put a bit of town bronze on two very green boys. And it wasn't like he was the worst of the lot among the *ton*. There were a number of men he could name who were truly depraved! He paused as he straightened his cuff. There was that. He had familiarity enough with the whorehouses and gaming hells of London to know of such depravity and the men who practiced it. He shook his head and giving his coat one final brush went to his wife's chambers to escort her. She was nowhere to be found, and when he queried Lara was told that she had already gone downstairs. So that's how it was to be.

When he entered the drawing room it was to Jacqueline's throaty laugh. She had her hand on Mr. Miller's arm and Philip Gladstone, whom Gideon had asked to join them this evening to make seating arrangements even, had turned his puppy-like adoration on her. It took a good deal of restraint not to pull the younger men away from her. Really, he had never been possessive of a woman before, once even trading off mistresses with Robert. But that rational reflection didn't keep his blood from boiling and his collar to seem suddenly tight, undoubtedly from his muscles clenching. Was it going to be worth a lifetime of this? Wanting to beat off admirers with a cane while his wife laughed and flirted with apparent innocence? It was hard to believe that she was as unaware of her impact on men as she claimed. He wanted to think that the adoring gazes she gave him were genuine, but she was now charming Mr. Miller and Mr. Gladstone with similar looks. He was burning with jealousy. He wished that he'd had Dibbs announce him if only to break the concentration of the small laughing group. Mr. Miller noticed him first and the bow he made for the earl alerted the other two to his presence. It disturbed him that Jacqueline's expression of joy drained to one of blank politeness when she saw him. He wished that he could dismiss the two men at her side so that he and his wife could have out whatever argument was brewing here. She walked toward him and held his eyes as he bowed over her hand. She seemed as cold and distant as he had ever seen her.

Dinner and whist afterwards seemed a dull affair with Jacqueline's spirits so dampened. His own mood was sour and he was sure that he seemed older than his years. Perhaps a wife nearly ten years his junior wasn't such a good thing after all, if she made him feel an old man. By draw of straws he and Jacqueline had been paired against the two young men and although this was their first time playing together they easily fell into a *simpatico* rhythm that trounced their opponents, but with the pallor of the evening it was difficult to enjoy the victory.

CHAPTER TWENTY-FIVE

After dinner he escorted Jacqueline upstairs in silence, escaping to his own room immediately. He wished that he had thought to bring up some brandy and considered sending his man down for some. He was yanking off his cravat when he heard footsteps coming through the connecting door.

"What now?" he asked, knowing he sounded surly.

"I think I would feel better if you apologized."

He turned to look at her. She had already taken off her dress and was wrapped in a dressing robe with her feet bare on the wooden floor.

"Apologized for what?"

"For leading Robert and Charlie astray."

"Oh good God, woman, can't you leave it alone? They are grown men capable of making their own decisions. It's not as if I forced them to do anything, they followed me willingly."

"You're older than they are, they probably looked up to you."

Gideon took off his cuff links, tossing them on the dresser and shaking out his sleeves. "Do you do everything your elders do? Or do you have sense and judgment of your own?"

"What if we had decided to follow Robert and Charlie after Lord Lucifer? How would you feel if I had visited whorehouses and gaming hells trying to live up to what my elders were doing? I learned to race and fight because of them, why not drink and game and whore?"

Gideon had crossed the room to her by the time she had finished her diatribe and gripped her chin. "You would do no such thing because you have more sense than that."

He saw tears at the corner of her eyes. "So now you say that Robert and Charlie have no sense?"

"They were young men. We were all young men, just sowing our oats. We haven't done any of that in years." He walked back to his dressing room, too angry to stay close to her, but she pursued him.

"I know that you still drink so I have to assume you're referring to the gaming and whoring."

"Devil take it, woman, but you are plain spoken. I should be shocked my wife can even put these sentences together."

"I told you that I wouldn't be a simpering mouse."

He turned to blister her with a response but was stopped by noticing how pale and upset she looked. As he watched her uneasily, she took a deep breath and clasped her hands in front of her.

When she spoke again, her voice was softer and somehow grave. "Gideon, I want to ask you something and I want you to be honest with me."

"Yes?"

"Do you have a bastard child?"

He paused for a moment to ensure he had heard her correctly. "Do I what?"

"You seemed to have a deal of insight into the viscount's responsibilities *vis á vis* Justin, so it occurred to me there might be a reason why. And if you do, I'd rather know than not. And I wouldn't want that child to be treated as Justin was, ignored by his father and outright shunned by the viscountess."

This argument had taken a sudden turn that he hadn't been anticipating. "So you're saying that you worry that I might have a bastard child hidden away somewhere?"

"It had occurred to me," she said, starting to sound testy, "and a simple yes or no would suffice."

"No."

"No?" she asked, betraying some surprise.

"Not to my knowledge. And you can be fairly certain that an earl of my means would be approached to provide support if a woman thought she could even hope to foist someone else's bastard on me, much less my own."

His lovely wife expelled a deep breath as though she had been holding it and nodded her head, looking down at her feet. "Very well then."

Gideon looked at her, so serious and sad. She was truly bothered by the Lord Lucifer nonsense. He thought of how she and her friends had ensured that Mr. Miller had education and opportunity far beyond what the viscount had accorded, being a tremendously good influence on a young man who might have otherwise run wild. And that reminded him that Jacqueline had an impulsive, bold nature that he could easily imagine running wild under the wrong influence. It wasn't far off the mark to imagine her taking on drinking, whoring, and gaming if she decided to. She was already content to flaunt traditions, what were a few more masculine hobbies? It humbled him to think where his influence might have led.

He approached her slowly and put his hands on her hips. "If it helps any... I'm sorry."

She looked up at him, her expression a mixture of hope and longing. "For what?"

"For being the Lord Lucifer that Robert and Charles were seeking. For it affecting you and lowering their esteem in your eyes."

She nodded and he saw tears glinting again. "And for missing the club trick in the second round?" she asked with a weak smile, referring to their whist game earlier.

"No, you beast, not for that. Who leads with a two as a signal to take the second trick?"

She settled against his chest and his arms went around her. As much as his mind might still be disturbed with their argument, his body was relieved to have this woman pressed against him. Relieved and aroused. Good God, would he never tire of her scent, her touch? He ran his hands lightly over her back, knowing that she would likely not be in the mood for bed sport after their afternoon of disagreement, but unable to keep from some small attempt at seduction. His body craved hers again.

Perhaps she was similarly afflicted because she snuggled deeper into his embrace and wrapped her arms around him. He leaned back to look down into her face. Her eyes were damp but she smiled up at him. He stroked her cheek and she leaned her face into his hand. He kissed her, lightly at first, and she responded. When he swept his tongue into her mouth she suckled it like the sweetest nectar. Now he wished he had brought the brandy up so that she had something worth suckling. But those thoughts quickly evaporated as his wife continued to respond, pressing her breasts into his chest as she strained to be closer to him. As he carried her to the bed he thought, even if they had nothing else, they had this.

In the morning Jack went riding with her husband and ate breakfast with him as though everything was normal. But somewhere at the back of her mind she knew that it wasn't. The revelation that he was Lord Lucifer didn't sit well with her at all. Robert and Charles had both changed after meeting Lord Lucifer. Tales of their drunken debauchery had reached even out to Derbyshire. The Haberdashers had at first defended the reputations of their beloved big brothers, but before long it had become too much. By the summer they were fourteen the three girls had admitted that their former inspiration, their heroes, were now tarnished.

In the meantime she needed to reconcile for herself how she could be disappointed in Gideon, yet also find herself unable to resist the physical nature of their relationship. It was as though coming within two feet of him rendered her unable to think rationally. Even now the memories of their lovemaking had her body responding with tightness and aches that Gideon's touch was designed to soothe. Rather than seek out her husband to distract herself from her thoughts and the perfidy of her own body, she had the footmen help her set up for something that always cleared her mind. Archery. Within an hour she was focused on the twang of the string and whistle of the arrows.

When Gideon hadn't seen his wife at luncheon he was informed that she was on the south lawn practicing archery. At least, he thought, of all her hobbies it was the one permissible for women. Taking some choice bits from the luncheon tray, he walked out to the south lawn to see how she was getting on and whether she was hungry. Rounding the manor, the first thing he noticed was a series of targets set out from fifteen feet to at least fifty yards. The next was that she drew the bow with an almost singular concentration. In the time it took him to reach her she had loosed five arrows, apparently practicing a pattern on one of the mid-distance targets.

"Poor bastard," he said, "what did he do to you?"

A mild quirking of a smile was the extent of response he received as she continued to loose arrows in quick succession at a more distant target. Finally out of missiles, she slung her bow over her shoulder and began collecting them from the nearest target. Gideon fell into step beside her. "Since you missed lunch I thought you might want something."

"I did?" she asked.

He nodded and handed her the napkin of items he had purloined for her. She stood sampling her light repast as the summer sun beamed down on her uncovered head.

Gideon found the silence uncomfortable. "You look like Artemis," he said.

She laughed. "It is a look I try to cultivate."

He pulled arrows for her as she ate, inspecting the tips and fletchings before putting them in her quiver.

"Does that make you Orion, then?" she mused.

"I don't remember my Greek myths very well, you'll have to tell me."

She squinted as she looked up at him, finally nodding. "Yes, you're probably Orion."

"What makes you say that?"

"He was the only one Artemis ever loved."

Gideon frowned and began pulling arrows from the next target. There it was again, that muddying and diverting concept of love. While his heart leapt in response to her words, his mind abhorred the idea. Rather than respond, he concentrated on the arrows. Once he had collected all of them she invited him to stay and shoot with her but he declined.

Jack watched her husband walk back to the manor. He had flinched again when she mentioned the idea of love. Was he so afraid of loving and being loved that he avoided the concept altogether? If true, it was the *idea* of love, not the actions of it. Who would expect the haughty Earl of Harrington to bring his wife a light luncheon by his own hand? He was often independent, she had noticed, eschewing his valet while out in the country and picking up after himself more than many of the upper class in her experience. But she had also seen him delegate a job to a footman more often than carry it out himself. He had brought her food because he wanted to see her, because he wanted to make sure she ate. That was an act of love.

She herself wasn't sure why she had brought up Orion and mentioned that Artemis had loved him, since she currently felt conflicted about her husband. But her feelings for him were strong, if shaken by the knowledge that he was also Lord Lucifer. In many ways it was hard for her to reconcile. Gideon didn't seem the type to carouse his way through London. Perhaps she needed to follow her own advice again, and instead of being irritated, she needed to become curious. To reconcile her considerate, responsible husband to what she knew of Lord Lucifer, she would need to know what had prompted him to act in that way. Of course her deepest fear was to discover that Lord Lucifer co-existed with the man she thought she knew and was perhaps even the greater portion of him.

She also realized she had best not tell him the full tale of Artemis and Orion, since in some versions of the mythology Artemis accidentally kills her love.

CHAPTER TWENTY-SIX

For Gideon, the business week proceded more like a week before Jacqueline. Certainly his life could always be measured in that way now, before Jacqueline and after Jacqueline. But throughout the week his wife was quiet and distracted, allowing him to concentrate on Mr. Miller's education. He also had Philip work with the Hobbes to execute his wife's wishes for placing the older children in service to support their mother and younger siblings in a small cottage in the village. And in his spare time, such as it was, he began compiling a list of invitees for the ball they needed to plan. He knew his wife was nervous about her first real duty as a countess. He searched his mind for a woman who could mentor her. Certainly there must be a society matron here in Kent who would take his wife under her wing to work out the details such an undertaking required.

He was contemplating the rather sparse list of women in the immediate area who might serve in that capacity when he noticed a gleaming black carriage with a smart team of four coming up his drive. As he might have expected from such a rich conveyance, the door bore the crest of the Duke of Beloin. Gideon stood and then realized he would rather receive Quince here than anywhere else in the house. He didn't have long to wait. The elder Dibbs announced the duke in a tone reserved for such august personages. Quince didn't often look out of sorts and the fact that he did now brought Gideon to his feet faster than the duke's title ever would have.

"Brandy?"

"Yes, please," Quince said, dropping onto the leather couch.

Gideon poured, bringing the duke's glass to him before pulling one of the chairs over to face the couch. "What's wrong?"

Quince inspected the brandy for a moment then tipped the glass back, drinking a goodly portion of the glass in his first swallow. "Liverpool is planning to bring the Corn Laws up for vote tomorrow."

Gideon was silent for a moment. "You know I'm not likely to vote as you will."

"Strange," Quince said tiredly, "that thought occurred to me as well. But I said to myself if the situation were reversed, would I want Gideon to tell me that a vote was imminent on one of the most significant pieces of legislation? And would Gideon tell me? When I told myself the answer was yes on both counts the course of action seemed clear."

Gideon shrugged. "You could have just sent a note."

"Notes can be misplaced or just ignored. I find the same isn't true of a duke."

Gideon smiled down into the brandy glass that he realized he hadn't drunk from yet. In his own way, Quince was extending an olive branch. An opportunity to begin bridging the rift that had started when Gideon's father had died. When Gideon had taken on a crushing amount of responsibility that he hadn't been prepared for at the age of seventeen. He had reacted, possibly predictably, by overindulging in every vice he could imagine. After pulling Gideon out of quite a few gaming hells and potential scrapes Quince had put his foot down and refused to go carousing. As that was Gideon's primary entertainment they had drifted apart. Gideon had become more, well, self-destructive and began to avoid Quince because he knew that his friend would take any opportunity to lecture him. And, God help him, Gideon was sure that he would still be indulging his baser nature if his friend Charlie Bittlesworth hadn't pleaded with him to use his position in the House of Lords to support the Cruelty to Animals Bill back in '09. Through that Gideon had accidentally discovered a love of Parliamentary procedure and governance.

Quince himself had ascended four years ago, after watching his father suffer a lingering illness. As the older duke's first marriage had been barren, Quince had not been born until his father was in his fifties. Somehow, Quince had completely avoided inheriting his father's dour disposition and conservative views. The first had been a blessed relief in the House. The second had caused Gideon no end of headaches. Their political clashes had proved to be more intense than their personal ones, and more than one conflict had resulted in shouting matches on the floor.

When Gideon didn't speak the duke continued. "I suggest you go back with me tonight."

Gideon, roused from his thoughts, nodded. "That would be fine. It will give me a chance to settle my new clerk."

"Oh, you've finally chosen a new clerk?" Quince gave him a wry smile. "I thought you enjoyed doing all your paperwork yourself."

"You know I don't, but I'd rather do it myself than see it ruined. However, let me tell you about Mr. Miller. This isn't for common knowledge but, well, it isn't something I would want you to be surprised by since we are known in some circles as being close."

"You're making me curious. Out with it."

"Mr. Justin Miller is Viscount Bittlesworth's bastard son."

Quince sank back against the cushion with a sneer. "Bittlesworth. Delightful."

"Don't judge Miller by his father."

"How do you know you aren't embedding an asp in your office?"

"I don't believe so. You can make some judgments about him yourself. He will need to ride to London with us tonight."

"He's here?"

"He's a friend of my wife's."

"Ah," Quince said lightly. "I see. It proves to be good to be a friend of your wife."

Gideon bristled. "I wouldn't have hired him if I didn't think he was competent."

"Time will tell," Quince said, raising his glass of brandy in a mock toast.

"Would you care to dine before we leave?"

"Of course. How could I miss an opportunity to see your lovely wife while I'm here?"

"We will dine early. I also assume fresh horses are in order."

"Yes, if we hope to get there in proper time."

"I will have Dibbs show you to a room where you can rest and refresh yourself before we dine."

With that Gideon and the duke parted company. Gideon to make preparations, and Quince to rest before dinner and the long carriage ride back to London. As soon as Gideon entered his chambers to direct packing for his journey, his wife descended on him.

"The servants say the Duke of Beloin is here."

"Yes. We'll be dining early with him and then I must go with him back to London."

"Whatever for?"

"A vote in Parliament that I can't miss. It was very kind of Quince to come tell me the vote is likely tomorrow. I wasn't expecting it for another week yet."

"I'm not going with you?"

He kissed her forehead. "No, love. I won't be gone long. There's no need for you to rush back and forth to London with me."

"When will you return?"

"Within a day or two. Besides, this gives me a chance to settle Mr. Miller. He seemed hesitant about going on to London without me."

His wife's brow was still adorably furrowed with her frustration that he was leaving and she was picking at nigh invisible lint on his jacket. He bent his head to whisper in her ear. "I have to leave directly after dinner. If there's anything you'd like to do...?"

She took his hand and led him away from the servants busy with his packing, into her room of blue skies and sunshine. He found that it didn't remind him so much of his mother anymore, but of his beautiful wife and new memories. They joined with a sweetness and intensity that made it feel like the first or last time. Gideon kissed her belly and dozed half on top of her while she ran her fingers through his hair, content in his knowledge that this was far from the last time he would make love to his wife.

Jack doubted the wisdom of the seating arrangement her husband insisted upon. The duke sat at the head of the table of course, as he was the highest ranking person, and her husband sat the foot. She sat to her husband's right and Justin sat to the right of the duke. She wasn't entirely sure of the protocols, but *was* fairly certain that seating an unrecognized bastard next to a duke broke all of them. Due to the length of the table this meant that either end was encouraged to talk privately, as conversation for the full table required one to raise one's voice.

Justin looked appropriately overwhelmed to be paired with a duke as his dinner companion and Jack wanted to be able to save him from the fear and embarrassment. But the affable duke soon had the young man enthralled in conversation and Jack was able to turn her attention to her meal.

"There's no need to fear for him," Gideon said for her ears only. "Quince is no Lord Lucifer."

Jack raised her brows at him. "It beggars the imagination to know why you're bringing up Lord Lucifer."

"Why wouldn't I? It's a common reference between us now. Although to me it is a teasing nickname from friends and to you it symbolizes a man with the power to lead others to perdition."

"And you doubt such a power?"

"You can't lead anyone somewhere they didn't already want to go."

"That's a convenient lie to tell yourself."

Gideon's brows lowered with irritation but any retort was cut off by the duke raising his voice to be heard across the table. "I find your assessment to be correct, Lord Harrington. Now that you have him trained perhaps I will steal your clerk from you."

Justin blushed to the tips of his ears with the compliment.

"Don't be ridiculous, your grace. Harrington men are known for their loyalty."

"But his grasp of the issues is startling. Especially for one so young. Perhaps you will share him with me?"

"What one man could work in both of our offices and not find himself conflicted?"

Jack looked at Gideon questioningly and he said, "Quince holds the opposite view from me on everything of consequence."

"Untrue," the duke said, swirling his glass of wine, "I knew from the start that Lady Harrington would be the perfect wife for you and I can see that *you* now know it to be true."

"We'll consider that the exception that proves the rule."

Jack blushed at that but asked, "What are the most notable items you conflict on?"

"Import taxes," Gideon said.

"Aid for the poor," Quince countered, raising his glass in a mock salute to the earl.

"Agriculture policy," Gideon responded, returning the salute.

"Domestic taxes."

"Foreign relations," Gideon said with a raised brow.

"Business regulation," Quince reminded in a chiding tone.

"Crime."

"And let's not forget women's rights."

"Will you never let that go?"

"Doesn't seem likely. Why don't we ask your lovely wife her opinion on the subject?"

Both men turned their attention on her, Gideon looking irritated and the duke inquisitive. Jack realized that this was the first item she was going to have to navigate as a politician's wife. Honestly she was a bit annoyed with Quince. He had been the one to say that politics and friendship were two different things, yet here he was thrusting her into the center of a political debate. It wouldn't do for her to counter her husband's political position, but since she didn't know what it was, that was difficult. In an attempt to remain neutral she shrugged and said, "I would of course enjoy participating in the political process."

With a sly smile the duke said, "Oh but you won't if your husband has anything to say about it."

Gideon, running low on charity for his guest, pointed his fork at the duke. "You would do best focusing on the universal vote for men."

Jack was unsettled by the duke's comment but asked, "What is the universal vote for men?"

The duke answered, "It is simply that currently in order to vote a person must meet certain criteria such as owning property, which ensures that we continue to have a government for the rich and by the rich. For instance, your young friend Mr. Miller here, who demonstrates a comprehensive understanding for current issues, can have no more influence on how the country is run than a newborn babe in arms."

The earl countered, "Yet you would let thousands of uneducated men access to the vote in order to allow Mr. Miller the privilege? What would our country be like if the majority of voters were uneducated and easily manipulated?"

"Most men are easily manipulated," Quince answered. "Except for you, of course, Giddy. A more stalwart man has not been put on earth by God."

Jack began to wonder if the two men would pull swords from the walls of the gallery and have at each other. However, one thing still bothered her. "I don't remember anything making the papers over the past few years about the House of Lords debating a vote for women's rights. When did this happen?"

The duke was swirling his wine again. "Of course it never made the papers because it was never publicly debated. Your husband made sure of that."

"What do you mean?" Jack looked back and forth between the two men. Gideon was thunderous and the duke icy.

"You see, my dear," the duke explained, "before a bill is written it is wise to chat with other Lords and men in the Commons to see what appetite there is for the nature of the bill. Of course my good friend, the Earl of Harrington, was one of the first people that I talked to about it. Not expecting that he would immediately begin a counter-campaign to ensure the bill never found sponsorship."

Gideon was stabbing the vegetables on his plate with more force than necessary. "It was a ridiculous item for you to bring forward as your first policy issue."

Quince raised a brow. "Ridiculous? You can fend off progress for now, Giddy. You may have even put it back a hundred years. But progress cannot be held back forever."

"And then who will you fight for to get rights? Dogs?"

Jack felt herself go cold. "Pardon me, did you just compare me to a dog?"

"I think you rated slightly higher than a dog," Justin suggested, his first contribution to the conversation and one designed to break the tension.

Still stabbing at the contents of his plate, Gideon said, "The typical woman rates lower than the typical dog in my estimation."

Jack pushed her chair back with a sudden scrape and rose, "If you'll excuse me I think I've developed a headache."

The gentlemen stood with her and bowed to her as she left the room. She needed to collect herself and think. Who... no that was the wrong term. *What* exactly had she married?

CHAPTER TWENTY-SEVEN

As soon as Jack had left the room Gideon turned his ire on Quince. "That was why you wanted to see my lovely wife? To upset her and push your own political agenda?"

"My dear boy, I don't think that I was the one to upset her."

"Bringing up that issue in her presence was unconscionable."

The duke turned to Mr. Miller. "You're her friend. Are women's rights something that Lady Harrington cares about?"

"She has never mentioned it before," Justin hedged.

The duke smiled. "Good man, Miller. You will have a future in politics yet. But based on Lady Harrington's intelligence, education, and independence of mind do you imagine she might?"

"I respectfully decline to speculate, your grace."

This caused the duke to laugh and Gideon said, "If this is how you're going to be all night, Quince, then I'll take my own carriage."

"Fine, I shall be on better behavior then."

"Mr. Miller, I plan for you to take Brier with you to London to be your mount. You may decide whether you would prefer to ride her tonight or ride in the carriage with us."

The young man looked back and forth between the duke and earl, finally saying, "I'll ride the horse, sir."

"An option I might take myself," Gideon said, downing the last of his wine. "You are dismissed to prepare, Mr. Miller. We leave within an hour."

After Justin left, Gideon turned to the duke. "I shall go take my leave of my wife. And find out how much your little revenge is going to cost me."

"I'm afraid to tell you Giddy, but she doesn't seem the type to be bought off with baubles."

"As you may find out when you marry, Quince, there are many forms of payment. Cash is amongst the easiest to make."

"Married less than a month and already you sound an old man. No doubt a circumstance I should endeavor to avoid."

Gideon dashed up the steps to face what was likely to be an unpleasant conversation with his wife. And he had thought Quince was extending an olive branch? Ah well, perhaps his days in London would allow this particular spat with Jacqueline to blow over. It would be a good deal longer before he would forgive the duke.

Jack was sitting at her vanity brushing her hair, and recognized Gideon's step entering her rooms.

"I don't want to talk to you," she said before he had a chance to speak.

"No tearful goodbyes and pledges that you will miss me while I'm gone?"

She glanced over her shoulder. "If you want that you should buy a dog."

Gideon chuckled. *"Touché.* I'm sorry I lost my temper at Quince and you got caught in the crossfire."

"Is that how you would describe it?" She felt herself becoming even more disappointed that he didn't consider his opinions or statements wrong in any way.

"This is an old argument between us, and he obviously hopes to win you to his way of thinking in order to either change my mind or at least make me uncomfortable."

"Is this the issue he mentioned from four years ago?"

"Yes, I suppose it was. It was his first year in the Lords after his father had passed. The former Duke of Beloin had been a staunch conservative. Even I was surprised by what a rebellious little progressive Quince turned out to be."

"He has such a reputation for being a snob. His politics surprise me."

"You see, my love, Quince is only snobbish among the *ton*. He happens to despise his own kind."

"And you're hoping that I despise my own kind and don't support rights for women?"

"That's not true. I hope that you don't undermine your husband's political ambitions by expressing opposing opinions."

"Doesn't that amount to the same thing?"

"I don't think so."

Jack clenched her fists in her lap and shook her head. How would she survive years of marriage to her Luddite husband as he dragged her from social event to social event expecting her not to counter his opinions. If she had known, if she had really understood, she never would have married him. She needed to talk to Justin before he left.

Gideon came up behind her to rest his hands on her shoulders and she twisted away from him, rising to put the chair between them. Finally seeing her expression he realized that there might be a good deal more trouble here than he'd assumed. Her eyes didn't have the wild fury that he remembered from the morning of the society article that necessitated their marriage. This time he saw resolve, rage, and more than a little disappointment. Perhaps he should just go throttle Quince now.

"No kiss goodbye, then?" he asked, still trying to maintain a mild manner to smooth the waters.

"Just get out," she snapped.

He nodded and backed away from her. Perhaps an extra day or two in London would be advisable.

As he settled into the carriage later that hour, he said to Quince, "Earlier this afternoon I was a happily married man. Now I'm not. You can expect a comeuppance for that."

"Come now, Giddy. By your own statement her opinion matters less than the dog's."

Gideon stared moodily out the window to the darkening landscape. "I don't have a dog. And don't call me Giddy. Only Jacqueline can call me that."

Quince raised his brows at that last, quietly added statement.

Gideon accomplished a great deal of work while in London. Debate for the Corn Laws raged for nearly a week, with passionate arguments both for and against. The House also took up the Treaty with America and discussed the Congress of Vienna. Meanwhile, with Mr. Miller's help he was able to catch up on his paperwork and correspondence. The young man was a godsend.

He ordered some wardrobe essentials for his wife, stopping short of sending her fabric and seamstresses since she would probably consider that more of an inconvenience than a treat. Then he tracked down the cabinetmaker with the best reputation in London and ordered a crew to be sent to Kellington to create whatever the countess might request. As the following week wound down he realized he couldn't put off going home any longer. It was a shock to know he had been purposefully avoiding Kellington, which made the third time his wife had put him in this position. He never delayed things, ever. His philosophy was to always deal with things straight on and that there was no time like the present to get things done. He would be damned if his prickly, opinionated wife was going to make him change how he did things.

In the spirit of not delaying, he went to the Walters house and bullied Mr. Walters into taking funds for Tyche and set off for Kent that very morning. No time like the present, he told himself. If she was still upset then they would argue about it until it was resolved.

Jack was in turns relieved that her husband hadn't returned, and annoyed that he not only hadn't returned, but also hadn't sent a letter telling her when he would. Things arrived almost daily from London. Clothing, craftsmen who measured her suite and discussed where to install shelves and cabinets, and miscellaneous household items that she supposed were from the earl but they didn't include any explanatory notes. She remanded the clothes to Lara, gave the foreman exact specifications for her room, and left Mrs. Gladstone in charge of the miscellaneous items. She also hadn't heard from Justin yet and hoped that a letter from him would arrive before Gideon did. Of course the list of bills he sponsored, and his voting record, wouldn't give her any insight into things that he killed at inception, like the duke's proposal for women's rights. She was loath to ask the duke for insight as he had his own political axe to grind. She didn't feel like she could even talk to her husband until she understood what she would be expected to support in this marriage.

By arriving to an event on his arm and simply remaining silent, she would be assumed to be in support of all his decisions and policies. It rankled. She had never been much for politics but she certainly had her own opinions and feelings! Was she to forever suppress them since to do otherwise could compromise his career? She hadn't expected marriage to make her less of a person but perhaps she should have. A married woman owned no property. It all belonged to her husband. She herself belonged to her husband.

To make matters worse she had been feeling poorly for the past few days. She had barely eaten and when she did, it seemed to all come back up. She knew that being upset made her lose her appetite, but this sickness combined with what could only be grieving for the marriage she thought she had was making her sleepless and grouchy. When she realized she had snapped at a chamber maid for no good reason, she took herself to her rooms to at least try to recover from whatever ague had laid her low.

Gideon strode into the front hall of Kellington and handed Dibbs his coat, gloves, and hat. "How fares the household, Dibbs?"

"Well enough considering my lady is ill."

"My wife is ill? Where is she?"

"My understanding is that she's been in her rooms for the last two days, my lord."

"Thank you, Dibbs. I shall go there directly."

"My lord," Dibbs said, gently halting Gideon on the first stair step. "Do know that she hasn't... been herself of late."

Gideon jogged up the steps. Well, then. Either Jack hadn't gotten over Quince's visit or she was quite ill. He knocked on the door to her suite and pushed it open. She was in the sitting room, curled up on the settee under a throw, and reading. She looked like death. Her hair was pulled back, there were circles under her eyes, and if he wasn't mistaken, she had lost weight. The look she gave him was somewhere between rage and misery. "So. You've returned."

Although irritated by her continued obstinance, he was alarmed that her health had changed so significantly in his absence. She needed to be in bed. She needed to be eating. She needed... he didn't know what. But he would figure it out and ensure that she received it.

"You should be in bed." He bent over to pick her up and she held up a hand to fend him off.

"I'm fine where I am."

"You should be in bed," he repeated, scooping her into his arms despite her struggles. Holding her, he could confirm that she had lost weight. Enough for it to worry him. "Are you not eating at all?"

Her struggles became more pronounced until she finally wriggled free and landed on the bedroom rug on her hands and knees. He dropped down beside her to check her for scrapes but she scrambled away from him. "Stop it. Leave me alone."

"Jack, you're not being reasonable."

"No, I'm not being reasonable. Just go away and leave me alone." She had pressed herself against the wall, pulling her knees up to and curling herself over so that her face was hidden.

"I'm not leaving until you tell me what's wrong."

This brought her gaze back up to his. "How can you even ask me that?"

"I am asking you that. Is this still about that foolishness that Quince brought up?"

"Foolishness? You think it's foolishness?"

"Yes," he said, rising to prowl her room. "I think it's foolishness. I don't see why you're still worried about it."

She pushed herself up the wall. "You arrogant ass."

"Fine, are you going to stand here and defend all of your sex to me? All those empty headed little fools and manipulative vipers? Women like you, who are educated and intelligent, are beyond rare."

"As if your sex is any better? The *ton* has scores of fops and rakes and vicious men whose only pursuit is wealth and influence regardless of whom they hurt. How am I supposed to feel better knowing that each of them has the right to direct the flow of governance?"

"At least men are expected to be educated."

"A bloody lot of good it does! And why couldn't women be expected to be educated as well?"

He threw his hands in the air. "Now you want better education for women! Well, you'd best write a letter to Quince, I'm sure he would be happy to take that issue forward to the House of Lords for you."

" You make me feel as though I don't even know you! Why do you have to be so..." Her voice trailed off and she put a hand to her head then crumpled to the floor.

Gideon felt his heart lodge in his throat when she fell. Cradling her in his arms he moved her to the bed, then rang for Lara. When the maid appeared he demanded, "Has the doctor come to see my wife yet?"

The little maid shook her head, backing away from him.

"Send for him now, please. I will expect him immediately. And ask cook for anything that is good for fainting."

"Yes, my lord," she said with a quick curtsy and then fled the room.

His Jacqueline was starkly pale, the dark circles under her eyes standing out like charcoal. Gods, he felt like an ogre for yelling at her. She was upset but that was certainly something they could work out. Stubborn as she was, yelling at her wouldn't change her mind. He kissed her limp hands and waited for someone to come who could tell him what to do for her.

CHAPTER TWENTY-EIGHT

Jack awoke to a sharp smell that made her sneeze. She sat up rubbing her nose and saw a wizened, bespectacled man looking at her. "Hello, Lady Harrington," he said with the barest sketch of a bow, "I'm Doctor Galloway. How are you feeling?"

"Tired. Sore. What happened?"

He sat on the edge of her bed and patted her hand. "You fainted, my dear. Gave Lord Harrington quite a scare. Your maid says you have been feeling ill this week?"

"Yes. Exhausted, sick to my stomach. I'm sure it will pass."

"Most likely. When was the last time you had your menses?"

"What?"

"Your female bleeding, my dear."

She stared off toward the window. "Not since... before we were married."

"It's possible you may also have some other complaint but most likely it is just the early stages of pregnancy. This may be news you want to keep to yourself. Many pregnancies don't make it past the first month. Or, if you wish, I can tell his lordship the news. You're young and healthy, we have no reason to believe you won't carry to term."

"No, it's all right," she said softly. "I'll tell him. When we're more certain."

"Then I will plan to come back and see you next month to check on your progress, my dear. Send for me if you begin to believe you have a malady. Dibbs knows my direction."

She nodded. "Yes, of course."

As he prepared to leave she said, "Wait, doctor. What should I tell my husband when he asks what was wrong?"

"We'll just tell him you were overwrought. That tends to be a diagnosis that husbands don't press for too many details on."

She nodded again and went back to looking out the window. There had been a time when she would have been delighted to know that she carried Gideon's child but now it felt like another thing that would bind them too closely together. After the doctor left she stroked her stomach. "I'm sorry, sweetling, you don't deserve to be born into a house of strife."

When the doctor had told him that Jacqueline was "overwrought" Gideon thought to give her some time to recover. But a week had passed and he hadn't seen hide nor hair of her. Tired of having his wife avoid him, Gideon walked into her rooms to seek her out. She wasn't in her sitting room, where he saw some bookshelves had been added. It was fine work indeed with delicate scrollwork painted light blue and edged with gilt of such fine craftsmanship one could hardly tell it was not originally part of the room. Entering her bedroom, he saw that shelves and cabinets had been added in here as well. Undoubtedly her weapons lurked in one of those cabinets since he didn't see them on display. Perhaps having them inaccessible would ensure that the two of them didn't come to sword point. If he could find her. On cursory review of the room he didn't see her on the bed or in one of the chairs. Just before he was going to give up and search the library again he noticed two slippered feet on one of the window seats, the rest of the woman hidden behind a billowing blue and yellow curtain. As he approached the window, she was slowly revealed beyond the curtain in her yellow morning dress with a book open on her lap. She looked as though she felt better, her skin clear and rosy and her hair again in the soft, pinned waves she preferred. He leaned against the wall opposite her and looked down, his heart squeezing painfully in his chest. She was so beautiful.

"Yes?" she said irritably, without looking up.

"I thought to check on you since you've now closeted yourself away up here for nearly a fortnight. Mrs. Gladstone says you still haven't been feeling well."

She turned a page. "Indeed I haven't."

"I've missed you at breakfast." He found it gave his heart a bit of a lurch to admit as much. His statement seemed to give her pause, however, and her glance flicked up as far as his waistcoat before she trained her eyes back on her book.

"Have you? My apologies for leaving you without company."

"I thought you never missed the family meal."

Her brows furrowed. "That was when I had a family."

The statement lay there between them, revealing exactly how much her feelings had changed. For a moment Gideon couldn't breathe. A tight band of tension wrapped his chest, leaving his heart feeling like it had iced over as a pond does in winter. He slowly straightened from the wall. "I see." He walked across her room to their adjoining door and then through it, closing it with a very soft click. Staring at the handle for a few moments he finally reached out to engage the lock.

Jack awoke early and stared at the window as dawn lightened the edges of her curtains. Justin still hadn't written and she felt conflicted. She was afraid to resume a close relationship with her husband if his politics proved to be untenable to her. On the other hand, when he had stiffened and walked away after her comment about family, she had felt horrible. A man who was never close to anyone had admitted to her that he missed her company, and she had thrown it back in his face. It didn't help that pregnancy was making her weepy and emotional. Other than the morning meeting with Mrs. Gladstone over the household affairs, a meeting they were now taking in Jack's sitting room since her illness, she tried to avoid anyone else in the household. She found that the French novels and plays she preferred made her cry and was now reading scientific texts in an effort to keep hold of her emotions. She was afraid to write any of these details to her friends because Gideon might intercept and read the letters. She had never felt more alone in her life.

She knew from Mrs. Gladstone's updates that the earl had followed through on her suggestion to employ the four oldest Hobbes children and that they had arrived almost a week ago. She had asked Mrs. Gladstone to send Emmy home to help her mother until Jack was feeling better. Meanwhile, by the housekeeper's reports, it sounded like the other children were settling in well. She supposed she should see to having some appropriate frocks made for Emmy's role as companion. There were many things that needed to be done. But first she would start with breakfast. Throwing back the covers she prepared to go downstairs for the first time in almost two weeks. After many fights with her strong-willed best friends she knew that the best course when having done a wrong was to apologize as soon as possible. From what she had seen, the earl had Sabre's temper and George's capacity to hold a grudge. The morning should prove interesting.

When Gideon entered the breakfast room his wife was sitting at her place arranging items on her plate to her satisfaction. He considered turning and walking out. Strongly considered it. But, since that would be craven, he instead took a steadying breath and walked to his place at the table. The footman held out his chair and as he settled into it he could smell her soap. The least the damned woman could do was sit at the other end of the table now.

"Good morning, Gideon," she said, still not looking up from her plate.

That simple statement left him wanting to blister her with his response. He had hoped that the brutal gallop he had taken Falcon on over the Downs would have helped to settle his temper, but apparently not. After the initial shock had worn off he had spent the night pacing his room like a caged animal, torn between grief and rage. After finally falling asleep, he had awakened with a dream he hadn't had since childhood of walking all the halls of Kellington and finding everyone dead.

He still hadn't responded when she continued. "I wanted to apologize for what I said last night. It was petty and childish of me."

At that she finally raised her gaze to his and he saw that her eyes were reddened and sad. Even through his hurt and anger he hated to see her looking miserable, and that just served to irritate him more. It didn't do to allow her to affect him with her tantrums and changes of mood. He resolved to treat her as he would a peer in the House. He had never allowed any of them to unman him. Even Quince couldn't provoke him anymore while in the House.

"Think nothing of it," he said with a shrug. "Are you feeling better?"

"Some, thank you."

"You'll never recover if that's all you eat," he said, indicating the small portion of toast and egg she was pushing around her plate.

"If I eat any more it doesn't do well."

He shrugged again. "As you wish."

"Gideon, I wondered if I could ask of you a favor."

She still sounded pitiful and by the gods he wished that he had a tot of brandy. She was giving him a headache. "Ask," he said abruptly.

"If when next you go to London I could go with you to see my... to see my parents and sister."

He could tell that she had stopped from saying her family. To see her family, her real family. Rather than being with what she saw as a failure of a husband. He ground his back teeth together but responded with equanimity. "If you like."

"Thank you, Gideon."

He wished that she would stop using his name. "I thought that you might want to remove to our estate in Staffordshire when they repair to the country after the season, so as to be closer."

"Oh, they will be staying in London after the season."

"No, I saw to it. They will be returning to Derbyshire. My manor in Staffordshire is less than an hour by carriage and I thought you might appreciate the proximity."

He thought she was quiet for a suspiciously long time, He finally looked at her again to find she had a stricken expression and tears streaming down her face. "What?" he asked irritably. He had arranged all of this for her benefit and she was looking at him like he'd killed a puppy.

"I knew that I would eventually be banished to a minor property but hadn't expected it within the first month." She covered hcr mouth on a sob and lurched to her feet. With that, she stumbled to the door and fled the room.

When he had made the arrangements he had planned to go with her, but as he didn't imagine he would now, it hardly mattered to explain that. He was at a loss over what to do. Perhaps, despite her reaction at the news, she would be happier without him. He couldn't think of anyone close to him that he hadn't disappointed. Why had he expected it to be any different with her?

He hadn't cried since he was very small, but he recognized the hot, pricking feeling at the back of his eyes. He rose abruptly from the table, almost knocking over his chair. Certainly the stables had another horse in need of exercise.

Jack sobbed into her pillow until she was thoroughly sick of crying. Perhaps it was for the best that she hide herself away in Staffordshire. She would have her parents and Sam nearby when the babe came. Provided that all this emotional tumult didn't make her lose it. She wrapped her arms around herself and wondered what parts of Gideon that the child would have. His kindness or his arrogance? His eyes? His unruly dark hair? With these thoughts she drifted off to sleep again.

CHAPTER TWENTY-NINE

Jack awoke to Lara shaking her shoulder. "My lady, my lady, please wake up."

Her mind was muddled with a nap that must have lasted most of the day if the light from her windows was any indication. "What is it Lara?"

"The earl is in terrible trouble."

At that she sat up. "What happened? Where is he?"

"Please come downstairs to talk to Mr. Gladstone."

Not even bothering to straighten her hair or morning dress, Jack ran down the steps after Lara to find the front hall full of servants. Dibbs and Philip Gladstone were easy enough to spot in the crowd.

"What's happened? Where is my husband?" Jack demanded.

Dibbs looked coldly at Philip Gladstone and the younger man stepped forward, twisting his hands together and not looking up at Jack. "The owlers have him, Lady Harrington."

She felt her heart lurch in her chest. "The smugglers? How on earth... I thought those were old stories."

"No my lady," Philip said. "Since the war they have been bringing in French wine and fabrics."

"How did you know that?"

Philip began to look even more miserable and Dibbs prodded him. "Answer the countess."

"I've been helping them."

Jack heard a whimper from the sidewall and saw that Mrs. Gladstone was propped in a chair with two maids fanning her face.

Steeling herself to hear the story, Jack said "Tell me what happened."

Philip looked at the ring of angry faces around him, then swallowed and began speaking. "Well, the owlers, they've been using a cave in the cliff side for storage. The earl hasn't shown any interest in riding the cliffs for the last few years. But this afternoon... This afternoon he did."

"And then?"

"He must have been curious when he saw crates on our shore because he came down to the beach. One of the men caught him from behind. I was talking to Belfor... he's the uh, he's their leader, when the men brought him in."

"What is his condition? Was he stabbed or..." Jack trailed off and her heart was in her throat while waiting for the answer.

"He was unconscious. The man must have hit him with a club or some such."

She let out the breath she had been holding. Such a head injury could be terrible but not necessarily fatal. She turned to Dibbs. "Has the constabulary been called?"

Dibbs looked at Philip with a raised brow. "According to Mr. Gladstone that would be a mistake because they are, how did you phrase it? On the take."

Jack looked at Philip again. Her voice cracked as she considered the possibilities. "Are you here to ask for the ransom?"

Philip was traumatized. "No, my lady! As soon as I recognized the earl I snuck out to come back here so that we could determine what to do."

She looked around the room at the shocked and fearful faces of the staff. Her people. Their people. They loved Gideon and would probably do anything for him but they needed leadership if they were to do it. By the gods, why wasn't it Sabre here instead of herself? Sabre, who had won almost every game of war they had ever played. Jack took a deep breath and tried to control her rapidly escalating fear. Yes, Sabre had won every war. But Jack had won a good number of battles. And that was all this was. A battle.

"Dibbs, find out who among the staff have military service and have them meet me in the library, and then send for Dr. Galloway. We don't know what we'll be dealing with yet. Also, have my weapons brought down from my room. Lara can help you find them. Mrs. Gladstone, you and your maids make sure that there are clean bandages and other supplies readied. Mr. Gladstone, you are with me." With that she swept out of the front hall and toward the library, the staff springing into action behind her. Once they were alone in the library she spun on the young steward. "If you are lucky, my husband will deal with you. My current level of charity would find you face down in the marsh."

Paling even further the young man stuttered. "Y-yes, my lady."

She rifled through the desk in the room until she found a fairly large piece of parchment, which she laid out on the library table. "Now you're going to give me all the details you can about the geography and the owlers."

Jack spent the next half hour going over details with Philip. As much as she hated the delay, it was best to be prepared when walking into a situation such as this. Not that she'd ever been in a situation such as this. She searched her mind for advice from the Greek and Roman generals she had studied. Strategy and tactics that had only been of intellectual interest now had much more weight. She had to find some way to apply what she knew or she might be a widow before the night was out.

Six men from the staff had military experience and all were ready to serve. However, by Philip's account there were least eight owlers. While briefing the experienced men she sent Dibbs to find twelve more volunteers. Enough to overpower the owlers two to one, not so many that stealth wasn't an option. Once she had the men assembled she broke them into three-man teams with a former soldier in charge of each one. After setting aside her chosen weapons, she let the men augment their own supplies from hers. Although there were some murmured comments and raised eyebrows, they armed themselves readily enough.

She dismissed them briefly, instructing them all to change into dark clothing, running upstairs to change clothes herself. Meeting them again in the front hallway, she stood on a step and looked out over her assembled team. If the owlers were as vicious and brutal as Philip described them then it was likely that at least some of these men would die tonight. It was possible that she should wait for a ransom request. Surely the smugglers wouldn't murder a peer as they would all hang. But then, they would hang for smuggling if discovered.

No, she couldn't bear the thought of Gideon dying due to her inaction. The faces of the men here, some of them boys really, all showed a clear resolve. They were looking to her to lead them down to the beach and rescue the earl. Now was not a time to be frozen with indecision.

She caught the butler's eye. "Dibbs. Keep Mr. Gladstone contained until we return."

"Yes, my lady."

Her attention back on the volunteers, she spoke in a voice edged with steel, "This will be difficult and probably dangerous. But as we all know, it is something that his lordship would do for us so we cannot fail to do it for him." Her small speech was met with the ayes and nods she had been hoping for. Encouraged, she led the group out into the falling night. It had been over an hour since the earl had been taken and she could but hope that he was still alive.

Gideon awoke with the worst hangover of his life. He tried to put his hand to his aching head but couldn't move. Coming to his senses a bit more, he realized that his arms were secured behind his back and he was lying against a cold stone wall. The pain in his head was so severe that he felt like retching, but instead gritted his teeth and tried to get his bearings. There was dim light flickering from a lantern in another room. He heard the drip of water periodically and the murmur of voices at a distance. Gods, what was the last thing he remembered? Jack. His wife Jacqueline had been at breakfast and they had quarreled. Afterwards he had gone riding again to clear his head. Then what? He closed his eyes to concentrate. What happened next? He had ridden along the cliffs as they descended at the north end of his land. Boats. He had seen what looked like two crates down at the beach off the inlet. Then what? His concentration was broken by a voice rising high enough for him to hear.

"I don' plum care that he's Himself," a gruff voice growled. "As soon as they find that little rat Gladstone we'll be rid o' the both of 'em."

The second voice was more wheedling. "Gladstone went back to the manor sure as sure does. We'll have the sheriff down on us soon as anything."

"I done told ye not to worry about the sheriff!"

"I don' want no part in hushing the cull, er, I mean his lordship."

Gideon knew that the two ruffians were discussing killing him. He struggled against the ropes on his arms but couldn't work them loose. His wrists were raw and sticky with blood. If he wasn't free and able to defend himself soon then this might all be over. He didn't know how Philip figured into this, but could only hope the boy had made it back to Kellington.

"Ye fool," the gruff one continued, "ye hang just as sure whether you slip the knife or no. I'm done waitin', we need to move out. I'm gettin' that itchy feeling."

"Mr. Belfor, don' make me do it," the other voice whined.

A meaty smack echoed against the stone walls followed by a whimper. "Ye'll do as I tell ye and I want no guff from ye!"

Gideon peered through the dim light, trying to discern where the men were since their voices echoed on the stone walls. The rough walls, sea smell and dripping water made him think they must be in a cave along the cliffs but he didn't know one existed on his land. As he struggled against the ropes he saw the lantern light bobbing closer with heavy footsteps. Before the light could reach him he ceased his struggles and pretended to be unconscious. His hope now lay in surprise.

CHAPTER THIRTY

Jack and the men mounted horses and raced across the Downs. The sun was setting at their backs and casting uneven shadows over the rolling hills, but she knew that this was no time to hesitate. She had been relieved and almost moved to tears to see Tyche among the horses from the stable and now, bent low over the mare's neck, urged her to fly over the tufted grasses. The men were spread out on both sides of her and difficult to see in the failing light of dusk. Now that they were putting her plan into action she worried whether she had made the right choices. Did she wait too long? Should they not have come at all? Would the plans work? Had she brought enough men? Would they all survive? She forced back her doubts and focused on keeping herself and Tyche safe on this pell-mell race. She heard a muffled shout from one of the men and turned her head. The winds were blowing hard, whipping words away from them as they tried to call to one another. Perhaps the difficulty in hearing would work in their favor when they had to approach the smugglers. For now the wind and sound of thudding hooves drowned out their voices. She saw that one of her men was waving a hand to the south and, after a moment, saw the lantern that had caught his attention. He held up three fingers and pointed to the light in the distance. Jack nodded, assuming that he proposed his team investigate. He and the two young footmen assigned to him split off from the main group and galloped towards the light.

Jack took the rest of the men to the cliffs. As they neared their destination her heart was beating painfully in her chest, her breath harsh and burning her throat. It worried her to think that they might be too late, that Gideon might have already been killed by the owlers.

Surely not. Surely the criminals would be too afraid of the penalty they would face. But as she looked out over the darkened landscape she reminded herself that with their smuggling and brutish ways they tempted death, even a hanging, every day. It would perhaps be a little thing to kill and dispose of a peer. But not just a peer. Giddy. Arrogant, complicated, and oddly sweet Giddy. She set her jaw as they began to pull up the horses at the path that Philip had said led down to the beach and cavern the owlers used as part of their smuggling operation. She had to believe that there was still time left and that they would succeed.

Using Philip's advice on where the owler sentries would be, Jack and her men left their horses ground tied and moved stealthily down toward the beach. It was a risk trusting the steward after his perfidy. The whole of this was a terrible risk. They couldn't use a lantern to light their way, as Philip had said the ship would arrive after sunset to wait for a signal from shore. The moonlight barely highlighted the trail they needed to follow along the treacherous cliffs but they didn't hesitate.

One of the older soldiers, Hammond, led his men forward with Jack's group close behind. Shortly after Hammond rounded a rock outcropping, Jack heard a scuffle and muffled shout. By the time she came up with her men Hammond had the sentry down. Listening keenly she only heard the pounding surf on the night air. Most likely the guard's shout hadn't been noted. She let out a pent up breath. The first hurdle had been crossed. There would be at least four more men at the entrance to the cave. The plan was for Jack to target them with her arrows, then have her men rush any who remained in hopes of overwhelming them before they could call to the smugglers inside the cave or signal the boat. This seemed by far the riskiest part of the plan, but Jack knew that they needed to press forward and try to gain an advantage while they could. As they inched their way down the steep, uneven trail in the dark they heard the sound of skittering gravel and the occasional grunt when one of the men mis-stepped. A cold wind blew up from the sea to whip around them, at times pushing them forward and other times back. Jack stayed close to the cliff wall, and wasn't sure if the black void at the edge of path was more or less comforting than seeing how far they would fall if either the wind or an owler managed to send them off the side.

Finally gaining the beach, the group spread out in the pale light of the waning moon. Once they spotted the mouth of the cave, where the sentries stamped their feet and blew in their hands to ward off the chill oceanfront wind, Jack pulled her bow from her back and strung it. When her arrow was notched she nodded to her men to proceed. As they drew closer to the sentries she murmured a quick prayer and sent her arrows flying in quick succession. Three of the sentries were down before her men had to pounce, but the fourth sentry managed to cry out and dash back towards the cave. Hammond took him down with a brutal knock to the back of the head and her men pulled the bodies away from the entrance as planned. One man came trotting out from the cavern holding aloft a light to search for the sentries that should be at there, most likely having heard the cry but unsure of what it had meant. Jack waited for a moment to make sure that he wasn't about to be joined by another then loosed an arrow. Rather than strike the man solidly in the chest it hit his shoulder, spinning him away and making him drop the lantern. Jack drew another arrow but the flare up of the spilled lantern oil flashed in her eyes and cast dancing black shadows against the stone. She heard the man yelling as he staggered back into the cavern and knew that they had no choice but to attack while they still had some surprise on their side. She threw down her bow and drew her sword for the run into the dark maw of the cave, her men close behind her. Within moments they were in the tight, echoing corridor carved into the rock face. As they rushed forward in the darkness Jack could hear the man she had hit with her arrow running ahead of them through the chamber, yelling "Attackers! Attackers!"

As her eyes adjusted to the gloom, she could see a dim light coming from the area ahead of her. She feared stumbling through the dark, twisting passage but her fear of what had become of Gideon was far greater. One of her men shouldered past her. She pushed herself to move more quickly before she was left at the rear of the attack. A dim lantern burned in a larger cavern just ahead. As they entered the larger area she saw two other dark openings gaped at the other end of the rounded stone chamber. The man she had shot was here, along with four other men. A blunderbuss was fired in the small space, felling one of her men and deafening her. She and her men rushed the owlers, swords flashing. One of the owlers, the best dressed of them, retreated behind the others. He had the discharged blunderbuss and his eyes darted as he considered his exits. Jack sidestepped the melee to work on cornering him. He edged towards one of the dark openings.

"Where is the earl?" Jack shouted. She could hardly hear herself between the ringing in her ears from the gunshot and the clash of steel from the fighting around her. The owler seemed to understand her, however, giving her a sadistic grin and drawing his finger across his throat.

Jack felt her heart plummet and tears burned at the back of her eyes. She surged forward to slash at the man, closing the distance quickly with her long stride. She saw his hand come up, at first she thought in order to try to ward off her attack, but then she felt the grit and stinging in her eyes. She tried to keep them open, but a flood of tears started immediately and she couldn't see. She felt herself seized and a knife pressed into her throat.

The man holding her shouted, "Drop your weapons, what, or the bitch will get what's coming to her."

Jack heard the fighting slow and then swords hitting the ground. The man shook her. "Yours too, bitch, or you'll join Himself bleeding out on the floor."

It took her a moment, but she decided to drop the sword. It was doing her little use now.

"All right then," the man continued. "Seems as me and the lady will be making our way to the boat now. All of you back your way into that spot over there if you please."

Jack's face was streaked with tears from the grit, from frustration, and from a welling sense of grief over losing the husband she was only beginning to know. Her men backed away from the owler. She realized that all of the tears were slowly but surely clearing her eyes as she could see the looks of concern and frustration clear on their faces. Of all the things they had considered and discussed, how to handle her being taken hostage hadn't been in their plan. But she would be damned if this scoundrel was going to abduct her and the potential future earl. She slipped a hand into her jacket and slowly drew her tiny, jeweled Spanish dagger from its sheath, silently thanking Sabre for the gift. She tried to remember what George had told her about how to strike vital organs but knew that the way she was being held severely limited what damage she could do. It seemed there were three potential options. Strike over her shoulder and into his neck, a wound that could bring a bloody death within minutes, but a risky attack since she couldn't see and the motion would most likely give him too much time to react. Strike into his thigh which could also bleed out within minutes but the vein was harder to get to. Or strike into the abdomen. Unlikely to cause immediate death, but would absolutely cause death within a few days. And this last attack would be the easiest of the three. The only complicating factor was that he could respond by slitting her throat.

Jack took a deep breath, wrapped both hands around the hilt, and plunged the dagger into his side with all the force she could muster. She heard him exhale with a shrieking gasp, taken completely by surprise. She yanked the small dagger to the side for the most damage she could inflict. Rather than plunge his blade into her he grabbed her by the throat and spun her around.

His eyes looked pitch black in the lantern light, wide with surprise and anger. "Bitch, I want you to see me killing you."

He was holding her throat so tightly that she couldn't breathe. She thought that her vision was going spotty when she saw a shadow behind him. The shadow brought a large rock down on the owler's head and after a spasmodic clenching of his hand the man released her as he fell to the ground. Jack coughed and choked, trying to breathe again after having her throat nearly crushed. Then the shadow moved forward and resolved into a familiar shape.

"Gideon?" she wheezed.

Stepping over the owler he swept her into a fierce hug. She held on just as tightly. After a few moments he stepped back and took her hands, frowning at the blood on them. "What are you doing here?"

"Saving you?" Her throat was still raw from her struggle with the owler and burned with her unexpressed fear for his safety. She wanted to stroke his face, his form, to reassure herself that he was really here and whole, but his grip on her hands kept her from moving. When she looked into his eyes in the dim light she saw the unusual expression she had noted before. The one she had seen the first time they had made love. Unguarded. Intense.

Behind her she could hear the men scuffling and a pained moan. "Oh!" she said, coming back to the moment. "Derek was shot." She hurried over to the young man, pulling Gideon behind her, and dropped to her knees while wiping her hands off with the sleeve of her linen shirt. Gideon crouched down as well and helped her turn him over. There was a great deal of blood but the young footman was still breathing shallowly.

Jack looked up at Gideon hopefully. "It looks like it's mostly in his shoulder. He could make it."

Gideon nodded and then took her hands again. "Jacqueline-"

"We need to get them to signal the ship."

He frowned. "We need to do what?"

"Get them to signal the ship. Otherwise the ship will get away." Jack looked down at their joined hands and saw that her own were shaking badly.

"Jacqueline," he said, "I don't care about the ship."

"But then they might try to do this again."

"Let them try," Gideon said, sounding more fierce. "We'll be on the lookout for it this time."

Jack looked over her shoulder and saw that Hammond had the remaining owlers contained. They had even trussed up the man Jack had fought, and Gideon had clubbed, in case he still had some life left in him. She felt the shaking spread to the rest of her frame with the relief that the worst seemed to be over.

She looked at Gideon again. "You're not allowed," she said, her voice breaking.

Gideon raised a brow.

"You're not allowed to get yourself captured again," she finished.

"I'll keep that in mind," he said drily.

She pulled her hands free of his to grab his neck and pull him down for her kiss. As she threaded her fingers into his hair he drew back with a sharp gasp. She looked at the dark stain on her hand in the flickering lamplight. "Is this your blood?"

Gideon was still wincing and probing gently at his head. "I imagine so."

She blinked, feeling the room slowly tilt. "Oh, that's not good," she said softly.

CHAPTER THIRTY-ONE

Gideon managed to catch his wife before she toppled over. He wasn't sure whether to be scared that she had fainted again or relieved that she had some feminine weaknesses. Hearing her voice demanding to know where he was shortly after he had fought off his unwilling assassin had seemed a godsend. But lurching into the dimly lit cavern to find her in the grip of the leader of the smuggling ring had easily taken ten years off his life. Lifting her gently from the floor he clasped her against his chest and stood up to look around at his men. His footman Hammond approached.

"My Lord," he said solemnly, "tis good to see you alive and well. My lady...?"

"She fainted. When she saw that I was bleeding." Gideon looked down at his wife and added wryly, "I can only hope that means she can never take after me with one of her blades."

Hammond smiled briefly. "She's a plucky one, that. And one of the best commanders I've served with here or on the Continent. Not many Captains could put together a rescue as quick."

"Yes, the countess is a woman of... unusual talents."

"With your leave, my lord, we'll stay in our teams with each team in charge of a prisoner or riding flank guard."

"I... yes, that would be fine."

"And the countess's men serving as your escorts."

"Yes, and those would be?"

Hammond waved two of the young and burly stable hands forward. They seemed uneasy but took positions to either side of him. It entertained Gideon that the little tyrant who lay swooned in his arms was still very much in charge by way of the polite but confidant Lieutenant that she had in Hammond. The earl decided to test whether he had any authority left whatsoever. "I don't think we should signal the ship."

"As you wish, my Lord," Hammond said. But there was enough relief in the man's voice that Gideon was sure he had also given exactly the order that had been hoped for.

His men made short work of cleaning up the cavern, carting out the wounded, and marching out the prisoners. As Gideon started up the path to the downs, still carrying Jack, he was becoming concerned that she hadn't roused yet. Their protective guards stayed close for the climb. Gideon thought that they took surreptitious peeks at Jack, as though to confirm for themselves that she was all right, but it was difficult to tell in the darkness. Halfway up he consoled himself that it was good his wife had fainted. He had been on the edge of promising her anything, everything, if she would just stay with him.

What had started as a conviction that he would make her to stay with him if he made it out of the caves alive had changed to a cloying panic when he had seen her in the hands of the owler. His heart was still in his throat even now, with her warm body pressed against his own and her breath feathering across his neck. If it weren't for the need to press on, step after step, to gain the top of the Downs he was fairly certain he would sink to the ground and sob into her hair. That wouldn't do. He was made of sterner stuff than to be brought to his knees weeping over the idea of losing this ferocious little slip of a girl. Well, perhaps she wasn't a slip being as tall as she was, but she was light as a twig these days. When they were home he would make sure that she ate at every meal, not just pushing food around on her plate. And she needed to get her exercise. He didn't know the last time she had ridden for sport since they had stopped meeting at the stables in the morning. That was certainly a routine that should begin again. And-

"Giddy," she said faintly. "You're holding me too tight."

Not trusting himself to speak, he simply loosened his hold and kissed her on the forehead. Anything. Everything.

Jack felt slightly guilty letting Gideon carry her the rest of the way up the path after she awakened. He didn't seem bothered by her weight and she was able to enjoy the solid feel of him, to breathe in the scent that was uniquely Giddy, to know that he was safe. The future was uncertain. He could still send her away. He could bury himself in his work so that they might as well be living separately. No, the future didn't bear thinking upon. For now she would simply relish the feel of her husband's strong arms around her as they headed toward the safety of Kellington.

Gideon rode Tyche back to the manor with Jacqueline seated in front of him. With both of them wearing breeches the thin fabric was hardly a barrier and every step and shift of the horse jolted his wife's posterior against him. He hardly needed reminding of the healthy amount of lust he had for her, but each moment they drew closer to home his attraction was rather viscerally reinforced. As they drew into the stableyard he wasn't sure if he was more relieved or frustrated. He swung off the mare, hoping he could get to the ground and help his wife down before she dismounted herself but she surprised him by waiting patiently for him to reach up and assist her. Once she had her feet on the ground she leaned into him, wrapping her arms around his waist, and they simply stood there a few moments as the men and horses stamped and milled about them. The light of dawn was brightening the stable yard as Gideon pulled her to his side so that they could walk into Kellington together.

Jack continued to burrow into the warmth of Gideon's side, loathe to give up the security of his closeness. As they entered the main hall, she could see all the servants were waiting to greet the earl. Some of the maids had tears in their eyes they tried to dash away, and Mrs. Gladstone, huddled in a side chair, was openly weeping into her apron. Jack felt Gideon tense beside her and realized that the open emotion was uncomfortable for him. Stepping forward she took charge. "As you can see the earl is thankfully alive. Prepare a hot bath and then have a fire and brandy readied in the study. And a hearty breakfast for all the men as well. The rest of you, go about your business." After some quick curtsies and bows the maids and footman scurried to do her bidding. One of the young maids took Mrs. Gladstone off, the older woman's head still buried in her apron.

Gideon looked around the hall. "Where is Dibbs?"

Jack sighed. "Most likely with Philip Gladstone."

Gideon arched a brow. "And where is Philip?"

"I don't know, perhaps below-stairs? But Gideon... Philip was working with the owlers."

"He was what?" Shock quickly gave way to anger. "Where is he? I want to see him now!" Gideon marched down the hallway until he found a footman. "Find Dibbs and have him bring Philip to my study immediately."

The footman bowed and then nearly sprinted down the hallway.

Gideon turned back to Jack. "How do you know he was working with them?"

"Because he told me. He came back here to tell us that you had been captured." Jack looked down at her hands. "As much as I wanted to kill him at the time, if he hadn't come back and told us then we wouldn't have known where to look for you."

Gideon pinched the bridge of his nose. "And I most likely wouldn't have made it out past that many men by myself."

"Well, it's possible they would have ransomed you."

"No, that wasn't their plan."

Jack felt her lip trembling. "It wasn't?"

Gideon strode back across the hall to embrace her again. "It's all right," he murmured into her hair. "I had my bloodthirsty wife to ride to my rescue."

Jack gave a small laugh that she feared sounded distressingly like a sob.

"You impressed Hammond, you know," Gideon said. "He spent ten years fighting Old Boney on the Continent."

"He hadn't mentioned that. I probably should have put him in charge."

Gideon leaned back to look her in the eye. "You? Allow someone else to be in charge?"

Jack smiled wryly and fiddled with a silver button on Gideon's waistcoat. "I could have been the General instead of Captain."

"Why don't you go take that hot bath while I deal with Philip-"

"But your head-"

"Is harder than granite. I'll be fine." He took her hands and kissed her fingertips, dirty as they were.

She frowned. "The doctor should be here somewhere, but I'm not sure where."

"We'll find him." Footsteps sounded in the hallway. "That will be Dibbs and Philip. Upstairs with you before you decide to end my former steward."

Jack looked over to where Philip Gladstone walked with Dibbs. The young man's eyes were downcast and he looked a man set for the gallows. It was, perhaps, a conversation she would prefer to miss. Looking back at Gideon, she rose up on her toes and kissed him. Still raised on her toes she whispered in his ear, "Don't go too hard on him." She walked up the stairs, sore all over but glad to still be the Countess of Harrington.

Gideon watched his wife ascend the stairs and ached to go with her. He was certainly far from happy that she had ridden into danger for him, but the fact that she had made him hopeful. Perhaps she still cared for him. Perhaps she still felt the love she had confessed and he had rejected over and over. The thought that he could still lose her made his heart twist painfully in his chest.

He looked over to where Dibbs and Philip waited patiently for his bidding. The young man still hadn't looked up from the floor. This task made his heart feel no better. Setting his jaw, Gideon turned on his heel and walked to his study, knowing that the two of them would follow in his wake. Inside the fire had indeed been started and the brandy set out. Gideon poured himself a tot of the liquor before settling behind his desk.

"Dibbs, you may go."

The butler seemed to consider an interjection but stopped himself and withdrew. A tense silence settled over the room while Gideon stared at Philip, and the young man fidgeted while staring at the floor.

"Well?" Gideon said at long last. "What do you have to say for yourself?"

"My Lord, I-" Philip's voice cracked and he finally risked a glance at the earl. "I had no idea they would- I never meant..." He trailed off helplessly, a sheen of unshed tears in his eyes.

"You allowed," Gideon said, his voice soft but deadly, "perhaps encouraged, criminal activity here at Kellington and you never thought anyone would be hurt?"

Philip hung his head again. "I have no defense my Lord."

"No, you don't. Did you have any accomplices here at Kellington?"

"No, my Lord."

"You shall be turned off without reference or severance. I assume that the funds you received from this enterprise will more than tide you over."

"You... you won't be sending me to gaol?"

Gideon gave him a withering stare. "No. You will have an opportunity to redeem yourself in this world, but it will have nothing to do with me. I wish to never see or hear from you again." Philip was nodding his agreement and Gideon continued. "I will also pension off your mother and as for your siblings they will receive reference letters so that they may seek employment at other houses, preferably at some distance."

Philip's face drained to such a pale white that Gideon thought for a moment that the young man might faint. "You're turning off my mother and siblings as well?" he asked in a strangled voice.

"There will be no more Gladstones at Kellington. Or any of my properties for that matter."

"But my Lord, they had nothing to do with it!"

"You thought that bringing dishonor to your name would only bring dishonor to yourself?"

Philip dropped to his knees and began sobbing. "Please, my Lord, they don't deserve to be punished. It was my mistake, my fault. You shouldn't punish them."

Gideon launched to his feet. "You think I'm punishing them?" he roared. "Has it occurred to you what their lives will be like under the shadow of your perfidy? All the whispers they would suffer, all the slander they would forbear because they share your name? So much as a piece of silver goes missing and who will be suspected in this house? A Gladstone.

Establishing themselves in other houses is the only hope they have to not be punished because of your actions. Now pull yourself together and be a man. If you want to help your family you will need to make something of yourself."

Philip pulled himself back to his feet, wiping his eyes on his sleeve and sniffling.

The earl frowned down into his empty brandy glass. "I don't think I have to tell you that I'm ashamed of your actions. That your father would be ashamed of your actions."

Philip nodded silently.

"I want you out of the house by tonight. The rest of the Gladstones will have until the end of the week."

"Yes, my lord."

"You're dismissed."

Philip bowed and stiffly left the room.

Gideon continued to stare into his glass, not sure if he wanted to drink more brandy. His head had begun to ache terribly and just the small amount of liquor he'd consumed was making him feel dizzy. It made him chuckle, thinking that it would start quite the talk if both Harringtons took to passing out at odd hours for no apparent reason. That made him frown again in worry about why Jacqueline had begun to faint at the slightest provocation. She hadn't seemed the type to be susceptible to the vapors but then again he hadn't really known her very long. Less than two months, he mused. It seemed he should hardly know her at all.

CHAPTER THIRTY-TWO

"Is everything sorted out?"

Gideon looked up to see Jacqueline standing in the open doorway. She had washed off the blood and grime of the midnight raid, and now looked the part of demure countess again. Her pale brown hair was upswept in a simple style, and she wore the pale yellow gown that looked as though a ray of sunshine had decided to wrap itself around her. Holding onto the doorframe, she was watching him with curiosity and a bit of concern. In the early morning light he could see that her eyes were shadowed with fatigue but she stood with the easy grace that defined her. She had become impossibly dear to him. There was a spreading warmth in his chest, better than the best brandy, just from looking at her. And a fluttering, too, as though his heart wanted to escape its confines and go to her on its own. He set down the brandy glass and rounded the desk to move towards her.

"Everything will be all right, I suppose," he responded. She walked into the room and they met in front of the couches, not touching but standing so close that either had only to lean forward for a kiss or an embrace.

"I found the doctor," she said, her voice huskier than before. "You should let him see to you."

"I will. Eventually."

"I heard you shouting at Philip."

"Don't tell me you're going soft on the boy at this point."

"No, but all of the Gladstones?"

Gideon sighed. "Did you hear why? It will ultimately go easier on them than trying to keep them here."

Jacqueline nodded. "I understand the logic. It's just... sad."

He took her hand, running his fingers over the soft skin and straightening the wedding ring. "Is this ring too heavy?"

She shook her head. "No, I like it."

He spent a few more seconds in silence, absorbed in watching their hands together. Hers paler and smaller than his but possessed of just as many callouses from sport. "It is sad. I grew up with them all. I was never encouraged to play with the servants of course, but on a summer day all boys want to play swords with sticks or sail the seven seas in the pond. At times like those, if we could escape the adults, it wasn't about class or position. It was about who came up with the best games and who won them. Philip always looked up to me. He was like a little brother."

"Oh Giddy, I'm so sorry."

He met her gaze to see that a tear had splashed down her cheek and more were gathering in her eyes. Cradling her face in his hand he wiped at the tears with his thumbs. "No, love, don't cry."

"But that's terrible. You were betrayed by a friend and now have to hurt yourself and other friends because of it."

He closed his eyes and rested his forehead on hers. "A man must always do what's right, no matter how much it hurts."

Then Jacqueline was kissing him and the warmth inside his chest expanded while the fluttering began to feel like a dozen moths trying to fly free. After a few moments he could forget how much pain he was in and simply enjoy his wife.

Jack had known for some time that she was in love with her husband, but his admission that sending away the Gladstones was affecting him deeply made her see the lonely child he had been, and how natural honor and strength were to him. Even if they didn't agree on some things, she knew that he had the best of intentions. He just believed he alone could or would take responsibility for things. That it was his job to always be in charge and make the right decisions. But if he was a good man and mostly reasonable, surely they could come to some understanding on things that were important to her. She would need to convince him that she was a partner, a worthy full partner, whose opinions were to be respected. And that made her realize that keeping the news of their coming child from him wasn't something that a trustworthy partner would do. Much as she was loathe to break the kiss, especially with him now stroking her collarbone as their tongues brushed, she knew they needed to talk before his hands wandered further and she forgot what she needed to say. As she started to pull away he growled and held her tighter. She wedged her hands against his shoulders and pushed hard enough to gain a few inches between them and he frowned down at her.

"What?"

"I need to tell you something."

He waited expectantly and she lowered her eyes to the buttons on his waistcoat again. "Well?" he prompted.

"It isn't easy to say. Apparently."

He chuckled and leaned down to kiss the side of her neck. "Then I must guess? Hmm, you need more pin money?"

"No."

"More dresses? No, not dresses for you. More swords? Or arrows?"

"No."

"Or perhaps-"

"Giddy, I'm pregnant."

Straightening quickly he took a step back, hands still hovering near her but no longer touching. She swayed a bit at the sudden loss of contact.

"You're what?" he demanded. He looked quite shocked and that unaccountably made Jack feel cross.

"Pregnant. Did they not cover that in one of your lover's handbooks?"

"I... of course." He held her hands out to the sides and looked up and down her as though he could somehow divine the truth of it from her appearance. She felt like a filly at Tattersall's. He frowned again. "How long have you known?"

"A few weeks."

His expression darkened further. "A few weeks? And you rode out to the cliffs last night in your condition?" He grabbed her upper arms in an almost bruising grasp. "Have you gone mad?"

She pushed at him again, as well as she could while he held her arms so tightly. "No, I haven't gone mad. As you already admitted, if I hadn't come after you then you would most likely have died."

"You should have sent the men. Are you even supposed to be riding a horse?"

"Giddy, I'm not a fragile doll."

"Gods, that's why you've been fainting, isn't it? And the illness?"

"Yes, all that. It's rather embarrassing really."

"You are not to go riding again. And you need sleep."

"Giddy, calm down."

"When was the last time you saw the doctor?"

"Just before I came downstairs."

"What did he say?"

Jack sighed with the repressed urge to throttle her overbearing husband. "That everything appears to be fine but with the strenuous activity of last night that I should get extra rest."

"Don't ever do something like this again."

"What? Save you?"

Gideon's eyes narrowed. "Risk yourself or the child. Do you realize you could be carrying the future Earl of Harrington?"

"Of course I do. And if he can't bother himself to help save his father how good of an earl would he be?"

Her flippancy appeared to shred Gideon's last bit of patience. "Jacqueline, that is poppycock and you know it. I demand your promise that you won't put yourself or the child at further risk."

"No."

"No?" His voice rose with his frustration. "What do you mean no?"

"You have to stop being a demanding tyrant. I won't do something simply because you're shouting at me about it."

"I'm the Earl of Harrington-"

"And I'm the Countess of Harrington," she interrupted. "And I insist that my judgment be respected. I've always insisted on it, you just haven't been paying attention."

"Jacqueline now is the not time-"

His statement was interrupted by the sound of steel sliding free of its sheath near the door. The Harringtons turned to see a petite, dark-haired beauty in a dark red velvet dress holding aloft a bright silver epee.

"I see I've arrived just in time, Jack," the young woman said.

Gideon pushed his wife behind him. "I would be pleased if you would put that weapon away."

"And I would be pleased," she said, advancing on him with the sword, "if you would stop shouting at my friend."

"How did you even get in here?"

She shrugged. "The front door was open. From there I just followed the sound of a very irritated Jack." She pinned the tip of the epee against his waistcoat, just below his cravat, and he irritatedly brushed it aside with his jacket-clad arm. She whipped the flexible sword around again landing it against his throat.

"Sabre, stop it," Jack admonished.

"You don't want him killed then?"

"I just went to the trouble to save him last night, so no, I would prefer not."

"Really? What sort of trouble can an earl get in on a Wednesday night?"

"Smugglers," Jack said.

"Smugglers!" Sabre's mouth drew into a pout. "Why do I have to miss all the fun?" She flicked the sword away and had it sheathed in an instant. "So," she said. "This is your earl."

"Yes, so be on your best behavior. Gideon, may I present Lady Sabrina Bittlesworth. Sabre, may I present Lord Gideon Wolfe, Earl of Harrington."

Sabre made an elegant curtsey as Gideon made a brief bow, but then she looked the earl over thoroughly. "He isn't what I expected for you."

"I *can* actually hear you, you know," he said drily.

Undaunted, Sabre continued. "I expected someone pale and bookish. Someone happy to let you make all the decisions. This one is all..." she waved her hands around his form, "dark, brooding intensity. Almost sinister."

"Well," Jack said with a smile. "He *is* Lord Lucifer."

Sabre spun to look at her friend, wide-eyed. "No!"

Jack couldn't keep herself from chuckling. She looked up at her husband and realized that regardless of his history she did love the man he had become. "Yes, I'm afraid so."

Sabre shrieked and wrapped her arms around Jack while jumping up and down. "That is too rich!"

"Perhaps it's the blow to the head," Gideon interrupted, "but you ladies seem to have lost me."

The petite brunette turned to him. "You're Lord Lucifer. Jack hates you. She's hated you for years and now she's married to you."

"I... and that's funny?"

"One day you will no doubt understand the satisfaction of watching Jack have to eat her words," she said with a tremendous smile.

"Sabre," Jack said warningly.

Sabre danced away from the increasingly irritated Jack, grinning smugly as she spoke, "She has said, and I quote, 'he is a horrible, despicable man and I wouldn't marry him if he were the last man on earth.' And now here she is."

"If I may ask," Gideon interjected, "why were you even discussing marriage to Lord Lucifer?"

Sabre laughed. "Unlike our stodgy friend here, George and I were convinced that you must be quite dashing to have led my brothers astray. And obviously you are if you have also enthralled said stodgy friend."

"Sabre!" Jack protested again.

"Well," Sabre shrugged. "As the Bard would say, 'All's well that ends well'."

"I prefer the Greek perspective," Jack said. "Thucydides wrote, 'Hatred is short lived but that which makes the splendor of the present and the glory of the future remains forever unforgotten'."

Sabre rolled her eyes at Gideon. "She'll be like this all day if we don't distract her with swordplay."

"No," he said. "Absolutely no swords during the pregnancy."

Sabre squealed again. "Is that what you were fighting about?"

"And she needs sleep," Gideon added.

Sabre pulled Jack's face down closer to her own. "You do look tired, Jackie."

Jack sighed. "I missed you, Sabre."

"And I missed you, too, Jack. Go get some sleep and we can have a nice tea when you get up."

"The servants need-"

"I'll take care of the servants," Sabre said. "Your earl will make sure they don't argue with me."

"And Gideon needs to let the doctor look at his head wound."

"Duly noted. Anything else you need, countess?"

"No..."

"Then let your earl take you upstairs and I'll start by sorting out why the front door was open with no servants in the hall." Sabre leaned in towards Gideon and poked him in the chest. "No funny stuff. She needs sleep. And you need to see the doctor before I track you down to find out why you haven't." Then she whisked herself back out into the hall.

CHAPTER THIRTY-THREE

Gideon wrapped his arms around Jack and buried his nose in her hair. "She's...interesting."

"I believe I warned you."

"Weren't we arguing about something?"

"Undoubtedly, but I'm too tired right now to continue."

"I love you, Jacqueline."

"Oh," she said in surprise.

He straightened and looked into her eyes. "That was easier to say that I expected. I love you. The idea of you being hurt scares me more than anything that could happen to me."

Jack could feel tears gathering in her eyes. "Oh Giddy, that's how I feel about you."

He kissed her hand. "I guess we need to avoid any more confrontations with smugglers so that it isn't an issue. Come, I'm supposed to put you in bed before that pushy little friend of yours comes back."

"Tiny Wellington."

"Indeed. If the war starts again I'll recommend you both for duty."

"Why Giddy, I think that's the nicest thing you've ever said to me."

"So in lieu of poetry you would prefer a military service recommendation?"

"And arrows instead of flowers."

"I have married the strangest woman."

"Strangest? No. You obviously haven't met George yet."

"There should be a reward for this, you know."

"For what?"

"Marrying into the Haberdashers. If I'd known I was going to get all three of you then I might have been more reticent."

Jack chuckled. "Lord Lucifer, you didn't read the fine print of our contract?"

"I'm never going to live that nickname down, am I?"

"And the Haberdashers won't ever let me live down that I married you."

"No, the Lady Sabrina doesn't seem the forgiving type."

"Oh, you have no idea. And George is worse."

"My headstrong, impulsive countess is the most forgiving of the three?"

"Indeed. Think of all the things I've forgiven you for."

"Sassy minx."

"Giddy," she said, sobering, "there is one more thing I want to say."

"Another startling announcement?" he teased, wrapping his arms around her again. "Should I sit down first?"

"I asked Justin to send me your voting records."

"I know."

She leaned back to look up at him in surprise. "You know?"

"Your Mr. Miller is quite clever. Before I left London he handed me a packet, saying it was the records you had asked for. Thus he hedged his bets that I wouldn't directly ask him about it and make him choose which of us to betray. Yet by passing it through my hands he left the decision to me on whether I opened it before I gave it to you."

"And you did!"

"And I did. I have the right, you know."

Jack took a deep breath. As much as she wanted to rail at him over his high-handed behavior, she recognized an opportunity. She hoped she wasn't too tired to capitalize on it. "Yes," she said. "You have the right. What's mine is yours. I'm yours."

He nuzzled her throat. "And I couldn't be more pleased."

"You said the idea of my being hurt scared you. It surprises me, as such, that you don't support women's rights on my behalf."

He drew back and frowned down at her. "This again? Already? You have my name, my protection. You know I would deny you nothing it is within my power to give you."

"What if you had already fallen in love with me but events had forced me to marry another man?" she implored. "A cruel man. One given to beating me when I didn't behave as he thought I should."

She saw his jaw harden and he backed another step away from her. "I wouldn't have allowed it."

"Not everything is within your control, Gideon. What if we hadn't saved you today and my next husband was a cruel man?"

His expression had turned formidable. "Why would you need another husband?"

"Because I have nothing! I own nothing! If our child is a daughter, she and I would be at the whim of your heir, a cousin of yours that I've never met. Is that the life you want for me? For your daughter? To have to depend on the very good fortune of finding a kind man?"

Gideon found that he indeed did need to sit as Jacqueline barraged him with images he didn't want to consider. In his time he had seen cruel men. Most likely had a better understanding of them than she did. The idea of her having to submit to such a man, to be abused until she was only a shadow of her impulsive, fiery self... And the idea of a daughter suffering such abuse, having no father to protect her as she should. The pain of the thought was beyond bearing.

He sat rubbing his temples and realized that Jack has stopped speaking. Alarmed that something might be wrong he looked up at her again but she still stood there, watching him with a worried expression.

"What?" he asked.

"Your head is hurting you. Perhaps you should see the doctor now?"

He snorted a laugh and let his hands drop away. "I think I could take two or three cudgels to the head easier than arguing with you."

"I…" She let the statement trail off, apparently at a loss on how to respond.

Gideon stared at the carpet between his feet for a few moments and found himself resolved. He clasped his hands together. "I'll ask Quince if he wants to co-sponsor a bill."

She was silent for a long moment. "Oh Gideon, are you sure?"

He looked up at her again. "Yes, I'm sure," he said.

She still looked worried but a smile tugged at her lips. "Be careful how you tell him. The surprise might cause him an apoplexy."

Gideon chuckled, feeling more relaxed. "Where will the fun be if I cannot devil him at least a little bit?" He rose and offered Jack his arm. "Now I'd best get you into bed before the tiny Wellington realizes you are still up and about. Do you still want to see my voting record? That reading is sure to put you to sleep."

"Of course I want to read it. How else am I to know how to respond when someone asks me a politically charged question?"

He picked up a rather large packet of papers from his desk and handed them to her. "That would be simple. Just ask yourself 'what is the absolutely correct thing to do?' and the answer will naturally lead you to my opinion on the matter."

She laughed almost all the way up the steps and then tapped him on the arm with the packet. "Do you know what else I'd like to know?"

"I'm sure you have an exhaustive list."

"Who sold our story to the newspaper? I've gone over and over it in my mind and I think the most logical suspect is Lady Wynders."

"I'm fairly certain it was Lady Spencer."

"What makes you say that?"

"She was asking after our marriage plans the night before it was published."

"You saw her that night?"

"Don't sound so jealous. It was in the card room at the Yancey ball."

"Libraries, card rooms," she teased. "You're icorrigible."

He trapped her against the wall and kissed her throat. "Sitting rooms, even."

"Which reminds me," she said, looking at the pretty blue and gold room, "we really should send for the decorators."

He straightened again. "There's no need. It doesn't remind me of my mother now, just of you." He looked around the room before returning his gaze to her. "That was another life. Unless there was something else you wanted?"

"No, I fear that if I toured all the grand houses of England that this is the one room I would want for my own."

"Well," he said with a lopsided grin, "how clever of me to already have it here."

Jack stroked his cheeks, worrying over the dark circles of fatigue beneath his eyes. "I suppose when we get back to London I shall have to invite Lady Spencer to tea."

He frowned. "Why?"

"To thank her. Or perhaps I should let Sabre do it. She would undoubtedly bill it the 'Jack isn't always right' tea."

Gideon chuckled. "It doesn't seem to bother you when she points out your errors."

"She wouldn't be that way if I were wrong more often."

"Perhaps I'm starting to see her point."

"Gideon," she admonished. "As my husband you are supposed to support me in all things."

"Whatever gave you that idea? I did, however, write to my investment manager to ask why it had taken him three months to arrive at a recommendation on the Jones-Berry Mine that my wife was able to make after reading one article."

Jack drew back and tried to divine whether he was teasing her. "Are you saying…?"

"That I'm the Wolfe in Wolfe-Telford? Indeed."

"W.T. is Wolfe-Telford? You and the duke have a company together?"

"Yes. Or rather I should say that you and I have an investment company with the duke. Perhaps I'll let you manage fifty pounds of it."

"Don't be ridiculous. I'll start with no less than a thousand pounds."

"At last, feminine materialism has reared its ugly head."

"Pish! I could find more blunt by going through your pockets." She smiled. "But I warn you now that I plan to practice risky speculation with it and will probably lose it all."

"Somehow I doubt that."

Her heart blossomed at the simple confidence in his statement. "Gideon?"

"Yes, darling?"

"I do believe you love me."

He laughed. "As I've said."

She wrapped her arms around him and snuggled into his chest. She hadn't wanted to marry at all, much less would she have chosen the man known to her as Lord Lucifer. Yet here they were. They still had challenges to face, but they were in love and she had hope. As Aristotle had written, hope was a waking dream. "Thank you, Giddy," she said. "Thank you for not being who I thought you were."

"How could I be without horns and a tail?"

"Giddy, I'm trying to be serious."

He chuckled and kissed the top of her head. "So am I. And thank you for not being who I thought you were."

"You thought all women were empty-headed shrews. It wasn't a difficult conception to challenge."

"Be that as it may, it's time for you to get some rest now."

"And you to see the doctor."

"Of course," he said. "Dream of me?"

"Always."

AUTHOR'S NOTE

Thanks for reading the first book in the Haberdasher's series! Don't miss the first chapter of the second book after this note, *Athena's Ordeal*, featuring Quince and Sabre. Although they are Jack and Gideon's best friends they haven't met by the end of the *Trials of Artemis*. Let's see how that goes, shall we? <u>Link to *Athena's Ordeal* on Amazon</u>.

One of the things I particularly like when reading a historical romance is to find *history* in it. But sometimes it's hard to tell the difference between real history and something the author made up to facilitate storytelling (what I like to call historical fantasy). In case you were curious what parts of this book were references to factual history I want to give you some additional information. *Trials of Artemis* takes place February 11 to March 31 in 1815 and that nestles it right in the middle of a tremendous amount of historical happenings.

The early 19th century was quite busy in Europe. Prior to the beginning of our narrative we had the Napoleonic wars, which when we pick up in February 1815 our heroes might have assumed had ended with Napoleon being exiled to Elba in April 1814. But in case you wonder why Gideon stays so busy with his Parliamentary work, it's worth knowing that Napoleon escaped Elba on February 26, 1815. The famous Battle of Waterloo is coming up on June 18.

Meanwhile, in response to the chaos visited upon Europe by the Napoleonic wars (as well as the French Revolutionary War and dissolution of the Holy Roman Empire), the Congress of Vienna was called starting in September 1814. It was held primarily among the "Great Powers" of Austria, France, Russia, and the United Kingdom, and turned into a redrawing of the political map of Europe. The Final Act was signed on June 9, 1815. Yes, shortly before Waterloo.

In the United Kingdom a protectionist grain bill was being debated in the Houses. It finally passed the House of Lords on March 15, 1815 and followed in the House of Commons in June. By requiring hefty duties on imports of grains the landowners of the United Kingdom were able to reap extraordinary profits. This became a source of friction between landowners and merchants, and created a significant hardship for the working class who had to pay high prices for food.

Also in the United Kingdom the seeds of modern Women's Suffrage were being sown. Mary Wollstonecraft wrote *A Vindication of the Rights of Woman* in 1792, just a few years before our lovely Haberdashers were born. If you want to know more about the political environment of women's rights in the era it will be something we continue to explore in the Haberdashers series.

The last thing I would like to point out is that although Gideon Wolfe is a complete fabrication, a real Earl of Harrington did exist at that time. This novel in no way tries to use his actual history and I did not research the family at all. Giddy exists purely in the realm of historical *fantasy*.

Thanks for reading!

ABOUT THE AUTHOR

Sue London began writing short stories about horses and teen sleuths when she was seven years old. After that she traveled to distant worlds, fought with swords and sorcerers, and played with a few undead things. As you might have expected, this means she went into accountancy. Well, maybe that was an odd plot twist, but "that's the difference between real life and fiction – fiction has to make sense."

In her twenties she developed a deep affection for romance, especially enjoying the works of Nora Roberts, Mary Balogh and, most recently, Lauren Royal, Danelle Harmon, and Diane Farr. You can thank those authors for leading a sci-fi tomboy into writing historical romances set in the Regency period.

Keep up with Sue and the Haberdashers on these websites:

Haberdashers   on   Twitter:
http://twitter.com/haberdashersfic

Haberdashers   website:
http://haberdashersfic.blogspot.com

Haberdashers   Club   (email   list):
http://eepurl.com/Bicsb
Sue   on   Amazon:
http://amazon.com/author/bysuelondon
Sue   on   Goodreads:
http://www.goodreads.com/CmdrSue
Sue on Twitter: http://twitter.com/cmdrsue

For more on Sue you can check out her
Sueniverse or be her fan on Facebook.

If you would like to report issues in this version
of *Trials of Artemis*, or in any books from
Graythorn Publishing, please drop us a line at
publishing@graythorn.com. Many thanks to
sharp-eyed readers who found issues such as
typos and Prime Ministers that had been dead
for ten years in the first edition. Oops.

ATHENA'S ORDEAL (HABERDASHER'S BOOK TWO)

"The essence of fencing is to give, but by no means to receive." ~ Moliere

CHAPTER ONE

May 1815, London

Quincy Telford, Duke of Beloin, knew the importance of discretion. Even a duke's power wasn't absolute and at such delicate times as these, a man of discretion was invaluable. That was why, if anyone had been attentive enough to notice, the duke would have been found on the doorstep of Robert Bittlesworth this fine spring morning, knocking lightly but politely, without a servant in sight. Even the best servants might not be trusted to be circumspect and on this occasion he could not risk any talk of what he was about. The door was opened promptly by a manservant too young and burly to be a proper English butler. Since Quince didn't want to present a card he simply drew himself up in his best ducal stance and said, "I am here to see Mr. Bittlesworth."

The manservant, noting the overall look of refinement that the duke cultivated, bowed him into the hallway and asked him to wait a moment while it was seen whether Mr. Bittlesworth might, indeed, be in to receive him. As the hallway was better than the street Quince was content to cool his heels looking at the paintings on display. Hearing footsteps on the stairs he turned, expecting to see Bittlesworth, but instead saw a vision that made him catch his breath. A young woman was just at the landing, perfectly highlighted in a beam of light from the second story window. Her hair was the deep, warm sable of a mink and had been gathered at the crown to cascade in a riot of curls down her back. She was petite in stature, her figure a perfect hourglass emphasized by the low cut red dress that hugged her curves. The dress was Italian in design if he wasn't mistaken. Expensive, no doubt, but worth every penny to any man who was fortunate enough to look upon her. Bittlesworth was a lucky man indeed, and brazen to have given his Cyprian free access to his home. As he stared up at her she glanced down and saw him, stopping with a startled

"Oh!" She took the remaining steps slowly, and watching those hips coming toward him he had to admit that he would probably give her free rein of his home, as well.

"Good morning," she said after a moment, obviously entertained that they stood in the front hall staring at one another longer than was considered appropriate in polite company.

He had to admit that he was well pleased that this wasn't entirely polite company. Taking her hand to bow over he kissed her finger tips and, looking up, enjoyed another quite spectacular angle of her cleavage. For such a tiny thing she had simply acres of creamy white skin to admire, from her barely covered breasts to her shoulders, teasingly exposed by the drop sleeves of the gown.

"Good morning," he responded in as silky a tone as he could muster. As he straightened he saw that it had the desired effect, as she seemed to preen under his attentions. Her eyes were the color of bright sapphires and light danced in them from her good humor.

"You have me at a disadvantage, sir," she said, "as Bobbins has been derelict in his duties again and not announced you."

Still holding her hand and staring down into her beautiful face he came to an impulsive decision. He would have her, at any price. He had never wanted a woman, or really anything, quite like this. As though leaving without her was impossible, unconscionable. He rushed to claim her before his own fear, his inexperience in bargaining for such a woman, could stop him.

"Whatever Bittlesworth is paying you, I'll double it. Triple it. You'll never want for anything again in your life."

The change in her expression was so sudden it was almost shocking. The humor was gone and she was so expressionless as to be carved from stone.

"Pardon me?" she asked.

As Quince searched his mind for what to say to bring back the delightful fairy queen she had been and, better yet, to convince her to leave with him, his thoughts were interrupted.

"Your grace, I didn't realize it was you."

The Duke of Beloin released the young woman's hand and turned to see Robert Bittlesworth, who had apparently emerged from some room here on the first floor while Quince hadn't been paying attention. "That's rather the idea, old boy," his normal hauteur having returned to his tone.

Bittlesworth paused and then said, "Quite." He looked from the young woman and then back to the duke. "I trust my sister hasn't been too tiresome?"

The last time Quince remembered being this lightheaded was when he let his friend Giddy talk him into going three rounds with Gentleman Jackson. Apparently a sharp uppercut from a man nearly twice your size had exactly the same effect as deeply insulting the younger sister of a gentleman that you had hoped could save you. But just as he had borne up under Jackson's pounding as best he could, the duke barely faltered in his response now.

"She has been delightful." Quince's eyes swung back to the dark-haired beauty who remained expressionless. Holding her gaze he said, "And I trust she can be discreet as well?"

The young woman raised her chin a notch as though accepting his challenge while her brother said, "Of course. Perhaps you would be more comfortable in my study?"

"Indeed," Quince said. Nodding to the young woman he said, "Miss Bittlesworth."

Bowing into a low curtsy she said, "Your grace."

Quince doubted that he had escaped so easily after such an insult, but beggars couldn't be choosers so he let Robert Bittlesworth lead the way to a small but well-appointed study so that he could explain his issue to the Hero of the Home Office.

Sabre, or as she was more formally known Sabrina Bittlesworth, stood quite still in the hallway for a few moments after Robert and his guest had left. She had heard of having your blood run cold before but had never experienced it herself. Until today. Until this supposed duke had mistaken her for some sort of... some trollop. When Bobbins returned to the front hall she proceeded with her original plan to call on her friend Jack, who, as of earlier this spring, was now Jacqueline Wolfe, Countess of Harrington. As she rather precisely put on her gloves, bonnet, and pelisse, she thought that's what one's oldest and dearest friends were for, someone to take comfort in when the day wasn't going quite as planned, and Jack would certainly be comforting. Looking down the hallway toward Robert's study, Sabre wondered when her other oldest, dearest friend Georgiana would come home from Scotland. Rather than comfort, George would just sneak down the hallway and poison the dratted duke's tea. Or at least threaten to, and that would be heartening. With a final tug to tighten her bonnet strings Sabre sailed out the front door of her brother's house and into the waiting carriage.

Having shut the study door, Bittlesworth wasted no time on pleasantries. "How can I help you, sir?"

"You've gathered this isn't a social call?"

Bittlesworth remained silent at that, waiting politely.

Quince realized he was glancing around the room and being in general more awkward than was his usual mien. Taking a deep breath he consciously forced himself to relax. "I'm being blackmailed."

"I see," Bittlesworth said, pausing. "Brandy?"

"That would be lovely," Quince agreed. Bittlesworth indicated a comfortable set of matching leather chairs near the fireplace and Quince sat while the drinks were prepared. Shortly, Bittlesworth sat next to him, handing him the glass of sweet liquor.

"Sir, you can tell me as much or as little as you're comfortable saying and I will help you in any way that I can."

It was then that Quince became clear on why Bittlesworth was so valued in his position. Bittlesworth was seated there, polite, attentive, and giving the impression that no matter the trouble that he was the man to solve it. That combined with the fact that he was set to inherit a viscountancy, and therefore implicitly trustworthy to any lord of the empire, was enough to give anyone in Quince's position a profound sense of relief. Perhaps he really had found someone who could help him with this most delicate of problems. He found himself relaxing more naturally into the chair. "Well, as you might imagine, it started with my father..."

Sabre marched on the front door of the Harrington townhouse but was deprived of giving the door a solid, satisfying rap by the butler, Dibbs, opening it before she had even gained the last step. The austere butler bowed her in, gathered her bonnet, gloves, and pelisse, and then silently led her to Jack's morning room. With Jack in the morning room that meant her husband Gideon was already at his office. The Harringtons had only been in Town for just over a week and it seemed to Sabre that Gideon was always at the office, sunrise to long after dark. The fact that her best friend was still misty-eyed over the new husband that was obviously ignoring her struck Sabre as ridiculous.

"Miss Bittlesworth," Dibbs announced in a quiet tone, then withdrew from the room. Jack rose from her settle with a delighted smile that faded rapidly. The countess was gowned in a pale green muslin that set off her dark golden hair well, and the empire waist served to make her appear even taller than she was. Since she towered over Sabre by better than a head, it wasn't an effect that the darker-haired girl appreciated.

"Oh my," the countess said. "Who did what, and what are we going to do with them?"

Sabre held the sides of her skirt out, like a fashion plate. "How do you like my dress?"

Jack smiled carefully, "I like it quite a lot. Just as much as I did when we looked at all your new dresses the day after I came to London."

Sabre turned once and then settled the skirts again, twitching them into place. "Then you wouldn't look at me and perhaps offer to make me your private whore?"

"Oh." Jack's expression sobered considerably. "Well, now we have the what, I assume what we are going to do with them will be horrible indeed. So who was it?"

Sabre stalked over to a tiny damask chair and sat. She fingered the red silk of her skirts as she smoothed them out. "I don't know."

"Well that's certainly-"

Jack's voice was interrupted by the door clicking open again as the countess's young companion Emmy Hobbes stepped in. No more than eleven, the young Miss Hobbes was Jack's current project. "Miss Bittlesworth," the girl said, dropping a passable curtsy.

"Emmy," Sabre said with a polite nod.

Jack sighed. "Emmy, I'm afraid that today is not a social call. Sabre and I will need some privacy."

"Oh!" the young girl said, backing away. "My apologies, I didn't mean to intrude."

"Not at all," Sabre said, relenting her bad humor over the girl's apparent concern. "You know I adore you. Who couldn't love a child that takes to the sword so quickly? But this is... family business, and likely to be quite boring to you."

Jack nodded. "It's all right. Take a free morning. Perhaps practice your French?"

As Emmy nodded and pulled the door closed behind her Sabre leaned back in the chair. "Luds, Jack, do you even know what a free morning is?"

Jack's brow furrowed. "That's what I would do on my free mornings as a child."

Sabre laughed. "You were never a child. You were once smaller and you knew less, thank God, but a child? No."

"Tea?"

"You don't have anything stronger?"

Her friend raised a questioning brow and Sabre blew out her breath in a huff. "Yes, tea would be lovely."

Jack pulled the bell and then seated herself on the small couch that faced toward the chair Sabre was in. "And?" she prompted.

Sabre sat up straight again. "I need your promise, your vow as a Haberdasher, that you will not share this information with anyone."

"Except George, I assume."

"Yes, you may share it among the Haberdashers. If George should finally get herself back from Scotland you can certainly discuss it with her."

"But not with Gideon." Jack said it more as a statement than a question.

"No, not with Gideon." Sabre agreed.

Jack grimaced but nodded. "You have my pledge."

Sabre nodded just as a discreet knock announced a maid. The girls didn't speak again until the tea had been settled and Jack was prepared to pour.

"I assume three sugars today?" the countess asked.

Sabre smiled again. This was the comfort that she knew old friends could provide. Someone who knew that stress made her want sweets. Sweets that she regularly avoided since so much as an extra lump of sugar seemed to go straight to her hips. With her tiny stature it took diligence to maintain her figure. "Yes, three sugars today. And that tart if you don't mind."

Jack smiled sardonically. "I wouldn't think you would want to be seen consorting with tarts."

Sabre merely snorted. That was the other thing about old friends. They had absolutely no respect.

"So," Jack ventured, after handing Sabre the cup and saucer. "Where did you meet this man? In the street?"

Sabre nibbled at the tart. "I'd rather not say."

"Well, how are we supposed to find him?"

"He's a duke," Sabre ventured.

"Oh. Well. That certainly cuts the list down substantially. Are you sure he's a duke?"

"I have it on the utmost authority."

Jack narrowed her eyes, obviously wanting to question her friend further in a direction that Sabre didn't want to go.

Sabre sipped her tea and said, "Let's start with what we do know. He's a duke, about your height I would say."

"Many men are," Jack noted drily.

"Robert's age or a little bit older. Fair haired, almost as light as Charlie's," Sabre said, referring to her second oldest brother, the ever affable and horse-mad Charles Bittlesworth. "Cut in that fashionably tousled style. And his eyes are green. A very light green, a spring green George would probably call them. You would expect such innocently colored eyes to house a more wholesome soul." Sabre realized Jack had become suspiciously quiet and looked over at her friend. The countess had one hand clasped over her mouth, eyes wide with horror.

"You know who it is," Sabre accused.

Jack closed her eyes and let the hand fall away. "Oh Quince, what did you do?"

Sabre slammed down her teacup with a crack and jumped to her feet. "You're telling me the obnoxious toad that propositioned me this morning is the Duke of Beloin?"

Jack nodded, "I think so, yes."

"The same Duke of Beloin you have been raving about since I came back from Italy? That you have been bragging I will meet at your ball?"

Jack shrugged helplessly, "Are you sure you didn't misinterpret what he said?"

Sabre loomed over her seated friend and hissed, "Do you want to know what he said? It was, 'Whatever he's paying you, I'll double it. Triple it. You'll never want for anything again in your life.' Do you think I misinterpreted that Jack? Really?"

Her friend gasped in shock. "That's terrible! I can't believe he would say that."

Sabre stalked off to stare out the window. "Either it was the Duke of Beloin or he has a twin. Who is also a duke."

"And who was the 'he' that the duke was referring to? I'm confused, Sabre. Did this happen this morning? Where?"

Sabre turned back to her friend. "I've said all I'm going to say on that matter. Thank you for providing the information I needed."

Jack launched to her feet as well. "Sabre, I don't like that look. What are you planning to do?"

Sabre tilted her chin up. "I'm planning to defend my honor."

IF YOU LIKE THE
HABERDASHERS YOU MAY
ENJOY THESE BOOKS BY
ROSE GORDON

Intentions of the Earl—Faced with never-ending poverty, a gentleman is offered a handsome sum if he'll ruin a certain young lady's future—only she has other plans, and it might entail her ruining his.

Liberty for Paul—There's only one thing Liberty hates worse than impropriety: on Mr. Paul Grimes, and unfortunately for her, it's her own importunity that just got her married to him!

To Win His Wayward Wife—Not to be out done by her sisters' scandalous marriages, Madison Banks is about to have her own marriage-producing scandal to a man who's loved her all along.

Her Sudden Groom—When informed he must

19701372R00197

Printed in Great Britain
by Amazon